Damon wanted her

The knowledge flowed through Hannah as she yearned for this man who tried to do what was right. This scarred, angry man who felt compelled to hide how truly decent he was.

She'd never known, never believed, that she could crave a man with such desperation. But then, she'd never been desired the way Damon desired her. No man had ever touched her with such possession.

His big hands molded her, shaped her, drew her intimately against him. Still, it wasn't enough.

For she had fallen in love with him. Hopelessly. She could no more deny it than she could deny the fire he ignited deep inside her.

Everywhere he touched, she burned.

And he was touching her everywhere....

Dear Reader,

What would July be without fun in the sun, dazzling fireworks displays—or heartwarming love stories from the Special Edition line? Romance seems even more irresistible in the balmy days of summer, and our six books for this month are sure to provide hours of reading pleasure.

This July, Myrna Temte continues her HEARTS OF WYOMING series with an engaging story about best friends turned lovers. THAT SPECIAL WOMAN! Alexandra McBride Talbot is determined not to get involved with her handsome next-door neighbor, but he goes to extraordinary lengths to win this single mom's stubborn heart in *Urban Cowboy*.

Sometimes true love knows no rhyme or reason. Take for instance the headstrong heroine in *Hannah and the Hellion* by Christine Flynn. Everyone warned this sweetheart away from the resident outcast, but she refused to abandon the rogue of her dreams. Or check out the romance-minded rancher who's driven to claim the heart of his childhood crush in *The Cowboy's Ideal Wife* by bestselling author Victoria Pade—the next installment in her popular A RANCHING FAMILY series. And Martha Hix's transformation story proves how love can give a gruff, emotionally scarred hero a new lease on life in *Terrific Tom*.

Rounding off the month, we've got *The Sheik's Mistress* by Brittany Young—a forbidden-love saga about a soon-to-be betrothed sheik and a feisty American beauty. And pure, platonic friendship turns into something far greater in *Baby Starts the Wedding March* by Amy Frazier.

I hope you enjoy each and every story to come!

Sincerely,

Tara Gavin,
Editorial Manager

Please address questions and book requests to:
Silhouette Reader Service
U.S.: 3010 Walden Ave., P.O. Box 1325, Buffalo, NY 14269
Canadian: P.O. Box 609, Fort Erie, Ont. L2A 5X3

CHRISTINE FLYNN

HANNAH AND THE HELLION

Published by Silhouette Books
America's Publisher of Contemporary Romance

For Pat Warren, the best of friends

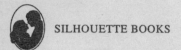 SILHOUETTE BOOKS

ISBN 0-373-24184-4

HANNAH AND THE HELLION

This edition published by arrangement with Harlequin Books S.A.

® and TM are trademarks of Harlequin Books S.A., used under license.
Trademarks indicated with ® are registered in the United States Patent
and Trademark Office, the Canadian Trade Marks Office and in other
countries.

Printed in U.S.A.

Books by Christine Flynn

Silhouette Special Edition

Remember the Dreams #254
Silence the Shadows #465
Renegade #566
Walk upon the Wind #612
Out of the Mist #657
The Healing Touch #693
Beyond the Night #747
Luke's Child #788
Lonely Knight #826
Daughter of the Bride #889
When Morning Comes #922
Jake's Mountain #945
A Father's Wish #962
*Logan's Bride #995
*The Rebel's Bride #1034
*The Black Sheep's Bride #1053
Her Child's Father #1151
Hannah and the Hellion #1184

*The Whitaker Brides

Silhouette Desire

When Snow Meets Fire #254
The Myth and the Magic #296
A Place To Belong #352
Meet Me at Midnight #377

Silhouette Romance

Stolen Promise #435
Courtney's Conspiracy #623

Silhouette Intimate Moments

Daughter of the Dawn #537

Silhouette Books

36 Hours

Father and Child Reunion

CHRISTINE FLYNN

admits to being interested in just about everything, which is why she considers herself fortunate to have turned her interest in writing into a career. She feels that a writer gets to explore it all and, to her, exploring relationships—especially the intense, bittersweet or even lighthearted relationships between men and women—is fascinating.

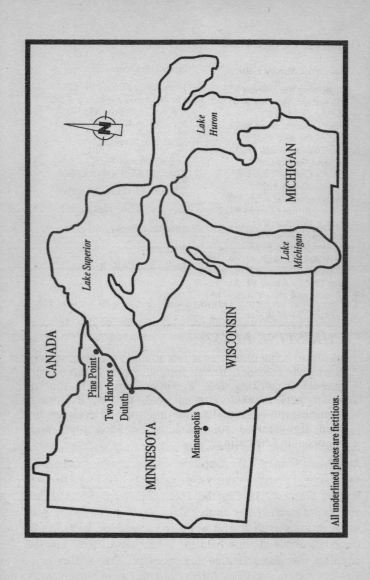

CANADA

Lake Superior

Lake Huron

Lake Michigan

MICHIGAN

WISCONSIN

Pine Point
Two Harbors
Duluth

MINNESOTA

Minneapolis

All underlined places are fictitious.

Chapter One

If there was anything Damon Jackson did well, it was block distractions. The distraction ahead of him, however, was driving him nuts. He wasn't about to acknowledge her. If he ignored her, she'd leave.

It was with that hope that he turned his broad back to the woman waving at him from the deserted dock and tried once more to start the *Naiad*'s engine. The old commercial fishing boat had been named for the young, musical nymphs once believed to inhabit fresh waters, but she was more of a croaking old hag now. The thirty-foot trawler he inherited from his father had battled Lake Superior's often perilous waters for every one of Damon's thirty-two years, and time had wreaked its own brand of havoc on them both. Damon considered himself impervious to any further damage. A man's scars were made of tougher stuff than wood and corroding metal. As for the boat, about all that held the dilapidated vessel together anymore was determination and duct tape. This winter, come hell or high water, he'd strip her down and refit her. If she didn't sink first.

The engine shuddered, coughed and quit. With an inventive curse, Damon hit the starter again. When the ignition fired this time, all cylinders kicked in and the crankshaft finally began to turn. The racket was deafening, and would be until the engine warmed up, but at least the thing was running.

Moving with the ease of a man who'd spent his life on the rolling deck of a boat, he swung out of the wheelhouse, deliberately overlooking the peeling paint and wood rot eating at the door frame. For the third time in two weeks, one of the two itinerant hands he'd hired for the season had failed to show for work. That had left him with only Marty, the more reliable but taciturn ex-dock worker who, like him, had his own reasons for staying out of trouble. He didn't know what those reasons were. He didn't ask. He didn't care. The other guy would get fired tomorrow, if he bothered to show up at all. As small as his operation was, Damon couldn't afford to be down a man.

"Hey! Can't you hear me?"

The woman's melodic voice rang out over the clatter and chug of the old workhorse of an engine.

Keeping his distance had become essential to his survival. Pretending he hadn't heard a thing, Damon snatched up a rag he'd dropped on the deck and headed for the open engine hatch. As he did, he glanced toward the parking lot beyond the dock for Marty. He'd sent him up the hill twenty minutes ago to buy another fan belt. The minute he returned, they'd pull out.

"Excuse me. Sir?"

The insistence in that single word had Damon uttering an expletive as short as it was succinct. He had no desire whatsoever to deal with some tourist who had more time on her hands than she knew what to do with, but ignoring her didn't seem to be working at all. The woman had the tenacity of a toothache.

Planting his hands on his hips, thinking a glare might work, he turned to face her. Occupied as he'd been, he'd barely glimpsed her when she'd hurried toward his boat. Now, prepared to ask her what in the hell she wanted, he found his glance moving over shining auburn hair that swung against the shoulders of a zippered sweatshirt, and skin that looked so soft it fairly begged to be touched. She had the face of an angel, the slender body of a dancer, and the way her lush mouth parted to suck in a breath when her deep blue eyes met his had a jolt of white heat slamming low in his gut.

The distinct, purely physical reaction added a whole new dimension to the morning's frustrations.

"You want the other dock," he called out, raking her with an appraising glance. She was clearly one of the summer people who swarmed up from the Twin Cities to invade Pine Point every summer. Even dressed in running shoes, jeans and the loose, zippered sweatshirt that camouflaged her curves, she was too polished to be a local.

A certain wariness preceded her hollered "What?"

"The fishing charters," he expanded, wondering if her hair was as silky as it looked. The breeze toyed with it like the fingers of a lover, pushing it back from her face, lifting it to catch the light of the sun. Strands of deep amber and ruby glowed in the depths of rich mahogany. He'd never seen quite that shade of fire in hair before. As his glance drifted down, he wasn't sure he'd seen anyone who could do what her long legs did for faded denim, either.

His jaw locked, the muscles there as tight as the unwanted ache burning low in his belly. The last thing he needed was a reminder of how long he'd been without the softness of a woman.

"They run from the new dock. Over there." He jerked his

thumb toward the pleasure craft moored on the other side of the inlet. "There's nothing for tourists here."

Most people would have backed off after such a curt dismissal. As he turned away, he thought for sure she'd have the sense to do just that. Not her. Apparently as dense as the pine woods growing straight out to the shoreline, she promptly tracked his path to the opposite side of his stern.

"I don't want to go fishing," she informed him. "I want to know if you know him."

"Who?"

"Him!"

Looking totally exasperated, she held her arm out toward the end of the weathered dock. All Damon could see was the abandoned bait house, until he noticed an elderly man leaning against its age-silvered siding. The muted greens and grays of his clothing made him nearly invisible against the greens of the lichen and moss on the warped boards.

"He was there when I got here a few minutes ago. He seems awfully confused, and I'm afraid he's going to fall into the water if he's left alone. Is he with you?"

Metal clanged against metal as Damon wiped grease from wrenches and tossed them one at a time into his toolbox. "No."

"Do you know who he is, then? There isn't anyone else around."

She held her arms wide, encompassing the line of empty slips. Only one other boat was still moored this time of day. An old derelict that made the *Naiad* look like a racing yacht.

The last wrench landed in the toolbox with a jarring clatter. Glancing toward the parking lot, wishing his man would hurry up, Damon unplugged the utility light and started coiling its thick yellow cord.

"His name's Lindstrom."

"Do you think he'll be okay?"

His brow furrowed, but he kept at his task. "How am I supposed to know?"

His response obviously gave her pause. It did not, however, get rid of her. "Since you know who he is, it stands to reason you might know something about him."

"Well, I don't."

"We can't just leave him here," she announced, unfazed by his lack of interest. "Do you know where he lives?"

Securing the end of the cord, he shoved it into a canvas duffel. "About a mile up the road," he told her, not caring at all for this "we" business. "Head south on the highway until you get to the sign for Verna Lake. Take a right and follow the road till it dead-ends. He lives in the last house."

Duffel and toolbox in hand, he disappeared into the hatch. A moment later, fervently hoping she'd disappeared, he re-emerged.

She hadn't budged. And she was still talking.

Making no attempt to listen, he lowered the hatch door into place. Rusted hinges screeched, the obnoxious noise cutting off part of whatever it was she said. All Damon caught was something about her car not being there.

"I walked down from the café," she continued, apparently referring to the little restaurant on the hill behind them. "I tried to get him to come back up there with me, but he won't do it. He just kept saying he missed his boat. What about yours?"

"My what?"

"Your car," she explained, somehow sounding exasperated and patient at the same time. "Is there any way you can take him home?"

The magnificently built ox with the lousy attitude finally looked up from what he was doing. As put off as Hannah was by his rudeness, she almost wished he'd continued ignoring her with his tasks. Meeting his hard glance head-on made her uneasy. *He* made her uneasy. He had ever since he'd turned around and given her the bold once-over that had made her feel as if he'd removed every article of clothing she wore—just before he'd dismissed her.

There was nothing even remotely civil about the mountain of granite-hewn male staring her down from the deck of the battered old fishing boat. From the dark sable hair falling defiantly over his forehead to the challenge in his wide-legged stance on the unsteady deck, everything about him radiated a kind of latent tension that told her to back away. Everything inside her warned her to listen to the silent message he was sending her, too. Tall and solidly muscled, he had a hard, hungry look about him that made her think him as dangerous and unyielding as the monoliths of rock farther down the shore. His eyes were the cool gray of a stormy sea, shadowed and fathomless. His handsome features were chiseled, the firm line of his mouth beautifully carved and frankly sensual.

Her glance jerked down, her heart hammering. That sensuality was as disturbing as his defiance. The latter impression was enhanced considerably by the dark, narrow tattoo circling his bicep and the sleeveless black sweatshirt that allowed the symbol to be visible.

With anyone else, Hannah might have thought the silent way he watched her meant he was thinking over her request. With him, she strongly suspected he was only waiting for her to finish checking him out.

"No," he replied flatly, apparently assuming she was through. "There isn't any chance that I'll take him home. Find someone else."

"There isn't anyone else." Common sense nudged hard for her to back away. Had she not been so concerned for the elderly gentleman, she'd have done so long before now. "And we can't just leave him here," she insisted, when the man on deck started to turn from her. "He isn't too steady on his feet and I'm afraid he's going to fall into—"

"Lady," he muttered, swiftly cutting her off, "*we* aren't

doing anything. I'm already two hours late pulling out, and I'm going to have to haul net twice as fast to get my catch in because one of my men didn't show. The minute my deckhand gets back, I'm out of here.''

''How long will that be?''

''Five minutes.''

''Then, you have time to take him home.''

''Are you deaf?''

She met his glare, her own expression considerably more tolerant. ''If he only lives a mile away, it wouldn't take that much longer for you to run him to his house. I'll wait here and tell your deckhand you'll be right back.''

For a moment, Damon said nothing. He just stood on his vibrating deck and narrowed his gaze on the woman who'd planted herself squarely behind his stern. Pretty as she was, she reminded him of a barnacle. She clearly had no intention of dislodging herself from the back of his boat until she got his help.

He was about to tell her that Lindstrom wouldn't want to taint himself by going anywhere with the likes of him when he saw the cause of this latest interruption push himself away from the bait shack and sway to the side. The woman was right. The old Swede was about as steady on his feet as a sailor on a three-day binge.

''He's drunk,'' he pronounced.

Hannah shook her head. ''I don't think he is. His speech isn't slurred, and he doesn't smell of alcohol. Even if he were drunk,'' she added, ''we couldn't leave him alone down here the way he is. Wouldn't you want someone to help you, if you needed it?''

The look he gave her was utterly bland. If it was her intention to appeal to his sense of guilt, sympathy or humanitarianism, she was wasting her breath. He possessed none of those qualities. Anyone in town could tell her that. Any of the locals, anyway. And the old man by the bait shack was one of them.

Ever since Damon had returned to Pine Point, he'd managed to avoid trouble by keeping contact with the town's "respectable" citizenry to a bare minimum. Trouble had a way of finding him, though. It always had. And this smelled like something he would live to regret. But he'd no doubt regret it if he didn't help. Not because she'd hit on some bit of decency lingering beneath his defenses. Because of plain old practicality. With his reputation, he didn't doubt someone would find a way to hold him responsible if the old man did happen to totter off the dock and drown.

He could hear the self-righteous accusations even now.

A woman tried to get him to help, but that Jackson boy just took off and left that poor old man....

What else can you expect from his kind? Thoughtless, nothing but trouble from the day he was born...

Frustration leaked from every pore as Damon headed into the narrow wheelhouse and shut down the engine he'd worked so hard to start. Jamming his keys into the pocket of his jeans, he strode back across the scrubbed planks of the long, wide deck, jumped onto the dock and headed for the shack.

For a moment, Hannah stayed right where she was. Tension radiated from him like sonic waves, seeming to increase in intensity with every step he took. That tension reached back to her even as he moved farther away, sending little shocks along her nerves.

Trying to focus only on the fact that he was helping, she hurried to catch up, then promptly halted on the worn planks when he stopped a few feet from the older man. She wasn't sure what caused it, but she sensed a sudden wariness in the big fisherman, something that made no sense at all because she couldn't imagine him being wary of anything. Or anyone. Certainly not a confused old man.

Unless it was the older man's attire that made him hesitate.

His gray eyes cut to her, then back to what the man was wearing. Mr. Lindstrom looked as if he were prepared to go fishing. Except he didn't have a pole or a tackle box, and there was a garden trowel and a small spade hanging from the utility loops on his fishing vest.

"You need a hand there?" he asked, sounding oddly defensive.

The elderly gentleman did a side shuffle as he looked up, causing the bigger man to grab his arm to keep him from shuffling himself right into the lake lapping on either side of them. Beneath the brim of a battered fishing hat, complete with brightly colored lures, pale blue eyes narrowed through clear-rimmed bifocals.

The guy from the boat looked as if he fully expected the man he was assisting to jerk away. Perhaps admonishing him in the process. It was that kind of defensiveness she saw in his stony profile as he helped the man gain his balance. But instead of pulling back, the wrinkled old man patted the big hand that supported him and focused his rheumy eyes on the fisherman's wary expression.

"Who are you?"

Incredibly, at the rusty-voiced question, that wariness eased.

"Just somebody who's going to take you someplace safer. You shouldn't be down here alone."

"I wouldn't be alone if I hadn't missed my boat."

"What boat?"

Mr. Lindstrom lifted his hand, clutching the bowl of a pipe in his fist. Rubbing his ruddy, spider-veined cheek with its stem, he knit his bushy gray eyebrows into a single slash. "The trawler I work on," he said, as if they should both know that. "I catch it here every morning."

The man she'd harassed off his boat glanced once more at the garden implements dangling from the fishing vest, then met her eyes with a puzzled frown. Lindstrom was eighty if he was a day, and while he looked to be in excellent physical condition for a man of his years, and he sounded quite coherent, it was apparent that something wasn't quite right.

All Hannah could do was hold that rather compelling gray gaze and offer a little shrug that said, *See what I mean?*

The frown, softening slightly, was turned to the old man. "Come on with me. I'll take you home."

"No need," Mr. Lindstrom informed him. "My nephew's wife will take me."

"Fine. Where is she?"

"Right there."

Looking fully prepared to divest himself of the matter, he glanced over his wide shoulder and up the dock. Hannah looked behind her, too, but all she saw were ring-necked gulls perched on pilings.

The instant she turned back, eyes the color of old pewter locked like a laser on hers.

"You?"

Bewildered, Hannah shook her head. "I'm not his nephew's wife," she whispered. "I've never seen him before."

Inching closer, he whispered right back. "That's not what he thinks."

"I can't help that."

The patience he'd exhibited toward the old man vanished like smoke in a stiff breeze. His voice went lower still, its rich, rumbling tones tinged with annoyance. "I'm not the one you need to convince. Tell him. Not me."

His face was inches from hers, close enough that she could see the flecks of jet in his quicksilver eyes. His dark lashes were ridiculously long for anyone so blatantly male. She could see the individual hairs of what looked like a night's growth of beard shadowing his stubborn jaw, too, and the sharply defined notch above his upper lip.

"Mr. Lindstrom," she began, jerking her attention to the man patting his pockets in search of his tobacco pouch.

"Kirsty," came the clearly disapproving reply. "You call me mister?"

"Sir, my name's not Kirsty. It's Hannah."

"Hannah?"

"Hannah Davis." Feeling a tad out of her element, acutely aware of the muscular, tattooed arm inches from hers, she gave a vague nod toward it. "This gentleman," she explained, priding herself on the fact that she didn't stumble over the word, "is right. You shouldn't be down here alone. Let him take you home."

"I don't know him."

"Maybe you just don't remember him."

"He's right," came the deep voice from beside her. "We've never spoken before. We know of each other, is all. This isn't that big a town."

Watery blue eyes narrowed on the younger man's face. "Who'd you say you are?"

He hadn't given his name when Mr. Lindstrom had asked before. At the time, Hannah thought he just hadn't considered it important. Now, seeing the muscle in his jaw work, she had the feeling the omission had been quite deliberate.

"Jackson," he finally said, the word sounding as hard as he looked. "Damon Jackson."

Shaggy gray eyebrows merged in concentration, but the name didn't appear to register at all. Oddly, that failure actually relieved the tension in Damon-the-Difficult's impossibly wide shoulders—something Hannah would have been more curious about had Mr. Lindstrom not balked just then.

Damon had repeated his intention to take the old guy home. Mr. Lindstrom, however, wasn't having any part of it. He wasn't actually pouting. At least, Hannah didn't think he was. But the way his fleshy bottom lip protruded from all the years he'd spent sucking on a pipe did make him look a bit like a four-year-old who wasn't getting his way. He wanted Hannah, whom he still believed was his nephew's wife, to take him home herself.

Acutely aware of the impatience in the gray eyes focused on her, she tried to explain that she couldn't take him because she didn't have a car. She also needed to stay by Damon's boat to tell his deckhand where his boss had gone.

Mr. Lindstrom missed the point completely.

"Skipper."

"Pardon?"

The old guy nodded toward Damon. "If he has a deckhand, he's not a boss. He's a skipper."

"His skipper," she conceded, though it didn't make any sense to her that he should be so clear on that point when he seemed so confused about nearly everything else. "But I still need to stay here. It really shouldn't matter who takes you home as long as you get there safely. Right?"

Logic wasn't going to work. Turning to the man who'd stepped behind her, she glanced up at a solid wall of chest. "Will you try to make him understand?" she asked on a whisper. "You might have better luck than I'm having."

The request was as unexpected as the quiet plea in her eyes. She was looking to him for help, clearly expecting that he would get through where she couldn't. Damon couldn't remember when anyone had looked to him to make something better. People always expected him to make matters worse.

Incredibly, he felt some of his annoyance ease.

Feeling naked without it, not trusting the lapse, he caught Hannah by the arm and tugged her closer. Beneath his fingers, smooth muscles tensed. He ignored her reaction, lowering his head to her ear. He wanted her close enough so she could hear him while he kept an eye on the old man who'd propped himself against the bait shack again.

He shouldn't have leaned quite so close. The way she

smelled, like something warm and innocent yet, oddly, in-
explicably, erotic, had the jolt hitting again.

"Listen," Damon grated, his voice a low rasp, "for all we
know, this guy's memory fades in and out as regularly as the
tide. If he thinks you're his nephew's wife, then that's who
you are for now. If you want me to help you with this, you're
coming along so I won't be any later than I already am. We
can try to reason with him on the way."

"What about your deckhand?"

He had been ready for her to balk at the idea of going with
him. He'd also been ready to tell her that was her only choice,
take it or leave it. Though he could definitely see wariness in
the delicate contours of her face, he wasn't prepared for her
unabashed concern about his situation. It was as real as her
consideration for the old man, and it disconcerted him as
much as the way his body kept tightening with every breath
he drew.

His glance slipped from the intriguing chips of green in her
deep blue eyes to the lushness of her blush-colored mouth.
The thought of burying his hands in that incredible hair and
tasting those inviting lips only agitated him more.

"He'll wait," he murmured, brushing his thumb over her
firm little bicep. "Get your 'uncle' and let's go."

Hannah's insides felt as unstable as a falling soufflé when
he slowly released her arm. The warmth from his hand lin-
gered, still searing like a brand as his shuttered glance moved
over her face. Over the pounding of her pulse in her ears, she
heard him tell Mr. Lindstrom that they would both take him
home, and for him to be careful walking because the boards
would be slick. Not to worry, though. He and Hannah would
make sure he didn't fall.

He was clearly interested only in getting this task over with
so he could get back to his job. Since she was now running
behind schedule herself, she concentrated only on what they
had to do, too. The old gentleman seemed a little steadier on

his feet than he had when she'd first come upon him. But she felt as if she held her breath the entire length of the long dock. She wasn't totally sure which man was actually responsible for that reaction. The one who kept edging her toward the water slapping at the wood, or the muscular mountain who muttered a curse when they topped the rickety wooden steps leading to the graveled parking lot.

With his hand still under Mr. Lindstrom's elbow, Damon stopped to watch the car coming down the hill.

"Is that your deckhand?" she asked.

The level look he gave her let her know that it was, indeed, the person he'd been waiting for—and that he could have been pulling out on his boat in a matter of minutes if it hadn't been for her. Considering how valiantly he'd tried to avoid the inconvenience, she actually thought it quite considerate of him to leave the thought unsaid.

"My truck's right there." He motioned to the shiny black four-by-four by a power pole a dozen feet away. "I'll be right back."

An old beater of a green station wagon with a primer gray front-right quarter panel continued bumping its way down the narrow, dirt-edged street leading down the hill. Spraying gravel, engine sputtering, it cut the turn short and angled into the lot ahead of them. Something loud and screeching from the psychedelic days of rock blared from its radio when it slipped between another pickup and a rusting white van sporting a Fresh Fish logo.

"That engine needs plugs," Mr. Lindstrom announced as she saw Damon's no-nonsense strides take him toward the wreck-on-wheels. "And the radio could use adjustment."

"I think that's just the music."

"Yah, Kirsty. And the adjustment I was thinking of is a stick of dynamite."

His memory might be shaky, but Hannah couldn't fault his flatly delivered opinion of the music that died just before the driver extricated himself. She told him that, letting the name-thing go, but most of her attention was on the men ten yards away.

The fair-haired hulk who worked for Damon was nearly the same impressive height, but built more along the lines of a tanker. Hitching up one of the suspenders holding his pants, he listened with a bulldog scowl to whatever his skipper said to him. She couldn't hear what they were talking about, but his response had Damon turning a deadly glare toward the top of the hill. His entire body seemed to grow bigger as something that bore a startling resemblance to fury corded the muscles in his neck. Seconds later, he whipped his billfold from his back pocket, pressed a handful of bills into the other man's hand and slapped him on the shoulder in a gesture that she could only describe as apologetic. Seconds after that, the big behemoth headed for the boat and Damon was bearing down on his truck as if he could chew the thing up and use the shards for ballast.

The moment she caught the hard glint in his eye, he pulled his glance. He knew she'd been watching him. He didn't seem too pleased about it, either. But by the time he'd unlocked his truck's doors, ushered her in and made sure Mr. Lindstrom got in all right, he'd buried his anger so effectively she might have thought she'd only imagined it. All that remained was the compelling, disturbing edge that had been there all along. That, and a rather weary determination when his passenger changed his mind about where he wanted to go.

"I'll walk from your house, Kirsty."

"You're going home," Damon said, pulling the powerful truck out of the lot.

Ignoring the edict of his driver, Mr. Lindstrom repeated his intention to Hannah, who occupied the bench seat between them. She could practically feel the scowl coming from her left, but she was more concerned at the moment with Mr. Lindstrom's request. She'd been prepared to go along with being his nephew's wife if it would help get him safely home, but with him wanting to go to her house, it became necessary to explain why that wasn't possible.

"You're confusing me with someone else," she told him, as gently as she could. "I don't even know where your nephew's house is. My name is Hannah," she emphasized. "Not Kirsty. I own the café. That one right there." She pointed toward the top of the hill as they approached it. "I was just out for a walk this morning. I try to do that between the breakfast and lunch rush," she explained, "if I get the chance."

His pale blue eyes blinked at her, confusion clearly visible in the craggy lines of his face.

"Lilly Sieverson owns the café," he insisted, though he seemed to be searching his memory even as he spoke. "She has for years."

"She used to own it," Hannah replied, watching him peer toward the sea green building that anchored the left corner at the top of the hill. "Lilly retired and moved to Minneapolis to be near her daughter. I bought the place from her about a month ago."

The discrepancy between what he thought and what he was being told clearly agitated him. Looking worried, he glanced from her in a way that almost made her think he was embarrassed, and stared down at the pipe he clutched in one gnarled fist.

His hands were freckled with age, the joints of his knuckles rounded, and his skin as thin as wet parchment. Blue veins stood out like rivers on a map. She didn't know the man from Adam, but that didn't stop her from placing her hand over his just because he looked as if he could use the contact.

She looked up as they reached the stop sign on Main, her glance moving to her left to check on her little establishment. Damon's dark head had turned toward it, too, and she could see the reflection of the black truck in the big, ruffle-curtained side window of the rustic Pine Café.

Damon said nothing, but when he glanced back, his eyebrows were bolted together. Giving her a quick, totally unreadable glance, he noted her hand resting on the gnarled old one, then eased through the pedestrian tourist traffic weaving in and out of the busy thoroughfare. She wasn't sure why, but she could have sworn she felt the tension in his big body escalate.

Just past the Moose Lodge, Mr. Lindstrom's confusion turned to distress. "Then you are not my nephew's wife?"

She opened her mouth, but it was Damon who spoke.

"Your nephew's wife is blond, Mr. Lindstrom. She's older, too, and not nearly as—" his voice trailed off, his glance totally impersonal as it raked the slender woman between them from the gentle swell of her breasts to her knees "—skinny."

Hannah's eyebrow shot up as she glanced toward him. Damon lifted his eyebrow to match hers, only where her expression questioned his conclusion, his challenged her to call him on it.

"So," he continued, pointedly turning his attention to his other passenger. "That trawler you said you missed. What kind were you talking about?"

The man was not only rude, he possessed the sensitivity of stone. His charming compliment to her aside, the gentleman they were escorting was more in need of reassurance than conversation about a flight of imagination. She'd have told him that, too, if Mr. Lindstrom hadn't been sitting right there.

The best she could do was aim a glare at his perfectly carved profile.

The look Damon shot back at her said he didn't care what she thought. Yet, within a minute, as Damon prodded for an answer by asking more questions, she could feel the hand beneath hers relax. Some of the strain even left Mr. Lindstrom's voice when he started talking about how long the vessel was and how much tonnage it held. Damon then hit him with questions about the type of nets he'd used, and the two proceeded to discuss the pros and cons of trap versus gill.

The debate sounded like a legal case to her rather than methods of netting fish, and she was quite obviously omitted from the conversation. But all she cared about was that the elderly man's distress had eased considerably—and that she had greatly misjudged Damon Jackson.

He wasn't being insensitive at all. He'd simply changed the subject to one he knew the man could remember, using something Mr. Lindstrom was familiar with to calm him down and, maybe, assure him that not all of his memory was as faulty as it appeared to be.

As rough as he was, as rude and difficult as he'd been, she never would have dreamed he possessed such perception.

It only took another minute to turn onto Verna Lake Road. The long, gravel-lined street served only two houses, and both were nestled in the dense stands of pine and spruce that edged nearly every lane and lake in northern Minnesota. They passed the larger of the two, a relatively new, two-story faux-Georgian that looked a tad pretentious in a community where more modest architecture prevailed. Past a dense stretch of spruce and scrub brush sat a square white cottage with fading red trim and a steeply pitched roof, looking like a forgotten stepchild. The little house, with its lace curtains in the windows and pots of geraniums on the porch, looked as old as Lindstrom himself.

When the truck stopped in the narrow driveway, the old man opened the door and slowly unfolded his lanky frame.

"Do you want us to come in with you?"

Her keys jingling in her pocket, Hannah scooted across the seat after him—only to be yanked to a halt by a manaclelike grip on her arm. Damon had obviously used up his quota of sensitivity for the day. Frowning over her shoulder, she met his meaningful glare.

"You've got one minute."

He didn't have time for this. That message was obvious as he let go.

"A minute is all I need. I just want to make sure he gets inside all right."

"I'm not going inside." From where he stood with his hand on top of the open door, Mr. Lindstrom nodded behind him. "I'm going to rest on my porch for a while."

"Will you be okay?"

Puzzlement added a few creases to his jowly features. "Of course," he said, as if he couldn't imagine why she would ask. "Thank you, Hannah." He ducked his head to glance across the seat, fishing lures bobbing. "And you," he added, seeming to have already forgotten Damon's name.

With a faint smile, he closed the door and lifted his hand in a wave. A moment later, he'd hitched up his pants and turned to amble up the alyssum-lined walk to his house. From the looks of the small vegetable garden and the profusion of flowers and well-tended bushes, he clearly knew what he was doing when it came to growing things.

Still concerned, Hannah dubiously eyed the trowel swaying from its loop on his fishing vest. "Does he live alone?"

"That's what I hear."

"Maybe we should call someone to stay with him."

Damon was already backing out of the drive, his attention on avoiding the banks of purple lupine edging the road. "His nephew's family lives there," he said, dipping his head dismissively in the direction of the faux-Georgian with its sweeping cement driveway and huge gray pots of ivy that had been tortured into topiary. The place looked as quiet as the mausoleum it resembled when they passed. "If you're that worried about the old guy, call Neil Lindstrom. He works at the marine supply store on Lake Drive. But if you do talk to him, don't mention my name."

"Why not? If it hadn't been for you, his uncle might have

been hurt. I know you didn't want to be bothered with this,
but you were very nice to—''

"Lady," he muttered, cutting her off, "I've been called a
lot of things before, but nice isn't one of them. Now, I'm
going back to the dock. Do you want to go back there, or do
I drop you off at the café?''

From the corner of his eye, Damon saw her lift her hand
to the base of her throat. The motion seemed graceful to him,
and decidedly protective.

"The café," she murmured, turning her head to the window. "Please."

He heard the faintly injured quality in her voice, and felt
it strike a nerve he didn't even know he had. It was apparent
she hadn't heard of his reputation. But, then, according to
what she'd said a while ago, she'd only been there a month,
and he hadn't done anything lately to make the natives restless. She'd hear about him eventually, though, and once she
did, she wouldn't want anything to do with him, anyway. She
was a member of the tightly knit community he went out of
his way to avoid. Yet, pushing her away first hadn't given
him near the satisfaction it should have.

Already defensive, he glanced over to where she studied
the blur of blue-green fir trees flying by her window.

"What's a woman like you doing moving to Pine Point,
anyway?'' She looked like the country club set to him. Or,
maybe, an urban professional. It was the cut of her hair, the
subtle makeup that didn't look like makeup at all. It took
money to look like that. Or breeding. Never would he have
pictured her owning a nondescript café in a place where, in
winter, church bingo was the highlight of the week. "I could
see you as a tourist, but as for living here, you don't belong
here at all.''

The look she gave him was amazingly eloquent.

"You have no idea what kind of a woman I am,'' she
quietly informed him. "You don't know a thing about me.

I've spent most of my life in the city, but this is where I spent all my summers growing up. I didn't belong where I was,'' she told him in that same soft voice, ''and if you say I don't belong here, then just where do you suggest I go?''

There was no heat in the question. No defense. Just a request for an honest answer that hit Damon harder than he was prepared to admit. He knew all too well how it felt to not fit in anywhere. He knew, too, how it felt to have someone deliberately prod at a vulnerable spot. He'd lived with jibes and taunts all his life. He'd developed calluses in most of those places. But there was nothing tough about the woman beside him. If anything, she looked as if he'd just added a bruise to a wound. One she tried very hard to pretend wasn't there.

Suspecting he'd just ridden roughshod over sensitive ground, feeling like a jerk for protecting himself at her expense, he said nothing. Even when he pulled into the gravel lot below the café to avoid the congestion on the street, he didn't trust himself to say a word. Being physically attracted to her was bad enough. Feeling empathy was downright dangerous.

She opened the door the moment he stopped. ''Thank you for not answering that,'' she murmured, sounding as if she'd fully expected him to respond to her question by telling her to go to hell. The breeze grabbed her hair as she slipped off the seat, flicking the shining strands around her face. She grabbed it right back, catching it at her nape, and turned to face him. ''And thank you for your help with Mr. Lindstrom. I know it was an inconvenience, but I appreciate it. Despite what you think, it was nice of you.''

With that, she closed the door and turned away. It seemed she couldn't get away from him fast enough as she headed for the flight of stairs leading to a back-door marked Deliveries Only.

The slope of the hill put the café's front door at street level. The back of it sat over a vacated welding shop. Situated as the building was, its view of the lake from there was unrestricted. But the only view Damon cared about was of the woman quickly ascending the green-railed stairway, her steps so light she scarcely seemed to touch the wood at all. It took a supple kind of strength to move that way, and it didn't help matters at all that the way she moved had the same effect on him as her scent and her spirit.

His hand tightened on the gearshift knob as he jammed his truck into reverse. She wasn't the only one anxious for distance. It had taken years for the lesson to sink in, but he knew the only way he could keep any peace in his life was to stay as far from involvements as he could.

Chapter Two

You don't belong here.

Hannah hurried up the last few steps, telling herself with each one to put the too-familiar phrase from her mind. There was no reason for the awful anxiety knotting her stomach. Not now. The words meant nothing.

I don't love you, Hannah. I never did. You don't belong here.

The words would have been so much easier to forget had they not been emblazoned in her brain. Even now, nearly a year after the fact, she could visualize her ex-husband's neat, precise handwriting on the note he'd left on her pillow. He hadn't even had the decency at first to tell her to her face that it had never been her that he'd wanted; that she'd only been a substitute for someone he'd thought he couldn't have.

She could still visualize the note. Yet, as she hit the landing, she knew it was only the sentiment Damon Jackson had echoed that still carried the power to shake her. That lonely sense of not belonging, of no longer being part of something that mattered, still left her empty and feeling more than a little lost. She'd been doing just fine all morning. All week, for that matter. Now she could almost hate the man for resurrecting the feelings his charming opinion had evoked.

She could hate him if she'd let herself think about him, she told herself. And that was not something she chose to do. Damon was cynical, mercurial and confusing. He also happened to be the hardest man she'd ever met. Not that she'd ever met anyone remotely like him.

He bore no resemblance at all to steady, uncomplicated types such as her father and uncle. Or, the stoic, salt-of-the-earth sort, as her grandfather had been. And he was the absolute antithesis of the urban professionals she'd known in Minneapolis, her ex-husband included. Not that that was a drawback. The point was simply that he unsettled her in ways that didn't merit defining, and she'd had enough upheaval in the past year to last her a lifetime. She needed to concentrate on running her business. The Pine Café was her life now. It was all she needed. And this town that she'd loved as a child was now her home. She might not truly belong there yet, but she was working on it.

She opened the kitchen's back door, mentally changing gears as she hurried inside and past her small office. She was late returning from her walk, and judging from the sounds filling the slightly rundown, stainless-steel-and-white space, the lunch rush had started early. That meant there was a good possibility Inga, her relief cook, would be in a snit.

Sure enough. The fifty-two-year-old scion of local gossip was up to her coiled, graying-blond braid in prawn salad sandwiches and looking none too happy about life in general when she caught sight of Hannah whipping around the corner.

"Well, there you are," the woman muttered, scarcely sparing her a glance. "I couldn't imagine what was keeping you. You simply have to talk to that girl," she continued, jabbing a spreader into the butter bowl. "She's just like her sister, slower than spring thaw and getting more behind by the minute. There's six orders sitting here to be delivered. If I'd known you were going to be late, I'd have had Brenda or Astrid come in early. They're more interested in working than flitting around the boys the way those two do."

Brenda and Astrid usually took turns working the supper shift. Like the cook, the women, one slightly older than Hannah, the other older than dirt, were as much a part of the rustic little restaurant as the heavy maple tables and pine green gingham curtains out front. That was one of the reasons Hannah had kept them on after she'd bought the place. It wasn't unusual for the new owner of a restaurant to hire new staff so she could put her personal stamp on the operation. But firing three locals from jobs they'd held for years would hardly have endeared her to people who were already afraid she'd "citify" the comfortable old café. As it was, had her grandparents not lived there all their lives, Hannah knew she wouldn't have received the welcome that had been extended to her so far. The locals' acceptance was only tentative, though. She'd have to work hard to keep it.

"I'll take care of her. Just give me one minute," Hannah told the scowling woman as she unzipped her sweatshirt. Inga hadn't liked the idea of hiring high school students from day one. Hannah, however, thought the Holmes twins were doing just fine. Erica and Eden, both blond and bubbly, did tend to bat their baby blues at the young male customers who came in, but they were fast learners, their attitudes were good and the patrons in general seemed to like them. "I need to make a phone call and wash up and I'll be right there."

Impatience flashed as Inga deftly arranged pink shrimp on buttered sourdough. "Can the phone call wait? I'm backed up seven orders. Eight," she amended when Erica shoved another ticket under a peg on the order wheel. "I'm running low on cucumber salad and I need three yellow pea soups and a chowder to go with these.''

Going four directions at once was nothing new for Hannah. A person didn't survive the restaurant business without learning how to put out a fire with one hand while garnishing a plate with the other. She also had a knack for swallowing personal irritations and concerns until the crisis of the moment was over—which was why she overlooked the older woman's proprietary instructions and picked up the portable phone on her way to the washroom. She never liked to keep customers waiting, but her conscience wouldn't let her do anything until she'd contacted someone about Mr. Lindstrom.

Her concern was real, but her motives weren't totally altruistic. The sooner she made the call, the sooner she could put the entire encounter with Damon Jackson out of her mind.

The familiar din of customers' conversations and cutlery clatter drifted through the service window above the work station. After quickly securing her hair in a neat knot at her nape, she tied her burgundy apron over her white Pine Café T-shirt while she held the phone to her ear with her shoulder to get the marine supply store's phone number from directory assistance.

Seconds later, waiting for Neil Lindstrom to be summoned to the phone, she was scrubbing her hands with the thoroughness of a doctor preparing for surgery. By the time the brusque-voiced Neil came on the line, she'd made her way to the tall stainless steel pots simmering on the stove, ladled up four cups of steaming, savory soup for Inga's order and snagged the next order from the wheel.

Inga asked for another chowder.

Now was not the time to remind the woman who worked for whom. Hannah ladled up the soup, then finished two chef's salads while she introduced herself to Neil Lindstrom and told him about her encounter with his uncle that morning. She didn't mention Damon. Partly because he'd asked her not to, but mostly because she had the distinct feeling there was no love lost between him and the man she was speaking with now. She didn't know who had the problem with whom, but it wasn't *her* problem, so she wasn't going to worry about it. She cared only that Neil said he'd check on his uncle. Since she didn't know the man, she could hardly judge his reaction, but she could have sworn he sounded more annoyed than concerned by her call.

Having done what she could, wondering vaguely if it was enough, she punched the button marked End Call on the phone. After dropping it into the wide pocket of her apron, she picked up the three plates for table five and backed out the swinging door.

She delivered that order and two of the others, refilled water glasses for the diners at the counter, then slipped up behind Erica to tell the tall, wholesome-looking high school senior that she was doing great, but she needed to hustle with filling the orders and clearing dead tables. The little café only seated twenty-four, twenty-seven if she counted the three high chairs, but when it filled up all at once, even the most experienced waitress could get behind.

When she had everything under control in front, she headed back into the kitchen and snagged the next order from the wheel.

Inga was dealing out slices of cheese like a card shark. "So that's why you were late," she said, as if there hadn't been a two-minute lapse since she'd overheard Hannah's telephone conversation. "It's too bad about Mr. Lindstrom," she continued, her nose back in joint now that she understood why Hannah hadn't returned on time. "You hear of old folks losing their memory and being confused and such, but I never thought it would happen to him. Up until a month or so ago, you'd never have known a thing was wrong. He was getting a bit crochety, mind you, but he was sharp as a tack." The bright overhead light caught the diamond weave of her gray hairnet when she shook her head. "This would be the second or third spell he's had now."

"Do you know what's wrong with him?"

Inga lifted a rounded shoulder and started dealing tomato slices. "Just getting old, I suppose. Lucky he has Neil to look after him. Never married, you know."

"Neil?"

Inga's expression held enormous patience. "Mr. Lindstrom. Neil married Kirsty Swensen. Didn't your mother or grandma ever mention the people around here to you?"

Turning from the big stainless steel refrigerator, Hannah murmured that they hadn't. All her mom had ever said about the residents of Pine Point was that they were salt of the earth, but that a person couldn't sneeze without someone spreading the word that he or she had a cold. As for her grandmother, Margretha Olson had been so into her painting and pottery that she'd rarely left her quiet woodland home long enough to hear what was going on with anyone, much less take the time to repeat it.

"Well," Inga confided, more than happy to fill the gap in Hannah's knowledge, "the only Lindstroms around anymore are Neil and his uncle, but Neil was the town's favorite son for a while. He was captain of our hockey team and went to the university on a hockey scholarship some fifteen years or so ago. The professionals were even looking at him in college.

"Nothing ever came of it," she hastened to add, sounding as if his failure had been a disappointment to the whole community, "but he and Kirsty got married before they found out he wasn't going to be picked or drafted or whatever it is they do. She was homecoming queen that year, I think. Or maybe it was Miss Snow Daze for the winter carnival.

"It was Snow Daze," she said decisively, getting side-tracked with the details she prided herself on keeping straight. "I'm sure it was because I remember her being pregnant with their first baby when she crowned the Jansson girl the following year. That was when she brought a torte that was tough as a hockey puck for the cakewalk. Poor thing still can't cook to save her soul. About poisoned us all at the Good Shepherd Christmas smorgasbord one year. But she gives her time to charity and her father owns the marine supply store. Everyone knows that's why Neil is the manager there.

"So," she went on, having dished out that gossipy bit of history along with the plates she set in the service window, "just how confused was Louie?"

Keeping up with Inga required a playlist. Unless Hannah was mistaken, Mr. Lindstrom's only local relative worked for his father-in-law and his wife couldn't cook. Somewhere in there someone with the same last name as the local sheriff had succeeded Neil's wife as Snow Daze queen. "Louie?"

"Lindstrom."

The problem with Inga was that Hannah couldn't always tell when the woman was looking for fodder for the gossip mill, or when she was truly concerned about the welfare of another. It was entirely possible that with Inga and her ilk, there wasn't that much difference.

She wanted to give Inga the benefit of the doubt. But she also felt oddly protective of the elderly gentleman she'd met that morning. If what Inga had said was true—that Mr. Lindstrom was usually quite together, his "spells," as she'd called them, had to be extremely upsetting. If he even remembered them after they happened.

"I'd say he seemed a little foggy on details," Hannah returned by way of compromise. Meat sizzled as she placed a chicken breast on the hooded grill behind her and sprinkled it with seasoning. "He seemed better when we got him home. Maybe that was because he was around familiar things again. I know Grandma always did better at home when she was having one of her bad days."

"Who's we?"

Hannah could practically see Inga's antenna rise on either side of her coiled braid. "We?"

"You said by the time 'we' got him home. Who were you with?"

Talking to Inga was like fishing with a gill net. Nothing got past her. Hannah hadn't even realized what she'd said until the woman picked up on it. Even then, the question was innocent enough. It was the image the question put in Hannah's mind that caused her to hesitate.

"A fisherman," she finally said. A very big, very…disturbing…fisherman. "I didn't have my car, so we used his to drive Mr. Lindstrom home.

"You know, Inga," she continued, deliberately motioning toward the few remaining orders to be prepared, "I think you can handle this now. I'm going to run down to the freezer for more stock and put on another pot of soup. We've already gone through the yellow pea."

If Inga found anything suspicious in the abrupt change of subject, she didn't let on. She just kept turning out sandwiches and salads and frowning at the youthful waitress who was doing a far better job than Inga wanted to admit.

Hannah was frowning herself as she turned away. Partly at Inga. Mostly at the image of the fisherman that had fixed in her mind. Determined to ignore the latter, she concentrated on how the older woman's uncompromising attitude toward Erica and her sister kept getting worse instead of better. If staff didn't get along, the business itself suffered, and she didn't want that kind of stress in her establishment. Before she talked to Inga, though, she needed to know if the woman had always had a problem with teenage staff, or if her picky attitude was a subtle form of rebellion for Hannah having taken over the café.

She'd no sooner decided to ask her evening waitress, the level-headed Brenda, her opinion when the image she was trying to block fixed more firmly in her mind—the image of muscular shoulders, a wicked-looking tattoo, storm gray eyes and a mouth that could make a woman go weak in the knees.

The man definitely wasn't one a person easily forgot, she conceded, and turned into her office to retrieve the keys for the lower stairwell door and the freezer.

She thought she'd left her key ring in the pocket of her sweat jacket. Obviously, she hadn't. She checked the other pocket, and the pocket on her apron, in case she'd been so preoccupied that she hadn't paid attention to what she was doing and put her keys in there. Considering what she'd been thinking about when she'd come in, that could certainly have been the case.

They weren't in her apron, either.

She checked her desk. The kitchen floor. The backstairs. Beginning to appreciate the frustration of the contentious fisherman she'd met that morning, she tried to recall when she'd last had them. She remembered hearing them jangle in her pocket when they'd left Mr. Lindstrom's house, so she checked the gravel lot below the café where Damon had let her out. When she didn't find them there, frustration gave way to an indefinable sort of unease.

She could think of only one other place they could be.

It was five-thirty the following morning when Hannah hurried down the hill toward the dock. Pebbles skittered in front of her on the cracked and narrow street, the small sounds magnified by the stillness. Sunrise was nearly half an hour off, but the eastern sky already revealed the first threads of pink morning light on the horizon. She didn't know what time Damon normally arrived at the dock, but she knew that many of the commercial boats left before sunup. Her first week in Pine Point, she'd often watched their lights disappear beyond the breakwater from her apartment above the café, grateful that the night was almost over. Since she opened the café at seven, she figured her best bet was to get to his boat early so she wouldn't miss him. If he wasn't yet there, she'd just leave a note taped to the door of his wheelhouse.

The single street lamp at the end of the road cast its spare glow over the gravel parking lot. At the fringes of that pale light, she spotted a dark truck among the other cars and vehicles nosed up to the horizontal logs defining the space. The truck was parked in a different place than Damon's had been yesterday, though, and she didn't know trucks well enough to be absolutely certain the one she noted was his. The one vehicle she did recognize was the white van with the Feldsons' Fresh Fish logo on the side. She bought fish from Axel and Jen Feldson for the café. Offering a smile and a wave to the couple as they pulled on waist-high rubber pants beside the van, she jogged down the worn wood steps and headed purposefully past the trawlers being loaded with coiled ropes and cooler chests. The boat she wanted was moored near the far end of the dock.

Few of the dozen or so fishermen going about their morning routines paid her any mind as she hurried along. Or, if they did, she didn't notice. Her attention was on Damon's dark shape as he moved around behind his battered boat. As she drew closer, she could see that he was loading a pile of gear from the dock behind the *Naiad*'s stern.

In the reflection of the wheelhouse and running lights bouncing off the inky water, she saw him reach for a thick, coiled cable, loop it over his shoulder, then snag two heavy red fuel cans in his expansive grip. Without missing a beat, he turned to the back of his boat, clamped his hand over the stern's thick lip and stuck his booted foot on the third rung of the short ladder tagging the boat's name. In one fluid motion, he swung himself up and over the stern's peeling wood. With that same economy of motion, he disposed of his load and swung his tall, powerful body back onto the dock.

The oddly graceful choreography stopped Hannah in her tracks. He moved as easily as if he'd been weighted down with nothing more than a sack of air, hard muscles bunching and shifting effortlessly beneath worn fleece and fatigues. The man was obviously no stranger to hard work.

"Good morning," she said, watching him reach for a long, rolled-up tarp.

The hesitation in her greeting was reflected in her expression when his head snapped up.

Seeing her, seeing the unease she tried to hide, he suddenly looked a little hesitant himself.

"Isn't this a little early for you?" Defensiveness marked his compelling features as he shouldered his load. "You told Lindstrom you don't come down here until sometime between breakfast and lunch."

It was apparent from the annoyed edge in his tone that he rather wished she'd stuck to her schedule. Sympathizing, since she would have liked to avoid him, too, she started to tell him why she was there, but he'd already turned his back to her and was calling for his deckhand.

"Marty," he shouted, his deep voice carrying over the slap of waves along the thirty-foot length of the boat. "Stow this and start her up."

From where Hannah stood ten feet away, she saw Damon's employee, the one with the square build of a tanker, emerge from below the deck. Without a word, the taciturn sailor took the tarp when Damon held it up and set about the tasks he was paid to perform. He never looked at her or at his skipper, his bulldog expression giving the impression of a man who did his job only because he had to work, and who could easily be bought by another operation for another buck an hour. Men like him showed up on the docks every spring and departed like migrating birds when winter ended employment. There was nothing for outsiders in Pine Point once the commercial season was over.

Had she not known that Damon owned the boat, she'd have

been hard pressed to think of him as anything other than a rough vagabond himself.

"I know you're in a hurry," Hannah called out, thinking him rough, anyway. "I just need to know if you've seen my keys. I think they might be in your truck."

He'd picked up a large green-and-white cooler. Stopping long enough to surreptitiously eye the way her breasts plumped over her tightly crossed arms, he shook his head. The cool breeze slashed strands of dark hair over his forehead, making him look as rakish as he undoubtedly was when he carried that disturbing glance up the long line of her throat to her mouth.

"I haven't seen them."

"Would you mind looking? Not now," she hurried to add, easing one hand to her shoulder to block his view when his glance drifted down again. "I have my cook's set, so I don't need them to open the café. But if you'd check your truck when it's convenient and let me know, I'd really appreciate it."

For a moment, he said nothing. He just watched her, his eyes glinting hard as diamonds in the reflected lights. Hers was a simple request, and he'd either do it, or he wouldn't. Yet, as his shadowed glance moved over her face, he seemed to be considering something far weightier than letting her know if he had her keys.

"I'll look when I get back," he finally said.

Her soft smile held relief. "Thanks. A lot." Anxious to be on her way, she took a careful step backward, lifting her hand toward his boat as she did. "Good luck."

His dark eyebrows darted together. "What?"

"With your fishing," she expanded, unable to imagine what else he thought she was talking about since she'd been pointing at his boat.

It was a moment before he slowly lifted his chin in acknowledgement, but his eyes remained locked on hers, no longer quite so cool, so dismissing. Hannah wasn't sure exactly what it was, but something about his questioning look made it seem as if he wasn't accustomed to anyone wishing him luck with the day's catch, and that he simply hadn't been sure how to respond.

That such a small, everyday consideration should catch him so off guard made her wonder if he wasn't accustomed to anyone wanting anything good for him at all.

Uneasy with that thought, unnerved by the way his gaze tugged at something deep inside her, she turned with a squeak of her sneakers on the dew-dampened wood and hurried back down the dock.

The feel of those fathomless eyes branded her back all the way.

Damon didn't move until he saw Hannah reach the stairs. It was only then that he remembered the other fishermen. Many of them were watching her, too, but curious glances had also turned in his direction, most of the latter belonging to owners of the other boats.

He'd bet the day's catch that they were wondering what a woman like Hannah Davis was doing talking to the likes of him.

Skimming his glance past old Ernie Pedersen three slips away, he blocked out the stares and the speculation as he always did. He had a job to do, and as long as he concentrated on getting it done, no one had any cause to find any more fault with him than they already did. He liked his work, anyway. When he was out on the water, it was just him and the elements and that suited him just fine. He needed nothing else.

He found her keys that evening, wedged between the seat and the seat back of his truck.

Two days later, he still had them.

Damon didn't fish on Sunday. The practice had nothing to do with any religious conviction. He hadn't set foot in a church since his father's funeral six months ago, and he couldn't begin to remember when he'd been in one before that. He didn't fish because the broker who bought his catch didn't work on Sunday, so he usually spent the day tending the *Naiad*'s infirmities or working on the ramshackle house where he'd been born. The old shake-roofed structure had been in worse shape than the boat and it still needed a ton of work. But at least the roof no longer leaked, the front porch no longer sagged, and he'd patched the gaps around the windows.

Today, though, he couldn't seem to concentrate on the house or the boat.

He leaned against the sidewall of the *Naiad*, his feet braced on the scrubbed deck and a can of beer dangling from one hand. The breakwater at the mouth of the tiny inlet cut the force of Superior's oceanlike waves, but, like him, the water was never truly calm. The boat rocked gently, the motion as familiar as the cry of the loons farther down the shore. He should be greasing his wench. Instead, he stood studying the keys the woman from the café had come looking for.

A small fob dangled from the crowded silver ring. It was one of those novelty items a person could buy at a fair or in a souvenir store, the kind that held a card in clear plastic and told the meaning of a name. The card was pink, the flowing script on it spelling out Hannah. On the line below the name it read Gracious And Merciful.

He didn't know if she'd bought the thing to remind herself of what she should be, or if someone had given it to her because they thought she already possessed those qualities. But from what little he knew of grace or mercy, and having seen her with the old man, he couldn't help thinking that she'd been named well.

His fist closed over the keys, metal biting into his palm. He needed to stop thinking about her. Mostly, he needed to stop thinking about how she'd looked just before she got out of his truck and practically bolted for her back door. He hated that what he'd said to her bothered him as much as it had. It *still* bothered him. And he hated that, too.

Raising his beer, he drained the can and crushed it in his fist. He didn't know where she lived. Only that she owned the café, and he really didn't want to go there. As long as he stuck to his boat and his house, he was fine. In town, he could seldom go anywhere without raising an eyebrow or being whispered about. He didn't care what the locals thought of him. He was irredeemable in their eyes, and they might well be right. He just didn't want to create the opportunity for someone to accuse him of something he didn't do. Half the locals were looking for any excuse to see him gone, but he hadn't done anything in the months since he'd returned except mind his own business. That was all he intended to continue doing, too.

He decided to wait until midafternoon, when the café was likely to be the least crowded, to return Hannah's keys.

The decision made, he pocketed the keys, grabbed another beer from the cooler and headed for the cable wench.

Damon had miscalculated. He realized that even before he stepped inside the little restaurant. Beyond the ruffled gingham curtains on the windows, he could see that most of the café's tables were full. Thinking only that he wanted to get this over with, he walked in, anyway.

The tinkle of the bell over the door sounded seconds before he breathed in the tantalizing aroma of good, hearty food. Reminded by the savory scents that he'd worked through lunch, he glanced from the customers at the short counter to those at the tables along the windows.

The place was smaller than he remembered it. But then he hadn't been in the café since its previous owner had kicked him out some fifteen years ago because "his type" wasn't welcome there. The frilly green curtains looked new, but the heavy maple tables and chairs seemed vaguely familiar. So did the silence that fell over the small group seated at the counter.

He figured most of the diners were summer people—couples and young families that had come up for the day, the weekend or the week. The middle-aged couple at the nearest table and the two older men downing hamburgers at the counter were definitely locals, though. They were the ones who'd stopped talking the instant he'd set foot inside the door. As if prompted by some invisible signal, their glances simultaneously raked from the tattoo visible below the short sleeve of his dark olive T-shirt to his worn khaki fatigues.

The waitress, a petite, thirty-something brunette in slacks and a white T-shirt with The Pine Café embroidered above her right breast, turned to see who'd interrupted her conversation with the couple. She hesitated, her hazel eyes widening just enough to let him know she recognized him, too. He thought he might have gone to high school with her, but he wasn't sure. All he cared about at the moment was that he'd stepped into a place where he didn't belong, and his reception was the same as always.

The few defenses he hadn't already raised locked firmly into place. He hated the suspicion and hostility he'd always encountered in this town. Even now, after having been gone for years, it was still there, fueling the anger building inside him. He hadn't realized until that moment just how much of the rage he'd once battled still existed. It wasn't usually so close to the surface, so demanding in its need to be acknowledged.

That anger burned like acid in his gut when the door from the kitchen swung open. The woman he'd come to see was suddenly there, two heaped plates in her hands. She hesitated, too, but more out of surprise than wariness.

"Hi," Hannah greeted him, suddenly aware of the quiet descending over her busy little establishment. The clatter of silverware continued to lessen. Conversations turned to murmurs. Only the kids were talking in normal tones.

She moved closer to the rugged man blocking the door, offering him the same smile she skimmed past the couple at the table beside her. She had no trouble understanding the hush falling over the room. Damon was not the sort of man a person could ignore. There was a powerful, rather intimidating air about him that tended to stop people in their tracks, make them want to back up a step. But, at the moment, the raw tension he radiated made that power seem downright…dangerous.

She deliberately masked a flash of unease. "Are you coming in to eat?"

"I came to see you."

At the deep rumble of his voice, even the children fell silent.

Not caring to interrupt her customers, or provide them with a sideshow, she signaled Brenda with the lift of her chin. "Come on back," she told him, then handed her curiously silent waitress the plates, smiling at the two ladies they were intended for, and headed back the way she'd come.

On the other side of the kitchen door, the muffled hum of the stove fan met the scrape of a metal spatula against the grill.

"As I was saying," Inga continued, picking up her interrupted conversation as deftly as she flipped the burger, "Elsa and the deacon got into an argument over the ladies auxiliary using the church hall for bingo on council meeting nights, and the whole congregation…"

Within a split second of peering up from her task, the woman cut herself off. Suddenly looking as if she was about to choke on whatever she'd left unsaid, she bounced a startled glance over Damon.

Had Inga been anyone else, it would have been logical to think it was the unexpected sight of the tall, decidedly tense stranger that made her forget what she'd been saying. Knowing the opinionated woman as she did, Hannah was more inclined to think it was Damon's appearance that earned him her quick, thin-lipped disapproval.

Looking quite disgusted, the cook ran her narrow-eyed glance from the strands of dark hair tumbling over his forehead to the grease streaks on his pants. It was as plain as oatmeal that she didn't think a man in soiled work clothes belonged in what she not-so-secretly regarded as ''her'' kitchen.

''Excuse us for a minute,'' Hannah said, more than willing to remove him from her presence.

Touching Damon's arm, thinking a chunk of marble would have more give to it, she motioned him into her office. The dishwasher was directly across from its door. Since it was running, she pulled the door to cut the noise and to block Inga's patently nosy glare, and turned to face him.

The instant she looked up, she wished she'd left the door open.

The room was little more than an oversized closet, barely big enough for the desk and file cabinets crammed into it. Even with each allowing the other as much space as possible, only three feet of floor space separated them.

It might as well have been three inches. His brooding presence seemed to fill the space, touching her with a force that was almost physical.

''I found your keys.''

''You did?''

''They were wedged in the seat.''

She watched his hand slide into the front pocket of his pants, then slip back out, past a small, mended rip in fabric worn soft from washing. His belt loops sported a few stray threads and the fabric near his zipper was faded from wear. Rather than looking as if he couldn't afford better, his clothes gave the impression that he simply took care of what he was comfortable with.

She was trying to imagine his big hands mending that tear, finding the thought totally incongruous, when she realized she was staring at the front of his pants. With a mental groan, she jerked her glance to the middle of his impossibly wide chest. The view there was only marginally less disturbing.

"When I didn't hear from you, I thought that meant they weren't in your truck. I couldn't imagine where else they could be." She met his guarded gray eyes, her smile coming more easily now that she knew why he was there. "I know how busy you are. You're very kind to bring them."

Seconds ago, Damon's only thought had been to hand over the keys, tell her he'd have returned them sooner if he'd known where she lived, and to head straight back to his boat. But she'd called him kind. Again. What amazed him more was that she looked at him as if she actually believed he was.

The anger he'd felt a minute ago receded like an outgoing tide. No one had ever called him kind before. No one had ever before looked to him for help, either. Not the way she had done with old man Lindstrom. He'd wanted to believe that hadn't mattered. But it had. And he couldn't deny how good it had made him feel.

All he'd done for her in return was make her feel bad when he'd told her she didn't belong there. The unwanted and totally unfamiliar empathy he'd felt for her refused to let him forget that.

Feeling big and awkward, he reached for her hand, hesitating a moment before he set her keys in her palm. Even as badly as he'd treated her, she'd still been gracious enough to wish him well with his catch.

"You asked me something the other day. About where I'd suggest you go if you don't belong one place or another. Please," he said, stopping her when she started to pull her hand away. He relaxed his grip, trying to get past his own guard. "I shouldn't have said what I did."

He looked down at her hand, drawn by the softness of her skin, the delicacy of her bones. Her nails were short and unpolished, her fingers long and tapered. Her hand looked so small in his, so fragile. He'd scrubbed his own hands before he'd come there, but they were still rough, callused, scarred. Like him.

"Some people never fit in anywhere, Hannah. Or they try to fit where they can't." He skimmed his thumb over the delicate veins in her wrist, felt the flutter of her pulse. "If you ever find that happening, you just make a place where you do belong." His voice dropped. "Even if you're the only one in it."

He hadn't realized how badly he'd wanted to touch her until he'd felt her soft skin against his. And now that he was touching her, he didn't want to let go. But he was good at denying himself what he wanted. He'd had a lifetime of practice.

He slipped his hand away before she could pull back herself, a little surprised that she hadn't already.

"I better get out of here."

"Damon. Wait."

She stopped him as he took a step toward the door, her hand catching his arm. The top of her head barely reached his chin, and she had to tip her head back to look up at him. When she did, the vulnerability in her lovely face nearly stole his breath.

It seemed he'd done it again, touched on something she related to all too well. But at least hurt wasn't clouding her eyes this time. This time, she held his glance with an openness that gave her no defenses at all.

Hannah didn't know what to say. She didn't even know why she'd stopped him, except that she couldn't just let him go. As she searched the gray eyes steadily holding hers, all she could think was that she'd had no idea he'd realized how badly she needed to find a new place for herself. Or how she'd once tried so hard to fit where she had never belonged. She couldn't imagine him sharing something so telling about himself, either. It seemed as unlikely as the patience he'd shown a confused old man.

A dull thump sounded from the other side of the wall. The instant the sound registered, Damon's guarded glance moved to where her hand rested on his arm.

Aware of the tension creeping into his body, she slowly eased her hand away. It was entirely possible that he didn't even realize how much of himself he'd just revealed. Or maybe he knew exactly what he'd done and that was why he again looked so defensive. But, because of the advice he'd just given her, she had the feeling that Damon had been forced to create a world for himself—and that he was very much alone in it.

Deeply touched, oddly shaken, she finally murmured a quiet "Thank you."

His response was nothing more than the tightening of his jaw. Looking as if he wished he hadn't come there at all, he reached past her and pushed open the door

Inga, on the other side, promptly backed into the steaming dishwasher.

"Where's the back way out?"

At Damon's low demand, she aimed her spatula toward the end of the short hall. "Right there."

Hannah scarcely noticed her cook's dour expression. She wasn't aware of much of anything except Damon as he disappeared into the bright sunshine outside, and the totally unexpected understanding he had offered. He knew nothing about her. Yet, he knew everything that mattered.

She opened her hand, staring at the keys he'd folded into her palm. It was possible, too, that he had just told her everything that mattered about him.

"Good Lord, Hannah. Do you know who that is?"

Chapter Three

Hannah had worked with Inga Olafson for over a month. It had only been after she'd asked a few judicious questions of Brenda about her, however, that she'd really gotten a handle on her relief cook. The fact that she'd overheard the twins refer to her as Brunhild the Hun had more or less confirmed her conclusions.

Inga was a woman who had an opinion about everything, and who spared no one her thoughts. She loved to meddle, and since her children were grown and had moved away and her husband worked a freighter out of Duluth for a week at a time, she had no one around to castigate, dominate or irritate. As a result, she tended to make up for that lack by pouncing on any impropriety, real or perceived, with the zeal of the newly converted. At the moment, however, there was definitely something more to her censure than disapproval of a man's physical appearance. Her demand had bordered on incredulous.

"His name's Damon," Hannah replied, though it was apparent Inga already knew that.

"What on earth was the likes of him doing here?"

"He was returning my keys," she replied, quite reasonably. "They fell out in his truck when we took Mr. Lindstrom home the other day."

"He's the one who helped you?"

"I asked him to. I couldn't manage Mr. Lindstrom by myself." Hannah's frown now mirrored Inga's. She was hardly accountable to her for her actions, but she had no reason not to answer, either. "What do you mean by the likes of him? What's the problem?"

"The problem," she pronounced, since Hannah was so obviously clueless, "is that Damon Jackson is nothing but trouble waiting to happen. He's looking for trouble right here, too," she insisted. "I could tell when I watched him follow you into your office."

"You could?"

"Absolutely. He was looking at you like he wanted you served up for his supper or something. That was pure lust in that man's eyes." She crossed her arms over her ample chest, seeming to shudder at the very thought. "No decent woman would have a thing to do with that one."

Hannah had gone utterly still. It was hard for her to tell which disconcerted her more: the woman's observations, her conclusions or what she meant by "trouble." Since the latter almost seemed safer, she decided to start there. "What has he done?"

"It's more like what *hasn't* he done," Inga muttered. Looking more like a mother hen now than a wet one, she lowered her voice as she always did when she was getting into something truly juicy. "That boy was always raising Cain, getting into fights, destroying property. He'd get to drinking and use that highway out there like it was a race-track." Her rounded features pinched, giving her the appearance of a plump, desperately anemic prune. "He has the morals of an alley cat, too. He nearly ruined the reputation of a nice girl from a fine family here. Heaven only knows how many others he led astray.

"He never had any respect for anyone," she continued, lumping all his transgressions under that one glaring flaw. "He still doesn't. I can't believe he'd come in here as dirty as he was. And I could smell beer on him. Couldn't you?"

Hannah ignored the query. She also didn't bother pointing out that Damon had obviously been working before he'd stopped by, or that he'd appeared quite sober. She didn't mention, either, that having a beer or two was hardly cause for criticism. Half the fund-raisers in town would suffer if there wasn't a keg to go with the polka band and spiced herring. Inga's other accusations had raised more disturbing questions.

What had he fought about? Who was the girl? There was *lust* in his eyes? "What did he destroy?"

"A row of mailboxes for one thing. I remember that Ollie Sieverson had just put up a new one. Damon plowed right through the whole line of them with his car, drunk as a skunk. You wouldn't have known Ollie," she added, apparently thinking that Hannah had frowned because she didn't recognize the name. "He was the oldest brother of Ernie Sieverson, who comes in here with the sheriff. He passed on years ago. Ollie, not Ernie. Heart attack." She paused, concentrating. "Or maybe it was a stroke. It's strokes that run in their family, I think."

Hannah held up her hand, cutting Inga off before she could get any further into the Sieversons' medical history. Privacy was a pipe dream in Pine Point. "You said Ollie had just put up a new mailbox, but that he'd died years ago. How many years are you talking about?"

"I don't remember," Inga muttered, not sure what that had to do with anything. The offense was what counted. "It must be fifteen or so, by now. But I do remember that they put him in detention for a few months…the Jackson boy, not Ollie,'' she clarified, planting her fists on her hips. ''He was more trouble than ever when he got out. Of course, that father of his was half the problem. If he'd made the boy go to school instead of working him on that eyesore of a boat, something might have come of him. He died here last winter. Late February, it was. That's when Damon came back.''

''He'd been gone?''

''For years. Must have been ten at least. Pity he just didn't stay wherever it was he'd taken off to.''

That conclusion was delivered just as Brenda called a brisk ''Order in'' through the service window. Inga's head snapped around. Turning the rest of her body in the same direction, she headed for the window and pulled the ticket from the wheel.

Hannah followed more slowly. ''So these things he did…'' she prefaced, wanting to make sure she understood what she'd heard. ''They happened when he was a kid?''

''That and more. If there was a problem at the high school or the docks, you could darn near bet money that Jackson boy was at the root of it.''

The outspoken cook had missed the point of the question, but her response provided enough of an answer to give Hannah pause.

''What about lately?'' Everything Inga mentioned was in the past tense, and she kept referring to Damon as ''that Jackson boy'' as if the years that had turned him into a man counted for nothing. A hard man, granted. And a disturbing, confusing one. But he was definitely no longer a kid. ''You said he'd been gone for a long time. Has he done anything since his return?''

''I haven't heard of anything, but it's hard telling what all he got himself into while he was away. Or what trouble he's going to cause,'' she added, making it clear she thought it only a matter of time before his past repeated itself. ''Once a hellion, always a hellion. You can't change a person like that.''

She punctuated her pronouncement with the clap of the heavy lid on a soup pot and set the bowl she'd just filled on a plate.

"Don't worry. People will understand that you didn't know who he was." She offered the assurance with a benevolent smile, making it apparent that, under the circumstances, Hannah would be excused for her association with the man. "But now that you do know, you'll be well advised to keep him out of here."

From the day Hannah had taken over, Inga had clearly regarded herself as having certain advantages over her new boss. She knew the town better. She knew the customers better. She knew the vendors better—points Hannah willingly conceded. But Hannah had rapidly gained ground in those areas herself. Because Inga was an amazingly good cook, and good cooks could be amazingly difficult to find on short notice, Hannah tended to overlook the woman's terminal chattiness, her nosiness and, for the most part, her tendency to want to run the café. She would not, however, allow her to dictate who she would and would not serve.

She moved closer, deliberately adding the garnish she'd repeatedly told Inga to put on each plate, but which Inga consistently "forgot" because she'd never done it that way before. Hannah considered herself a fair person, and her willingness to give second chances, and third if need be, had earned her the loyalty of many an employee. Her ability to listen to complaints and concerns had also, on more than one occasion, kept temperamental chefs and staff from skewering one another. That was why her ex-husband, one of those temperamental chefs, insisted she run interference between the kitchen and the front of the house in the elegant restaurant they'd owned together.

She'd had little experience, however, with this particular circumstance.

"I appreciate what you're saying, Inga, but we don't discriminate in this establishment. Unless Mr. Jackson gives us a specific reason to keep him out, he's as welcome here as anyone else."

The woman's eyebrows merged. "You can't mean that."

"I can and I do. I always reserve the right to refuse service, but he hasn't given me any reason to do that."

"I just gave you reasons."

"You told me about what he'd done before he left. You said yourself that he'd been gone for years and that he hasn't done anything since he returned. All *I've* seen him do is work on his boat, help an elderly man and return something to me that I'd lost." It wasn't necessary to mention that she felt a little threatened by him herself. Or to comment on the edge he possessed, the defensiveness he wore like a shield. There was a principle to defend. Just because he'd shared what he had with her, just because she suspected there was more to Damon than first met the eye, had nothing to do with anything. "I doubt he'll come back here, anyway, considering the reception he got. But if he does, we treat him like anyone else."

"Well, he'd better not come on my shift," she muttered when Hannah stepped away. "Because I'm not cooking for a Jackson."

From the set look on the woman's face, it was apparent that she felt quite comfortable with her position. The way Inga saw it, Hannah needed her to keep the place going. After all, she'd been the summer cook for the previous owner for more than twenty years and Hannah could hardly handle lunch and dinner alone. What she failed to realize was that Hannah didn't back down when a principle was involved.

"If that's the case, then you're free to leave anytime," Hannah said, and picked up the next order herself.

* * *

Inga quit. Hannah wasn't particularly surprised, but she wasn't pleased, either. Especially when it became clear that the woman expected her to beg her to stay, then left in a huff when she didn't. But she didn't have time to worry about the ramifications of letting the loquacious woman go. The last two weeks of August were the busiest Pine Point had seen. The café was open from seven in the morning until nine at night, seven days a week through the summer months. Without another cook to spell her, Hannah practically lived in the kitchen.

If she wasn't working on an order, she was preparing food for later, ordering meats and produce, checking deliveries or cleaning. There were always dishes and pans to wash, a floor to mop, a grill, a stove or a rest room to clean, a linen order to count, a vendor to pay. The thought of taking a break, much less getting out for a while, was a fantasy she didn't even have time to indulge. The only break she managed was the six hours between falling asleep as she hit the bed in her apartment upstairs and dragging herself into the shower the next morning to start all over again.

She didn't know what she'd have done without Brenda and the twins. When Astrid quit out of loyalty to Inga, Brenda volunteered to work double shifts and Erica and Eden went from part-time to full. Between the four of them, they managed to survive with no real problems at all right through Labor Day.

It was then that the face of the town changed overnight. The people who owned summer cabins closed them for the winter and returned to the cities. The pleasure boats were trailered away, leaving the new dock all but abandoned. Many of the locals who owned the quaint little antique, curio and art shops along Main boarded them up and headed off to stock up for next year, or took a vacation themselves before spending a winter creating the paintings or pottery to be sold once the tourists returned.

Only the nine hundred locals remained. They were the true "lake people," and they seemed to emerge as if they'd been in hiding, coming out to enjoy the crisp air now that there were fewer cars to pollute it, and to venture into the establishments the summer people had overrun. Bowling leagues started up. The community theater posted notices in the businesses along Main for tryouts for its winter production. High school football was the focal point of every Friday night. And the biggest crowd in the café, if a dozen people at any given time could be called that, came at breakfast.

Morning was when people would stop by for a cup of coffee, a plate of Swedish pancakes and news of their neighbors before heading on to work. Dinner was more sporadic, but she had a small group of regulars at lunch, too. It was through those people that the bedrock of the community was exposed, and through them she learned that, in Pine Point, people were definitely judged by the strength of their character, who they were related to and the company they kept.

She hadn't seen Damon since he'd returned her keys two months ago. But thanks to Inga, word had spread like a swarm of honeybees that Hannah had been "friendly" to him in her café. The result of that behavior had been all manner of unsolicited advice from good people who wanted to protect her from what they thought she didn't know. She'd nearly lost count of well-intentioned locals who'd stopped in to see what she'd done to "their" café and to share a memory of her mom and her grandparents along with their warnings.

Fortunately, by mid-October, comments about Damon were limited mostly to brief mentions of someone having seen him at a gas station or down at the old dock. Inevitably, the mention of his name would get someone going about an old transgression, but for the most part, the warnings had ended.

At least, they had until Dorothy Yont, the retired postmistress, stopped in for a slice of Hannah's Tosca cake.

"I remember when you were not more than six or seven

and your grandpa would bring you and your big sister into town to show you off,'' Dorothy said, methodically dipping a piece of the tender, almond-crusted pastry into the decorative swirl of whipped cream beside it. "He was so proud of you two. And protective,'' she added, eyeing the bite through the bottoms of her blue-rimmed bifocals. "I'm sure he'd be spinning in his grave if he knew you'd been talking with that Jackson boy.''

Dorothy was presently between her visit to the beauty shop, where her short gray curls had been teased into a bubble, and her trip to the grocery store. She'd heard at the Curl Up and Dye that Hannah had Tosca cake, Danish apple pudding and chocolate torte on her dessert menu today. Since she hadn't had good Tosca in ages and she always spent more when she shopped for groceries on an empty stomach, she'd headed over the minute her spray was dry.

"That was two months ago, Dorothy.''

"Well, I've been in Springfield with my sister. She got a new hip, you know. So I only heard about it last week. And your grandmother,'' she went on, since the news was still fresh to her, "she never was one to pass on talk. You remind me of her that way,'' she confided, "but surely she'd warned you about the less savory characters on the docks. My son's a fisherman, and the stories he tells of what goes on in that tavern on the south shore during the season is enough to keep a parent on her knees for a week.''

Hannah's only response was a forbearing smile as she refilled the woman's coffee. She didn't recall any warnings from her grandparents about the docks. But they probably hadn't thought them necessary. Her grandparents' house had backed up to one of the bizillion little lakes in the area, and the dock where she and her sister had played and swam and tanned had been a ten-foot floating plank where their grandpa had tethered his rowboat. The only unsavory character they'd encountered had been the marmot that kept making off with their potato chips.

"Of course, Peter doesn't patronize that tavern," Dorothy qualified, speaking of her son. "But I understand Damon does."

"I don't imagine Peter's fishing today, is he?" Hannah didn't want to talk about Damon Jackson. Every time someone mentioned him, she inevitably found herself remembering how he'd stood brushing his thumb over her wrist, making her skin tingle and her pulse leap, while he'd shown her an understanding she would never have expected him to possess. And every time she thought of that, an indefinable longing would begin to fill her. She'd never felt so drawn to anyone in her life as she had at that moment. "It's getting pretty nasty out there. Don't you think?"

She nodded toward the wide, plate-glass windows. Outside, the rain turned the morning a dull, glistening gray. Dorothy didn't seem at all suspicious of the deliberate change of subject. Weather was more than just an idle topic in the north country. During fall and winter especially, the elements ruled everyone's life.

The burly man at the end of the counter looked up from his newspaper and plate. He was one of the truckers she'd discovered among her regulars, a guy named Rick who drove a twice-weekly route from Duluth to Grand Portage on the Canadian border.

"This could be more than a typical blow," he said, using the native term for the fierce wind and rain that swept in from the northwest this time of year. "I heard on my radio that it might turn into a gale. It seems the fall storms are on us."

Looking as if her appetite had suddenly disappeared, Dorothy set down her fork without taking her last bite. "I always hate this time of year. Ships go down when the weather turns, you know."

"They sure do," the trucker added, hefting his girth from

the stool to remove his billfold from the back pocket of gray work pants. "Last I heard there were three-hundred-and-fifty wrecks on the lake's floor. The *Edmund Fitz* is down there, you know?"

That sobering bit of common knowledge had Dorothy paying her check and gathering her purse and her umbrella. There wasn't a person living near Superior who didn't know about the lives the lake had claimed.

Years' worth of worry lines had creased the woman's brow by the time Hannah handed her her change and she'd removed her raincoat from the rack by the front door.

"I can't imagine that my son would be out today, but I think I'll run by his house and see on my way to the store. I suppose I should get my shutters up, too." Pulling a plastic rain bonnet from the pocket of her coat, she tied it over her freshly coiffed hair. "Lovely Tosca, Hannah. Thank you. You're doing a nice job here."

Having left his money on the counter, Hannah's only other customer shrugged into his jacket. "Catch you later," he said, just like he always did, and snatched up his cap.

She thanked them, told them both to be careful on the road, then watched the husky trucker hold the door for Dorothy and her umbrella before they headed into the downpour.

Normally, she would have set to work bussing the counter and rinsing dishes. Instead, after putting the meal checks on the spindle and the trucker's money into the cash register, she stuffed her hands into the wide pocket of her burgundy apron and rounded the counter.

She stopped at the front window of the empty café, watching the rain and thinking of how worried Dorothy had looked at the thought of her son being on the lake. She couldn't see the water from where she stood. It disappeared beyond the horizon behind the building, stretching as far as the eye could see in either direction, a body of water so vast and unforgiving that thousand-foot-long freighters were swallowed whole.

She had never seen a storm on Superior, but she'd heard that the waves sent forty-foot sprays crashing against the high cliffs to the south, and that those waves could be as powerful and destructive as any to be found on the seven seas.

Damon could well be on the lake—in a boat that had looked to her as if it were falling apart. She had the distinct feeling there wasn't anyone out there worrying about his welfare the way Dorothy was worrying about her son's. Or the way the other fishermen's friends and family were undoubtedly worrying about them. She had the feeling, too, that was exactly how Damon wanted it.

Her arms tightened over the hollow feeling in her stomach. Try as she might, she hadn't been able to forget what he'd said the day he'd returned her keys, or the absolute conviction in his voice when he'd said it.

You make a place for yourself, even if you're the only one in it.

A year ago, she wouldn't have understood the need for creating such a place. She did now. Her ex-husband had shown her how much safer it was to pursue solitary dreams, to simply not allow yourself to count on someone else. Getting past the loneliness was the hard part. Even when she was surrounded by people, new friends, actually, that hollow feeling was often still there.

She was wondering if Damon experienced that same feeling when she noticed Bill Andersson across the street. Looking like a giant lemon drop in his yellow sou'wester, he was nailing boards on the front window of his appliance store. Glancing up the street as a pine bough skidded down the sidewalk, she noticed that the florist and barber shops were already shuttered. Hattie, the florist, even had a Closed sign taped to her door.

Two minutes later, Hannah had changed the movable hands on the little clock-shaped sign on her own door to indicate that she'd be back in five minutes, and was in the cavernous space below her restaurant. The area had once housed a welding shop. Now it held only the café's freezers and the sheets of plywood used to shutter the building. The previous owner had made a point of showing her the tracks above and below the plate-glass windows where the boards were supposed to fit.

In theory, putting up the boards shouldn't be much trouble at all.

Damon was halfway up the hill when his glance automatically cut to the left. He didn't know why he checked out the café when he drove past it on his way home, but he always did. He never saw her. Even if he had, he wouldn't have done anything about it.

Or so he was thinking when he noticed one of the wide double doors below the café's back stairway hanging open. A woman was backing through it, the wind tearing at her bright blue raincoat as she dragged out a piece of plywood as tall as she was and twice as long. She was too slender to be the cook, and too tall to be the waitress he'd seen in there before. He couldn't see the color of her hair. Not with her hood pulled up. And though he couldn't see her face, either, something about the way she moved put a knot of recognition in his gut.

His reaction wasn't conscious, but the moment the knot formed, his foot lifted from the gas. Since he was going uphill, the truck immediately slowed. As it did, he watched Hannah prop the wood next to another sheet just like it at the side of the building.

The wind promptly blew both boards over, then grabbed at her hood, blowing it back enough to confirm what his instincts had told him. That he had recognized her when he could barely see her was something he didn't take time to consider just then. She'd covered her head again and had left the boards so she could close the heavy door banging against the back of the building. Moments later, she was lifting one of the awkward sheets to drag it up the wet sidewalk.

His glance darted ahead, past the blur of windshield wipers trying to keep up with the downpour. Except for a couple of cars parked on the street, the area was deserted. Still, he fully expected one of her staff to come around the corner any moment to help her. It would be difficult enough to manage the cumbersome boards without the wind snatching at them. Getting them up alone would nearly be impossible.

He was less than ten yards from the café when he saw her edge the corner of the board into the groove below the side window. The power lines were swayed when the wind tore the board from her hands, overending it like a quarter flipped for a toss. Looking slightly stunned, she stared down at her palms as if the wood had abraded them, then promptly dragged the board back from where it had landed by the power pole.

The woman was nothing if not determined. He knew that for a fact. He'd butted heads with that determination the day he'd met her. He also knew she was going to hurt herself if she didn't get some help quick.

Swearing to himself, he pulled to a stop by the boarded-up art gallery across from the café. He wished someone else would show up so he could keep going, but there wasn't a soul in sight. It was him or no one. And he couldn't leave her struggling. Not with the power lines swinging the way they were.

Head ducked against the rain, knowing he was exposing himself to trouble just by being there, he jogged across the street. Each footfall seemed to echo that he was damned if he did and damned if he didn't.

That was the story of his life, he thought, coming up behind her.

He reached for the board.

"Let go." He muttered the order over the top of her hood,

spanning the width of the plywood with the full stretch of his arms.

Hannah's heart lurched. The voice behind her matched the low rumble of thunder in the distance. She knew that voice, and the jolt it sent down her spine caused her to step back, only to find herself bumping into the solid wall of his body. With her shoulders to his chest, she glanced up and around to find herself staring at the strong line of Damon's jaw. An instant later, he glanced down and she saw his dark eyebrows bolt together over his smoke gray eyes.

"Come on, Hannah. Move."

Too grateful for the help to care about anything else, she slipped out from between him and the board.

"I've never put them up before," she said, watching him shift the board into position. "If it wasn't for the wind I don't think it would be a problem."

"If it wasn't for the wind, you wouldn't need them." Her logic obviously escaped him. Beneath the bill of his black baseball cap, a scowl as formidable and dark as the sky slashed his carved features. "Why isn't your cook helping you? Or one of your waitresses?"

He held the board flat against the sea green siding and guided the lower edge into the narrow metal track below the window. Tipping his head back to see what he was doing, he caught the top edge in the slot of the upper track. As he did, rain sluiced down his face and ran in rivulets over the arms and shoulders of his heavy canvas jacket.

Seconds later, the window disappeared when he slid the board into place.

"I don't have any waitresses on during the day anymore. Not weekdays, anyway."

Hannah grabbed for the other board as the wind skidded it along the sidewalk. Damon stopped it with his foot, tipping it to take one end while she held the other. Walking backward, he rounded the corner, frowning at her all the way.

"What about your cook?"

"I'm the cook."

"The other one." He grumbled the words over the muffled roar of rain pounding the pavement, angling the board to cut its resistance to the wind. "She should be out here doing this. That old battle-ax has probably shuttered this building a thousand times."

Ducking her head against a sudden gust, fighting for control of the board, Hannah shot him an uneasy glance. He obviously hadn't forgotten how he'd been received by Inga the last time he'd been there.

"I'm sure she has. But she quit. I'm the only one here."

Because there hadn't been anyone else to help her, she would have told him how grateful she was that he'd stopped. She had no idea how she'd have managed the task by herself. But the wind wanted to make a Frisbee out of the board and she needed to concentrate on holding up her end while Damon wrestled the plywood into place.

She didn't mind the rain. And she loved the snows that would come in another month or two, though, like everyone else in Minnesota, she would grow a tad tired of shoveling it along about March. What she didn't like was wind and thunder. And thunder was exactly what she heard rumbling inland as the other board slid between its tracks and snugly covered her other big window.

The thunder kept coming, rolling in from the lake until it felt as if its power had gathered into a fist in her stomach. It cracked overhead like the snap of a whip, its vibration shaking the windows and Hannah with the same force. Lightning flashed at that same instant, eliciting a gasp from Hannah that had her dropping any pretense of bravery and bolting for the café's front door.

Damon was right behind her. The bell over the door was still tinkling wildly when she spun around to close out the weather. Damon apparently had the same idea. His big hand flattened an inch above hers on the wooden frame, pushing against the wind when a heavy gust blasted rain against the other side. She knew he was behind her. She just didn't realize quite how close until the door suddenly shut with a bang when the gust slacked off and she turned to sag against it.

Her heart was still lurching against her ribs when she realized that all she could see was his chest. Specifically, a strip of wet gray sweatshirt between the sides of his open coat.

The imposing width of that chest had scarcely registered when she saw him lift his hands and his fingers curled around her upper arms. Her heart had barely given another jerk when he pulled her forward so quickly that her head snapped back.

"You don't want to stand there." He practically growled the words as he reached past her with one hand to pull the shade over the narrow green pine tree painted on the window. "If something blows through that glass, you'll be digging splinters out of your scalp for a week."

The pressure of his hand increased, causing the heat of his palm to burn through her slicker and blouse as he pulled her a step farther into the room. "Are you all right?"

The demand sounded grudging, as if he didn't want to ask but couldn't help it. More convinced of his reluctance than his concern, she raised her glance to his face.

The lights over the counter and above the neatly set tables easily compensated for the gray light the shutters now blocked. In that brightness she looked from the water beaded on the shoulders of his heavy jacket to the strong cords in his neck. The hard angles and planes of his face were damp from the rain, making his chiseled features look as if they'd been hewn from polished marble. A night's growth of beard shadowed his angular jaw and defined the firm, sensuous line of his mouth.

As she gave him an uncertain nod, she couldn't help thinking that his beautifully carved mouth was the only thing about him that held the remotest potential to be soft.

"You sure?" he asked, sounding no more convinced than she looked.

"I'm sure," she told him, even though he had to feel her trembling. The reaction was from the chill she got in the rain and from the start the lightning had given her. Meeting the guarded look in his eyes, aware that he'd yet to let her go, she couldn't deny that the unsettled sensation had a lot to do with him, too. "I'm okay now that I'm inside, anyway. I've always heard about how bad the fall storms can be, but I guess I wasn't ready for this. I've only been here in the summer before."

"If it makes you feel any better, this isn't really a storm. It's somewhere between a strong breeze and a fresh gale."

She eyed him dully. "That's more than a strong breeze blowing out there. One of those gusts nearly knocked me over."

Something that almost passed for a smile glinted in his eyes when his glance dropped the length of her body. He'd called her skinny before. Almost certain he was considering a remark about a stiff wind blowing her away or some such thing, she tipped up her chin.

"I meant on the scale," he explained, the glint deepening at the hint of challenge in her expression. "A strong breeze is twenty-five to thirty-one miles an hour. A fresh gale is between thirty-nine and forty-six. You have to hit fifty-five to call it a storm."

"The scale?"

"The Beaufort Scale. That's how you measure wind."

Damon skimmed a glance over her face, her flawless skin, and settled on her liquid blue eyes. Beneath his hand, he could feel the slenderness of her arm, the supple strength in her muscles. "We'll get worse than this before winter's over. Just be glad you're not on the water. That's where it gets rough."

He should let her go. He knew that. But he figured there were a lot of things he should do, and didn't. For one, he should have forgotten about her by now. Yet rarely a night had gone by that she hadn't crept into his thoughts, invading his bed by haunting his dreams. In those dreams, he knew the taste of her, the feel of her body. In the cold light of day, he knew nothing but a burning frustration he tried his damnedest to ignore.

He hadn't realized he'd been running his thumb over her tight little bicep until he became aware of the question slipping into her eyes. Or maybe it was caution. Had she pulled back, he didn't know what he would have done. Stepped back himself, he supposed. But since she didn't, since he was tired of only imagining, he found himself lifting his hands toward her face.

Over the heavy beat of the rain, he heard her slow intake of breath when he lowered her hood. Her hair had been down the day he'd met her. She'd had it pulled back when he'd brought her keys. Seeing that it was pulled back now, too, he felt the briefest twinge of disappointment. Except for the strands that had loosened from the big clip holding the shining mass at the back of her head, her beautiful hair was as confined and prim as an old maid's.

The thought that she was deliberately restraining herself somehow was fleeting, but it lasted long enough to furrow his brow when he tucked back the strands of hair clinging to her cheek, and smoothed them into place. Her hair was even softer than he'd imagined, almost as soft as her skin when he let his knuckles drift to her cheek. She seemed to be holding her breath as he carried that touch to the fragile line of her jaw.

The air in Hannah's lungs felt trapped. She remembered Inga saying something about the way Damon had looked at her, as if he wanted her served up for his supper. She'd had no idea what the woman had meant until now. Damon was looking at her as if he could devour her. No man had ever looked at her that way. And no man had ever caused heat to pool inside her just by touching her face.

The thought had scarcely registered when she felt his thumb brush her bottom lip. His eyes held hers, the intent in them making him look every bit as dangerous as she'd heard he was.

It had just occurred to Hannah that he definitely *was* dangerous when a glass-rattling boom of thunder cracked overhead. She jumped, jolted as much by the intriguing sensations Damon's touch evoked as the storm raging outside.

Letting his hand fall, he eyed her as if nothing at all unusual had happened. "It's only thunder."

"I don't care what you say about this being nothing," she muttered, more rattled by her response to him than she was by the wind blowing outside. She'd allowed his touch as if she'd been starved for the contact. The thought that she might very well be didn't help matters at all. "Thunder scares the daylights out of me."

"It's the lightning you need to worry about."

A self-deprecating light entered her eyes. "I didn't say my fear was logical."

"No," he agreed, a little too easily, "you didn't."

Giving her a wry look, he used the back of his hand to catch a drip of rain running down his neck. A second later, aware of another one, he pulled his hat off to wipe at the damp hair at his nape. He hadn't even taken the time to button his coat when he'd come to her rescue.

"I'm sorry," she said, suddenly realizing how wet he was. How wet they both were. Pulling off her slicker, she backed toward the door to the kitchen. "Let me get you a towel. Would you like a cup of coffee? Or lunch? It's the least I can offer for your help."

Her smile lacked the ease he'd seen in it before. She was definitely wary, but he couldn't tell if it was because of the racket outside, or because of what he'd done. He could have sworn she'd felt the same awareness he had. It had been as obvious to him as the way she scrambled to cover that response now.

"Just the towel." He was feeling a little wary himself. If a woman was uneasy around him, he wasted no time on her. If a woman was part of the community, he had nothing to do with her at all. So, what was he doing there? "You don't owe me anything."

She didn't look as if she agreed with him on the latter, but she didn't argue the point when she emerged from the kitchen moments later, minus the cheerful blue coat. There was nothing at all seductive about the way she was dressed. Burgundy bib apron over a white turtleneck and slim, dark slacks. Neat, tidy, efficient. But the thought of untying those apron strings, peeling off that shirt and taking her hair down had the same effect on him as if she'd been standing there in red lace and garters.

Taking the rectangle of white terry cloth she held out, he rubbed it over his face and wiped the rain from the back of his neck. What he needed was a cold shower, or a dip in the lake. When he handed the towel back, he did the prudent thing and said he had to go.

"I really appreciate you stopping," she told him, hugging her arms, and the towel, to herself. "I hope the delay didn't keep you from something important."

"It didn't." He shook the water from his cap, the drops disappearing into the dark green indoor-outdoor carpeting. "I was just on my way back from securing my boat."

"Will it be okay?"

The unmasked concern in her expression hit him square in the chest. He wasn't accustomed to anyone caring about him, much less about his property. But her interest was evident in the faint pinch of her brow and in the depths of her expressive eyes. He didn't know which was more dangerous just then.

The way she'd responded to his touch, or the way she looked at him now.

"I battened her down and tied on a few extra bumpers." The old wreck had ridden out worse than this. "She'll be fine."

Tightening her arms when the lights flickered, Hannah murmured, "I hope so."

The lights flickered again as thunder reverberated through the building, causing the rows of glasses on the service counter to tinkle as they bumped together. She didn't jump this time. She simply gripped herself a little tighter, said she hoped the electricity didn't go out and gave him a smile that didn't quite work.

Had she not been alone, Damon would have been gone by now. Hell, he thought, had she not been alone, he wouldn't have stopped in the first place. But there was no one around to speculate about his presence, and he really didn't have anywhere to go but to an empty house. The thought that he didn't like the idea of leaving her because she was skittish about the storm was banished as quickly as it formed.

"There's no sense going out in this right now. If the offer's still good, maybe I will have that coffee."

The relief in her expression was as subtle as her reaction had been to the flicker of the lights. With a soft smile that did something rather interesting to the nerves at the base of his spine, she pointed to the dark, lacquered maple counter. "Just toss your coat on a stool and have a seat," she said, and headed behind the counter to pick up a steaming pot of coffee.

She had it poured and had just set the cup in front of him when he reached across the shining wood and caught her wrist.

"You should put some salve on that," he said, turning over her hand. "And check it for splinters."

Her glance darted to the abraded strip of skin at the base

of her small palm. He'd seen one of the boards chafe across it when the wind ripped it from her hands, but it seemed she hadn't even noticed the scrape until now. It wasn't much more than a red rash. Not even much of that. As he looked closer, he couldn't see any slivers at all.

He couldn't help noticing how still she'd gone. He couldn't help noticing the softness of her skin, either. Thinking it best to ignore both, he drew his hand back and curled his fingers around the heavy ceramic cup. "When did your cook quit?"

It seemed he'd knocked her a little off balance. Pulling her quizzical glance from him to her palm, she backed up, then moved down the counter to start clearing the dirty dishes there.

"A couple of months ago," she replied, stacking white ceramic plates and carrying them to the service window.

"After the season was over?"

She hesitated, then turned around with a cloth in her hand. "Actually, she quit before that."

"What happened?"

"Philosophical differences," she returned, taking the cloth to the crumbs. "You know how some employees can be. You have people working for you, too."

Damon slowly lifted the cup, contemplating the steam rising from it before he took a sip. He might have wondered at how easily she credited him with understanding, except he was more interested in the timing of her employee's defection. It had been just before the end of tourist season when he'd returned her keys. Not long before the end of it, in fact.

"What kind of differences?" he idly asked. "Did she want more money?"

"She seemed fine with what I was paying her."

"More hours? Less hours?"

Over the richly scented steam, he watched her move back and forth behind the counter as she set fresh green paper mats and silverware on the spaces she'd cleaned. She didn't glance up. She didn't slow down.

"Inga had a little trouble adjusting to some of the changes I made. They were just minor things, really. Garnishes and new recipes I've added. Changes to some of the specials the old owner used to serve."

The low sound Damon made was nothing short of derisive. "Nothing changes easily around here," he told her. "Especially the way people do things. And how they think," he muttered, because changing a mind was the hardest accomplishment of all. "But what you've said doesn't sound that serious." He eyed her carefully over the cup's rim. "Did you want her to quit?"

"Not really. She was a good cook."

"Then why did you let her go?"

The question was casual enough. But he knew when she suddenly stopped fiddling with the settings that were already perfectly positioned that the conversation wasn't as innocuous as it might seem. She was evading. As evasive as he could be, he had no trouble recognizing the tactic.

"Hannah?"

"She also had a problem with remembering who was boss."

"And?"

"And with who we will and won't serve."

He set his cup down with a quiet click. Keeping his hands locked around it, he watched an odd defensiveness slip over her face.

"Am I a 'will,'" he asked, his voice utterly flat. "Or a 'won't.'"

She matched the challenge in his eyes, but she didn't say a word. She didn't need to. The cook was gone. And he was there.

Disbelief shadowed his face. "You defended me?"

"It was the principle. I don't make decisions based on rumors."

Damon felt himself go utterly still. He was stunned. That she *had* defended him was incredible enough. But for her to let a cook she surely must have needed quit rather than back down on her position was unbelievable. Nobody around there stood up for him. Ever.

Except for being slightly mystified, he really wasn't sure how he felt just then. He was even less sure what to make of her. He did, however, question her comprehension.

"Have you considered that the rumors might be true?"

"You don't know what I've heard."

"No. But I can certainly imagine."

"So?"

"So, what?"

"Are they?"

The question slipped out before Hannah could consider the magnitude of what she was asking. With no way to retract the demand, all she could do was wait. Something inside her wanted very much to know what was and wasn't true about this man, and she knew the only place to discover that truth would be from him.

Looking at her as if he couldn't decide whether she was very brave or very foolish, Damon pushed his coffee aside and rose from the counter. His eyes were still locked on her face when he finally said, "Probably."

There was a warning in that single word. But there was no denial or explanation. As he reached for his jacket, the muscle in his jaw bunching, he clearly had no intention of offering either.

"Can you manage all right?"

"Manage?"

"Without an extra cook."

His concern for her ability to cope was the last thing she

expected just then. Wondering if he always took such confusing mental leaps, she replied with a quiet "Yes."

"How?"

The demand had her blinking at his frown. "I'd planned all along to do the cooking myself during the slow season. There's not enough business here in the winter to need more than a couple of part-time waitresses. I'm managing well enough."

"Then you've done this before?"

"If by 'this' you mean owned a restaurant, yes, I have. I owned one with my ex-husband in Minneapolis." That particular enterprise couldn't possibly have been more different from the café. Gregory's had been upscale and trendy and she'd never felt comfortable there at all.

"But this is mine. This is who I am," she added quietly, looking from the gingham curtains on the windows to the menus of unadorned regional fare sticking up between the salt and pepper shakers on the very untrendy maple tables. "I bought this place because I want something that no one can take from me. I'll manage if it kills me."

The conviction in her voice made his eyes narrow. He knew exactly what she was talking about. She could feel it. The same way she'd felt his understanding before. He knew how necessary it was for her to hang on to what she had. That same need had to be why he stayed in a place that held so little welcome for him. No one could live day in and day out just for spite.

She didn't have the chance to ask what it was that kept him there, or to wonder why he'd pushed her away, only to draw her back again. Wind rushed in when the door opened, the wild tinkling of the bell punctuated by the pounding of the rain on the sidewalk.

Moments later, the door was closed and Sheriff Jansson stood dripping on the rubber mat, his rangy frame camouflaged by a tent of olive-colored oilcloth. His attention was on his broad-brimmed hat as he whipped it off his head and slapped the rain from the plastic covering it. He was a friendly man who'd settled into middle age well, taking as much pride in avoiding the paunch sported by some of his cronies as he did in the town he'd lived in all his life. The only thing he took more pride in was his family, especially his oldest daughter and son-in-law-the-lawyer in Cleveland and his three small grandchildren. Every time he got new pictures of the brood, he shared them with everyone in the café.

He'd just run his hand through his barely gray, honey brown hair when he promptly froze where he dripped. The thick slashes of his eyebrows slammed together like lightning bolts.

Instantly guarded, his glance jerked from the man standing in front of the counter to the woman behind it.

"Is everything all right here?"

"Everything's fine." Hannah offered the assurance with a smile, only to feel the smile falter and her stomach knot when she saw Damon's jaw lock. "Damon was passing by when he saw I needed help with the shutters. We're just talking." She tried the smile again. "Come on in."

The sheriff didn't seem to believe that all was as well as she said it was. One instant he was searching her face as if looking for signs of distress. The next, he pinned Damon with a glare that would have had most people squirming their way toward the door.

Damon met that glare head-on, his eyes cool, unblinking and revealing nothing of his thoughts or intentions. Though his motions seemed normal enough when he pushed back his hair with one hand and pulled his cap on with the other, the tension in his body was almost palpable.

Hannah could have sworn she felt that same tension knot itself in her stomach when she saw his hands drop to his sides. He stood still as stone. Apparently, he wasn't moving until the sheriff did.

"Go ahead and have a seat." She motioned the sheriff toward the counter, thinking the weather had brought him in for an early lunch. "I'll get your coffee," she added with a cautious smile. "It's really bad out there, isn't it?"

"I'm not here to eat." He wasn't there for small talk, either. Looking as if he wasn't sure he wanted to take his eyes off Damon, he nodded toward the door. "Louie Lindstrom has wandered off again. I was wondering if you'd seen him."

Concern replacing caution, her glance darted to the man looming beside the counter. "I haven't. Have you?"

There was definite tightness to Damon's quiet "No."

"How long has he been missing?" she asked the sheriff.

"It's hard to say. He was home last night when Neil dropped off a prescription. When he called him a while ago to make sure he'd closed his shutters, he didn't answer. Neil left work to check on him and he wasn't there."

"I hope he didn't head for the dock," she said, not sure what to make of the way the sheriff was looking at her. His eyes had narrowed when she hadn't hesitated to turn to Damon. Now the concern she'd first noted was no longer there. Disapproval had replaced it. Thinking only of the elderly man they'd helped before, she looked back to Damon. "It's been a while since you were at your boat. Maybe he went down after you came up. We should help find him."

"I don't think so."

"But you were so good with him before. If you were to—"

The way his jaw tightened cut her off even before he spoke. "They don't want my help," he told her, his voice utterly flat. "If you want to go, that's your business. I've got other things to do."

She started to ask what he had to do that was so important that he couldn't help find an old man in a storm, but the sheriff's presence stopped her cold. There was something in Damon that responded to people when they truly needed him; something he fought and denied and probably even cursed when he went to battle with it. She knew that capacity was there, but she also sensed that he wasn't about to expose it now. At the moment, she sensed nothing in him but carefully banked anger as he started for the door.

He'd just passed the sheriff, when the sheriff reached back and caught his arm.

"You didn't pay for your coffee."

A knot of pure dread settled in her stomach as she watched Damon slowly glance down at the man's hand.

"Let go," he said in a voice so ominous that the hairs at her nape stood on end.

The sheriff's tone was barely a whisper. "Make me, hotshot."

The knot in Hannah's stomach coiled. Animosity fairly leapt between the two men. Damon looked intimately familiar with the emotion, but Sheriff Jansson had always seemed so laid-back to her. She couldn't believe he was goading Damon as he was.

"It was on the house." If she sounded a little frantic, she couldn't help it. That was exactly how she felt as she moved forward, only to draw to a halt when Damon's cool glare cut toward her. He wanted her to stay back, but that didn't keep her from trying to get the sheriff's attention. "It's all right, Sheriff. Really. He doesn't owe me anything."

"Are you sure?" he demanded, sounding as if he couldn't believe she wasn't being coerced into letting Damon off.

"Of course I'm sure." Her displeasure at his actions put steel in her tone. "Let him go."

It was with great reluctance that he released Damon's arm. Actually looking disappointed that Damon hadn't stiffed her on a bill, he didn't spare him so much as a glance before he jammed his own hat back on. He didn't say a word to Damon, much less offer an apology—something Hannah felt Damon definitely had coming. He had done nothing wrong. Yet, from the moment the sheriff had laid eyes on him, the older man's distrust and dislike had been glaringly obvious.

Small wonder, she thought, that Damon nearly took the door off its hinges when he jerked it open and stalked out into the rain.

"He had just helped me," Hannah repeated, hurrying over to shut the door when the wind blew it back. "There was no reason to treat him that way."

"I think I know Damon Jackson a little better than you do," the sheriff assured her, making it sound as if that were reason enough. "The next time you need help with your shutters, you call me or Bill across the street, or Brenda's husband. You don't need a man like him hanging around here and ruining your reputation.

"Now," he continued, as if he'd just put everything in order and there was nothing left to discuss, "if you want to help find Mr. Lindstrom, I'm sure Neil would be obliged. There's no sense you being out in this weather, so maybe you could do some calling around. Just let dispatch at the station know if you come up with anything. They'll get in touch with me."

Chapter Four

"It must be awful getting old like that," Brenda murmured, plates clattering as she placed them in the wash rack. "I saw Mr. Lindstrom at the hardware store a couple days ago and he seemed just fine. He was telling the checker that he'd been working in his garden, getting it ready for winter.

"I don't think the checker was much interested in chatting," she confided, shoving in another plate, "but the old guy really wanted somebody to visit with. I talked with him for a couple of minutes about how to prune back my shrubs, but other than seeming kind of lonely, he was just as normal as you and me." Lifting her arm, she rubbed her nose with the back of her wet hand. "I hear Neil was fit to be tied when he finally found him in his boathouse."

Hannah measured flour into a large aluminum bowl, trying to concentrate on both her task and on Brenda's running dialogue. The feat shouldn't have been particularly challenging. Doing two things at once was practically second nature to her, but there was a bit more than cooking and conversation on her mind at the moment. No matter how hard she tried, she couldn't shake the memories of how Damon had looked when he'd touched her hair, her cheek, and of the caged anger that had filled his body at the sheriff's affront.

"I heard that, too," she replied, thoughts of Damon's refusal to help the man they were discussing further straining her concentration. "Do you suppose he got confused again, or just went out to check on something and decided to wait out the storm?"

"It's hard telling. But as long as there's the possibility he did get confused, maybe Neil should get someone to stay with him."

"Or move him into a wing of that big house of his." Wondering if she should have tried to stop Damon when he'd left, not sure what she could have said if she had, Hannah reached for her measuring spoons. "There should be enough room. That place looks huge."

"It is. I served at their open house last Christmas," Brenda replied, spraying off another plate. "I got lost trying to find the bathroom. I swear I've never been in anything that size that wasn't a hotel. But Kirsty Lindstrom and Neil's uncle in the same house?" The sprayer snapped back into place on the wall above the stainless steel sink with an audible clunk. "I don't think so. As picky as she is about everything, she'd have a heifer the first time he came to the table in that fishing vest he likes to wear. And he's just stubborn enough to refuse to take it off. I think they all pretty much do their separate things."

Brenda shoved the rack into the washer and punched buttons. An instant later, the sound of water running through pipes joined the music coming from the disk player. After Hannah closed the restaurant, she usually changed from the quiet instrumental music conducive to dining, to alternative rock or the classics, depending on her mood. Brenda, who readily admitted being stuck in the eighties when it came to everything from music to makeup, insisted she could tell whether the day had been good or bad by the CD Hannah put on once the customers were gone and how loud she played it.

Tonight, since Hannah hadn't bothered to change the music or the volume at all, she supposed her mood could best be described as preoccupied.

"Is it Mr. Lindstrom who has you so rattled, or is something else bothering you?"

The question forced Hannah's head up. Brenda stood at the sink, her arms crossed and a frown threatening. Her own brow furrowing, Hannah reached for a box on the shelf above her work station. "There's nothing bothering me."

"Well, you're thinking about something, and it's not about what you're doing. I thought you were making your rocky road, double fudge brownies for that order."

The order Brenda referred to was a standing order of twenty sack lunches to be delivered to the owner of a tour boat first thing in the morning. It had already taken Hannah twice as long as it should to get as far along as she had. "I am."

The pint-size brunette gave a cryptic nod toward the box Hannah held. "That's paprika."

Hannah's glance darted back to the box. With a sigh of disgust, she traded the box for one of baking powder. "I am concerned about Mr. Lindstrom," she admitted, willing to concede that part of her preoccupation. "I know Neil is busy, but I get the feeling he sort of brushes his uncle off."

She'd met Neil Lindstrom several times now. He would come in to chat with the mayor over coffee about organizing Snow Daze, since Neil was annual chairman of that event. Or he'd have pie while visiting with someone about the Pine Point Boosters, since he was president of that organization, as well as the PTA and heaven only knew what else. He was always polite to her. She just didn't care for the subtle way he had of making sure people knew how hard he worked. In many respects, he was still the town's golden boy.

The exact opposite of Damon.

"He was having breakfast with the mayor this morning, and I got the feeling from what he said that his biggest concern about his uncle missing yesterday was the time he'd had to spend looking for him." She frowned at herself and blew a breath. Heaven help her, she was beginning to sound like Inga. "Ignore me, Brenda. I could have that all wrong. Maybe the next time Neil mentions his uncle, I'll ask if he'd like to get him involved over at the senior center. It could be that Neil's responsibilities are just stretching him to his limits."

"Maybe." Brenda repeated the word slowly, considering Hannah closely. "But now that you've got that figured out, do you want to tell me what else is bothering you?"

"What makes you think there's something else?"

The neat wings of Brenda's eyebrows lowered over the concern and curiosity in her warm brown eyes. "What about Damon Jackson?"

Hannah's fingers tightened around a container of salt. "What about him?"

"I understand he was with you when the sheriff came looking for Mr. Lindstrom. Come on," she prodded when Hannah's only response was to hesitate before she added salt to the bowl. "You've been preoccupied ever since I got here. And you haven't said a word about Damon coming in yesterday. I didn't even know he had until Bridget asked me a while ago if it was true."

"Bridget?"

"Sonnenfeld," Brenda added. "She lives next door to one of the deputies."

"There's nothing to say," Hannah replied, continually amazed at the extent of the grapevine. "He helped me with the boards on the windows, I gave him a cup of coffee, and

he left.'' Right after the sheriff tried to make like Clint East-
wood, she thought, but she wasn't about to add that bit of
grist to the mill.

"Bridget also heard that he had his arm around you when
you two came in here."

"What?"

Brenda held up her hands, palms out. "I'm just telling you
what I heard. Apparently someone in the appliance store saw
you two run in here, and whoever it was said Damon had his
arm around you."

"I ran in here because of the lightning," she explained,
exasperated. It was no wonder the grapevine was so tangled.
"I have no idea what Damon did right then, but it's possible
he grabbed the door when I pulled it open. Maybe from across
the street it looked like his arm was around me, but I know
it wasn't." Even now, more than twenty-four hours after the
fact, she could easily remember the heat that had pooled inside her when he'd done nothing more than touch her face.
Had his arm been around her, had she been pressed to his
very big, very solid body, she would have most definitely
remembered it.

She swiped flour from her hands onto her apron, wondering
if her myopic neighbor had also seen Damon leave. Remembering his quiet rage, she could only imagine what someone
would make of that.

The sensation in her stomach turned leaden.

"This is ridiculous."

"This is Pine Point." Brenda shrugged, catching Hannah's
irritation if not all the reasons behind it. "You get used to
gossip. Just be careful. Okay?"

Normally, Hannah would have taken the sincerely offered
advice and let the matter go. When it came to Damon, she
found that she would listen to what people said until she could
politely change the subject, and offered little comment about
him herself. Brenda was becoming a friend, though, and Han-

nah had discovered that the little woman with the big hair and toothy smile laid claim to broader views than those of her counterparts.

"Do you know him?" Hannah asked, needing insight she couldn't seem to find anywhere else. "I mean, have you ever had anything to do with Damon personally?"

"Like go out with him, you mean?"

"Did you? You're about the same age."

Coffee brown curls bounced as Brenda shook her head. "The only person I ever dated was my husband. Ron and I were a couple from eighth grade on. But even if I hadn't been stuck on him, I can't imagine having anything to do with Damon Jackson. He was too much of a loner, even before he started getting into trouble. And I think he's a year or two older," she added. "He must be thirty-two or thirty-three. We were in a lot of the same classes through school, but he'd been held back a grade somewhere along the line."

"Why was he held back?"

"I have no idea."

Common sense told Hannah she should let this go. Damon was not an easy man to know. She wasn't sure she even *wanted* to know him. There was too much about him that unsettled her. But she seemed to pick up things about him that everyone else was either content to ignore or simply didn't notice. Or, maybe, she acknowledged, unable to imagine why it would be, that he only allowed her to see.

"I'm just wondering how much of his reputation is earned and how much has been embellished. After all, this is the land of tall tales. You and I both know that the thousands of lakes around here weren't really made by the hoofprints of a big blue ox."

The mention of Babe, Paul Bunyan's bovine buddy, had Brenda nodding sagely. "I'd go sixty-percent truth, forty-percent elaboration. Damon was a rough kid who's grown into a tough man. He never did anything to me personally," she admitted, "but I remember him hanging around the bleachers smoking cigarettes at lunchtime...and that he'd fall asleep in class and get sent to the principal's office a lot."

"What about his mom and dad?"

"I don't know what happened to his mom. She wasn't from around here like his dad was. I heard she was one of the summer people, but that's all I know about her. Damon lived with his dad, and his dad was always sort of drunk."

The Jacksons had lived a world apart from her own family and their friends, Brenda went on to say, finishing up the pots while Hannah finished the large sheet of brownies. She did remember when he left town, though. It had been three or four years after graduation. The only reason she could recall it at all was because there'd been so much speculation about why Damon had disappeared. It wasn't as if anyone saw him on a daily basis. It was more a case of people suddenly noticing that he hadn't been around in a while. No one had heard his old, souped-up Chevy screaming down the highway in the wee hours of the morning. No one heard him and his dad fighting with each other on the dock. Nothing was missing from any of the other boats.

"I remember my dad saying he figured Damon left town because the fishing industry was doing poorly and one boat couldn't support him and his father. A lot of fishermen turned to other work about that time, so that could well have been true," Brenda continued. "But there was also a rumor going around that Damon took off when he did because Maryanne Jansson's father was going to arrest him on charges of statutory rape. I guess Maryanne's brother caught her and Damon doing the wild thing in the woods."

The thought of Damon doing the wild thing with anyone caused Hannah's heart to lurch. "Maryanne Jansson?" she calmly inquired.

"Sheriff Jansson's daughter."

* * *

The *Amber Waves* rocked gently in the calm little inlet when Hannah delivered the twenty sack lunches to Ole Nelson, its skipper, and started back for the café. The gleaming white vessel wasn't really a tour boat. The old, meticulously maintained trawler netted smelt all summer long. When Ole's sons went back to school in the fall, he cleaned it up and hung a sign on the highway five miles south of town advertising spectacular views of Superior's autumn shoreline on a real, working fishing boat. Word had passed on year after year and folks driving up from the Twin Cities for the day or a weekend to enjoy the fall color paid premium prices for the four-hour luncheon cruise.

With the weather growing colder, the nip of frost on the ground every morning now, Ole's little side business wouldn't last but another couple of weeks. And that was only if it didn't rain on weekends. The coming of winter meant weekend business at the café would be falling off further, too. Business would pick up again for the holiday festivals, but Hannah knew there would be some lean months before and after those few weeks.

She was considering that cheery thought, and wondering how she could possibly make up for that lost revenue, when she glanced toward Damon's boat. She'd noticed it moored at the end of the dock when she'd come down, but Damon hadn't been anywhere in sight. Now she could see him leaning against the sidewall. His head was down, his hand clamped over the back of his neck as if he were studying something on his deck.

It was possible that his engine was giving him trouble again. Or maybe he was staring at a leak and waiting for the thing to sink. The possibility wasn't all that far-fetched. The whole boat looked about as seaworthy as a sieve to her.

Common sense told her to keep going. But something about his posture kept her rooted right where she was. Always before, even from a distance, Damon had radiated a raw, elemental energy. Now, with his shoulders slumped as they were, it looked almost as if the life had been drained out of him.

The very thing that had held her in place now pulled her forward. It didn't matter that everyone kept warning her away from him. He had stopped in a storm to help her. The least she could do was make sure he was all right. She'd only be a minute, anyway. It was midmorning and there hadn't been any customers in the café when she left, but she'd told Brenda she'd only be gone five minutes. Ten, tops.

As usual, the wide stern of Damon's boat was backed up to the weathered dock. Stuffing her hands into the pockets of her navy pea jacket, she moved closer, looking past the flaking paint and faded blue letters that spelled out *Naiad*. His head was still down, his hand still clamped around his neck. The breeze ruffled his dark hair, the strands looking freshly washed and surprisingly soft. What gave her pause was the swelling visible around his eye.

"Damon?"

His head snapped up. His expression as dark as an oil slick, he promptly winced and turned his broad back to her. The lap of waves against the hull all but drowned out his muttered curse.

"What are you doing here?"

"Intruding," she called back, watching him push his hand through his hair. The muscles beneath his cabled charcoal sweater bunched with the motion. The temperature was barely thirty. Obviously his hide was thick enough that he didn't require a coat to ward off the chill. "I just wanted to know if you were okay. If you're feeling well enough to be deliberately rude, I suppose you're fine."

Damon turned on his heel, more aware than usual of the boat's rocking motion. He wasn't hungover. Not anymore. But his head still felt like little men were riveting boilerplate to the inside of his skull.

''What made you think I wasn't all right?''

The demand held more challenge than inquiry, but the fact that she'd cared to inquire at all took much of the edge from his words. The way she went still when she got a good look at his face put that edge right back.

''What's the matter? Haven't you ever seen a black eye before?''

Damon was sporting more than the everyday, garden-variety shiner. A bruise the color of a concord grape on his right cheekbone merged with the crimson swelling over his puffy right eye. A small cut slanted through his eyebrow, and the corner of his lip was abraded.

''What happened to you?'' she asked, the words rushing out on a breath. ''*Are* you all right?''

''I'm fine.'' He ignored her first question. He usually didn't care who witnessed the results of his temper, but for reasons he didn't care to question, he didn't want to share those details with this particular woman. He didn't want to be affected by her concern, either. He didn't want to be affected by her, period. If it hadn't been for her, he wouldn't have been at the café when that jerk of a sheriff had shown up. The mere thought of the man's condescension made his blood pressure spike.

The thought of his own stupidity made him angriest, though. He'd known better than to put himself where he didn't belong. Yet, he'd done it, anyway. Because of her.

''Have you seen a doctor?''

''What for?''

''What for?'' she repeated in mild disbelief. She moved closer, her head tilted, her eyes narrowing. ''May I come up there?''

He'd have shrugged to let her know it didn't matter what she did, but the motion would hurt. ''Suit yourself,'' he muttered, then made himself stay where he was when she grabbed the short ladder and swung her long, black corduroy-covered leg over the stern. Half of his instincts wanted to help her, to make sure she didn't slip. To touch her. The other half, the self-protective half, let her climb aboard on her own.

Her feet had barely hit the planks when he saw her glance from the long grooves on the deck that delineated the hatch for the fish hold, to the square boathouse near the front of the boat. He'd closed the door at its center, but the lower edges of the square windows on either side of it were propped open with sticks.

"Do you have a mirror in there?" she asked, her expression utterly innocent.

"Why do you want a mirror?"

"You asked why you should see a doctor. I want to show you."

He couldn't tell if she was frowning at the skinned spot by his lip, or if she was looking at the nick he'd put there last night trying to shave around it. He was just wishing she'd look someplace else when she glanced to the cut in his eyebrow.

"Did you clean that?"

"Of course I cleaned it."

If it was his intention to glare her down, Hannah thought he might well have succeeded—had he not winced when he started to plant his hands on his hips. Intimidation thwarted by injury, he lifted his hand to his ribs, gingerly holding his side as he blew out a slow breath. When his eyes locked on hers again, she saw as much discomfort as defiance.

"Stop looking at me like that."

"I can't help it. You look—"

"Like hell?"

"I was going to say that you look as if you're hurt a lot worse than you'll admit. But since you mentioned it, yes, you look like hell."

"Thanks."

She ignored his sarcasm, concerned with how carefully he

moved when he lowered himself to a long metal box along the sidewall that apparently doubled as a bench. She'd been told that he drove like a demon. Though he'd taken no risks at all the one time she'd been with him in his truck, he'd told her she should consider the rumors about him true. "Were you in an accident?"

"No."

That left only one other possibility. "A fight?"

Damon eyed her evenly. The discomfort he felt wasn't just physical. It was with her seeing him as he was.

Embarrassed, hating the feeling, he went on the offensive. "Yeah. I got into a fight. That's what I do. Haven't you heard?"

Locking his jaw against the pain in his side and shoulder, he reached into his shirt pocket for a packet of headache tablets. Any second now, he fully expected her pert little nose to wrinkle in distaste. She'd called him kind before. She'd even defended him. Or some principle he represented, anyway. It wasn't too hard to imagine what she thought of him now.

Not that he cared, he reminded himself.

"I've heard," she quietly replied, wondering at the weight of the chip on his shoulders. "But I've also heard that you hadn't had any trouble since you moved back here."

"That doesn't seem to be the case anymore, does it?"

The note of accusation in his flat tone made it sound as if she were somehow responsible for that circumstance, but it was apparent he neither wanted nor expected a reply. Having no idea what she'd done, she watched him rip open the packet with his teeth, then mirrored his grimace when he reached sideways for the open quart of orange juice he'd set on the deck.

The effort was too painful to witness. Intent on sparing them both, she moved across the gently rocking deck, unconsciously using his leg for balance when she hunched down to pick up the carton herself. With one knee on the deck, she glanced past his dark sleeve and held it out to him.

His eyes flicked to hers, then focused on her hand splayed over the worn cargo pants covering his upper thigh. Her heart hitched when she noticed that the tips of her nails rested scant inches from his groin.

It was impossible for her to tell what Damon thought of the unintended familiarity. Or if he thought anything of it at all. He simply took the carton and eased it from her grip.

"Thanks," he murmured.

The bone and muscle beneath her hand felt like granite. Thinking the rest of his body was probably just as hard, head included, she eased herself up and curled her fingers into her palm. She told him he was welcome, but he paid no attention to her as he popped the two white tablets into his mouth. Tipping his head back as far as he dared, he drank deeply from the carton, the strong cords in his neck convulsing with each swallow. When he'd drained the container, he lowered it, wiped his mouth with the back of his hand—and promptly hissed in a breath.

Dragging his fist across his lower lip had pulled at the abrasions in the corner. The acid from the orange juice probably didn't help matters, either. "You might want to stick with milk for a while," she suggested.

"I might do that."

"What was the fight about?"

For a moment, Hannah didn't think he was going to answer. He held the empty carton in both hands, dangling it between his wide-spread knees and staring down at the top of it. But instead of shutting her out, he moved down on the bench to make room for her.

His focus remained on the carton when she cautiously sat down a foot away. From somewhere beyond the breakwater came a long, deep blast from a tanker's horn. Damon barely noticed. His awareness had narrowed to the woman sitting quietly beside him, and the feelings gnawing at his insides.

He would tell her what the fight was about because it was simpler than dodging her questions. But he wouldn't tell her what he'd done beforehand that had made him force a fight in the first place. He wouldn't speak of how hard it had been to swallow his bitterness when the sheriff had tried to goad him into doing something stupid by grabbing him the way he had. And he wouldn't tell her that he'd gotten himself royally stewed in an attempt to forget how lousy he'd felt walking out when she'd asked him to help her find Mr. Lindstrom again. He didn't believe for an instant that any of the towns-people would have wanted him involved. But she hadn't hesitated to turn to him.

What he did say was that he'd driven to a tavern ten miles inland after he'd left the café, and run into Bud During. "He owns the building where my dad stored the boat every winter for as long as I can remember," he explained, his words tight. "Only I'm not storing it there this year. The lease Dad signed was up when I took the boat out of storage last April, but During said he wouldn't have a new one ready to sign until this fall. He wanted to make changes in the lease form or something. There were changes, all right. He decided to announce in front of everybody that he's doubling my rent and cutting my space. Take it or leave it.''

He gave a snort. This wasn't the first time a local supplier had decided to treat him differently from other paying customers. He took most of his business twenty miles up the road to Caribou Bay, not that he had much business to tend, other than at the grocery store, the bank, a gas station and, when his hair grew over his collar, a barber shop. But no one paid any attention to him in Caribou. He fueled his boat there, too, or at Two Harbors if he'd fished more in that direction that day. The only other close place to buy diesel was at the new marina, which happened to be owned by the marine supply store, and that was part of the world of Pine Point he avoided. Even if it hadn't been, his checks and credit cards weren't welcome there.

He'd discovered that the morning he'd met Hannah. He'd given Marty his credit card to buy a new fan belt, but Neil wouldn't accept it. Considering that the card hadn't been Marty's, Damon would have understood the store's refusal to take it. But Marty had returned with the message that the store didn't take checks or credit cards anymore. All business was strictly cash.

All of Damon's business, anyway.

The intention behind the practice was hardly subtle; make his life miserable enough and he'd leave. As far as he was concerned, Superior would turn into a hot springs before that happened.

"I suppose you could say we had a philosophical difference," he finally said.

He'd used the same explanation she had for letting her cook go, mostly because that was what the matter boiled down to. Hannah, however, didn't seem to see any similarity at all.

"So you hit him?"

"No," he replied, his tone as flat as the horizon. "That's not what I did. Contrary to what you may have heard, I've never thrown the first punch. I just told him what I thought about his business practices. He took exception to my way of thinking and tried to loosen my teeth." He unconsciously touched the angry purple bruise on his cheek. "All I did was stop him."

Bud had missed on his first swing. Damon hadn't. That circumstance hadn't set well with Bud, who didn't seem to appreciate that Damon wasn't in a mood to exercise restraint. Damon tried to tell him that when he'd shoved the big ox against the wall, but Bud's friends had joined in about then. The long and the short of it was that both men, along with two others Damon had never seen before, had wound up in a heap at the bottom of the tavern's stairs.

He was no longer welcome at that particular establishment. He didn't much care, since he'd rarely hung out there, anyway. His only concern was his boat, and where he would dry-dock it before the lake froze.

The nights were already cold, the days growing shorter. The snows would begin in November, and temperatures would range from double digits below zero to a couple degrees above. By January, Superior itself would be a vast sea of ice. The port of Duluth would be frozen in for a solid three months. So would the inlet at Pine Point. The frigid weather was simply part of life for the lake people, and being one of them in that sense, Damon enjoyed the relative isolation that would come. He just needed to find a place for his boat.

"Isn't there somewhere else to store it?" she quietly asked. "Or can you cover it and leave it on a trailer? That's what my dad does with his bass boat."

"I could winterize it and leave it covered out at my place if it didn't need so much work, but this boat won't last another season without an overhaul. I need indoor space big enough to tear her down and put her back together." He'd been on the phone all yesterday afternoon looking for space. "Any sheltered places around here that size and with electricity were grabbed up months ago. The only place I found that sounds promising is up in Caribou Bay. But I sure don't relish the thought of that drive every day in the dead of winter."

There would be days when he wouldn't be able to get to Caribou to work on his boat because of the inevitable blizzards. And days when he wouldn't be able to get back, and he would be stuck there. He didn't have to mention that for Hannah to understand why he didn't seem terribly pleased with the possibility he'd found.

"Why did you come back here, Damon?" Was it to prove

something to the town? To himself? Between what he'd told her about his encounter with Bud During, and what she'd witnessed between him and the sheriff, it was apparent that Damon wasn't the one trying to cause problems. Yet, he apparently had no intention of walking away. "Why do you stay?"

The hard look he gave her tightened the muscles in his bruised jaw and burnished his eyes with heat. Her tone held nothing more than a quiet need to understand, but apparently all he'd heard were the questions themselves.

Or so she thought, until some of the rigidity eased from his wide shoulders. Setting the carton on the deck between his spread thighs, he stared down at his hands.

"I was away from here for ten years," he told her, still amazed by how little had changed in Pine Point in that time. Contemplating his bruised knuckles, he was no longer sure he'd changed that much himself. "I worked freighters on the St. Lawrence and on the docks at Sault Ste. Marie. I had nothing holding me anywhere, so I spent some time on oil tankers sailing between the West Coast and Hawaii. But I hated punching someone else's time clock, and I missed Superior. It grows on a person. Sort of becomes part of him," he admitted, then cut himself off because he wasn't accustomed to sharing what mattered to him.

"So you came back because you missed the lake." Hannah offered the conclusion quietly, looking beyond the breakwater to the vast inland sea that had such a hold on him. As solitary as he seemed, she was surprised he'd admit that anything had a hold on him at all. She suspected he'd also fought that hold for as long as he could. "But the lake is huge. There has to be a hundred other places you could settle where you wouldn't be bumping into the past every time you left your boat."

"None of them are Pine Point." He looked at her as if he would have expected her to understand, seeming almost disappointed that she hadn't. "When my dad died, he left me this boat and the house where I was born. This is my home."

His tone dared her to challenge his claim to his turf. But it never occurred to Hannah to try. As tough as he was, as guarded and combative as he could be, he had come back to claim the only thing in the world that was truly his. That his home mattered to him so much touched her more deeply than she would have imagined possible.

You make a place for yourself. Even if you're the only one in it.

The laughter of children drifted across the water. Drawn by the sound, Hannah glanced up the dock to see a young family headed for the tour boat. An instant later, her glance jerked to her watch. With a mental moan, she grabbed the sidewall behind her and rose to her feet.

"You're late," he concluded.

"Am I ever. I told Brenda I'd be back fifteen minutes ago. She can handle soups, but not the grill. Look," she said, not quite sure when she'd made the decision she was about to propose. "The space under the café is big and it's vacant. It used to be a welding shop, remember? If you think it would work, you could rent it for your boat. You don't have to answer me now," she told him, holding her hand palm out when his eyebrows jammed together. "Just think about it and get back to me. I'll talk to you later." She looked from his livid eye to the scrape on his knuckles as she backed toward the stern. "Take care of yourself. Okay?"

Chapter Five

Hannah pushed the heavy mop across the kitchen floor, throwing her back into the effort and hoping she wouldn't throw it out in the process. All she wanted was a hot bath, a cup of tea and something to read that didn't have ingredients listed in it. Ten minutes more and that dream would be hers.

The café was closed for the evening, the salt and pepper shakers refilled, the grill scrubbed. Her secret apple walnut batter sat in the refrigerator waiting to be baked into fresh muffins in the morning, and Eden, who'd served the dinner shift, had taken the leftovers from the day's special to the church for its shut-in program to save Hannah the trip. The day had been a long one, but it hadn't been as profitable as the Saturday before. The stream of customers had been slow but steady from noon on, and there'd been no time for a real break since she'd come back from the dock.

The scent of green soap and chlorine bleach annihilated the cooking smells that had earlier filled the room as she attacked a section of institutional beige tile by the double ovens. If her friends in Minneapolis could see her now, they'd never believe it. Hannah Davis, wife and business partner of Chef Gregory Davis, whose artistry with a sauté pan was legendary among the Twin Cities' movers and shakers, scrubbing the floor. There had been no less than forty people on their staff. Ten on janitorial and back kitchen alone. She had gone from working as a sous-chef in his original restaurant to being the always fashionably attired manager and hostess in the popular establishment they'd owned together. Anyone who'd known her then would take one look at her now and think she'd hit rock bottom.

She pushed a swath of her hair back with the sleeve of her worn sweatshirt and dipped her mop in the bucket. The thought of how appalled those people would be pointed out one of the more glaring differences between herself and what she'd left behind. She didn't mind scrubbing. And while her ability to present lamb medallions on a bed of sautéed arugula and make the dish look like a flower was totally wasted here, she actually preferred preparing simpler, heartier fare. She was exactly where she wanted to be. If she was missing a few of the dreams she'd once had, she'd just have to learn to get along without them. The only thought in her musings that bothered her at all was that those people really hadn't been her friends. They'd been Greg's. Not until they'd parted had she realized how totally his circle had eclipsed hers.

She was still frowning at that thought when she heard the squeak of boards groaning under weight. When the sound came again, the focus of her frown shifted.

In the past few months, she'd become accustomed to the groans of the old building, as comfortable with them as she was her own skin. But what she heard over the classical strains coming from the CD player wasn't just the creak and moan of wooden beams settling for the night. The distinctive sound came from the back steps. Specifically, the third and fourth steps from the top.

She turned down the volume, still listening, and caught the sharp raps of a double knock. The back entrance was seldom used except for deliveries, and no supplier she did business with made deliveries at ten o'clock on a Saturday night. Had she still be in the city, there'd have been no way she would open that door. Not being there alone as she was. But this was Pine Point, and the odd way her heart was beating had nothing to do with the threat of physical danger. As she moved across the room, still clutching the mop, she had the feeling she knew exactly who was there.

The glass storm door kept out the cold when she pulled open the inner one. She wouldn't have noticed the deep chill, anyway. Damon stood on the small landing, a mountain of male skepticism in a black leather jacket. His hooded glance flicked over her frame, the lemony glow of the porch light turning the bruises on his face a sickly shade of charcoal.

She reached for the aluminum handle, flipped the lock and pushed open the glass door.

Damon stayed right where he was.

"Were you serious about that offer this morning?"

Her hand tightened around the mop handle. "I wouldn't have mentioned it if I hadn't been."

Something shifted in his gray eyes, but his tone remained as flat as a fly on a windshield. "Then I need to look at the space. Is this a bad time?"

Anyone else would undoubtedly have told him that the hour was hardly convenient for an impromptu tour. Had *he* been anyone else, Hannah might have mentioned that herself. But she suspected that Damon had come as late as he had on purpose. It was the only way he could avoid running into the sort of problems he'd encountered there before.

Wondering how often he went out of his way to avoid people, suspecting from the way he'd tried to avoid her and

Mr. Lindstrom the day she'd met them that he did it more often than not, she pushed the door open wider. "I'm just finishing here. Come on in while I get rid of this."

He hesitated a moment, his hooded glance darting over her shoulder as if he were checking to be sure she truly was alone. Seeing no one else, he grabbed the door when she turned and followed her in to close out the cold.

She could feel his silent scrutiny on her back when she dropped her mop in the bucket and headed into her office. She had started out fresh that morning, but she now felt as wilted as old lettuce. Wisps of hair had loosened from the clip at the back of her head and the faded World's Best Aunt sweatshirt and holey jeans she cleaned in looked like something a street person would reject.

Struck by the thought that she cared more about what Damon thought of her than she would have the people she'd once considered friends, she plucked a key from the corkboard above her fax. The realization that she wanted *him* to care about *her* caught her so off guard, she didn't have time to question it. "You can go ahead and look around downstairs if you want. There's a light switch about three feet to your right when you first walk in. The switch for the main lights is back by the electric box."

Damon stood just inside the door, his dark features masked as he glanced around the small, efficiently arranged room. Steam rose from the dishwasher next to him, the machine finally silent now that it had moved into the dry cycle. The white walls looked as if the paint had nearly been scrubbed off of them, and the stainless steel surfaces of the preparation areas and the grill had been scoured and polished until they gleamed as much as their age would allow. The kitchen wasn't modern by any means, but it contained the equipment she needed and it was clean. Anything that could sparkle, did.

When his glance finally returned to her, she couldn't help thinking that he looked as if he weren't sure he should touch

anything. Then she caught the tightness in his jaw and she
realized why he hung back by the door. He wasn't venturing
any farther inside because he didn't want to be there in the
first place.

The only reason he had come was because he needed a
place for his boat. As she eyed the scabbed-over gash above
his eyebrow, she wanted to believe that a sense of fairness
and practicality was the only reason she'd invited him.

"How's your headache?"

"Better."

"How about your ribs?"

"I never said my ribs hurt."

She eyed him evenly, wondering why men in general and
this one in particular regarded pain as an affront to their mas-
culinity. "You hardly had to." She dangled the brass key in
front of him. "You winced every time you took a deep breath
this morning. I'd be willing to bet that you've either wrenched
or bruised your shoulder, too. You didn't say anything about
that, either."

The firm line of his mouth pinched, but he didn't deny her
observation. He didn't even seem surprised that she'd noticed
as much as she had. Looking as if he just wanted to get his
business there over with, he palmed the key and turned to the
door. "I'll be back in a minute."

"Take your time," she told him, and turned to finish her
task.

The open space that had once housed a welding shop was
as cold as a meat locker. With a scuffed concrete floor and
illuminated by banks of fluorescent lights, it was just about
as inviting as one, too.

Hannah wondered what Damon thought of the area when
she entered it five minutes later. She'd used the inside stairway rather than the outer one he'd taken, and she'd found
him near the back of that large, empty space. He had his

hands planted on his lean hips and was looking from the large white freezer on the end wall to the long glass box on the table under the back window. He didn't look terribly pleased.

"I had the freezer brought down here so there'd be more room in the kitchen," she said, speaking quietly so her voice wouldn't echo. "And those are my herbs," she added, since his attention had settled on the portable greenhouse. "I like to use fresh ones, so I grow my own. If they won't be in your way, I'd like to leave them down here. This side of the building gets the afternoon sun."

"They won't be in the way."

Damon's attention slid from the table-size glass structure with its profusion of green and silvery-leafed plants. He hadn't a clue what any of them were. But they clearly thrived under her care.

"Do you think this would be big enough for you?"

It wasn't the size of the place that had him concerned. Though a higher ceiling would have been nice, the space would suit his purpose quite nicely. The previous occupant had obviously worked on large equipment and installed the double, barn-type doors by the entry door that would make access with his boat possible. The steel bracing at the ceiling would be perfect for his hoist. The lighting was even better than he'd expected. What bothered him was the woman who owned it.

He didn't know what to make of her. Unlike everyone else, she simply refused to cut him a wide berth. And when he tried to push her away, she simply pushed back. Her didn't quite understand her physical response to him, either. She hadn't pulled away from him that day in the café, but she'd seemed almost confused by the electricity between them. He could still picture the awareness that had been in her eyes, could still feel the way she'd unconsciously turned into his hand when he'd touched her face. The pull between them was as strong as currents in a flood. And those silent, eddying currents held the potential to be just as dangerous.

"Why are you willing to rent to me?"

Her eyes darted from his, her stance becoming protective when she crossed her arms over the jacket she'd pulled on over her cleaning clothes. "You know that winter business is slow here. I can make it through to summer if it doesn't drop off much further, but I could be in trouble if it does. Or if something breaks down and has to be repaired or replaced." Her shoulder lifted in a shrug that wasn't anywhere near as dismissive as it could have been. "I can use the money."

He wasn't sure what he'd thought he'd hear. He'd just hoped that her offer hadn't had anything to do with pity, or that principle she felt so compelled to defend. He didn't want it to be personal.

"How much do you want?"

"I have no idea what boat space goes for. You'll have to tell me."

She trusted him to do right by her. Determined to do just that, for his own sake as well as hers, he gave her the figure he'd paid last year, then told her he'd double it because he was getting so much more space then he'd had. He'd also pay whatever extra it cost to heat the area.

She was fine with the utility arrangement. It was the rest of his offer she protested.

"That brings it to more than what that During person wanted you to pay. You can just pay me the rent you paid last year."

He mimicked her frown. "You're a landlord," he reminded her, annoyed further by the fact that the expression pulled at his eyebrow and made the cut above it sting. "You're not supposed to turn down rent."

"Well, I'm not going to take double. How about paying what you paid, plus twenty-five percent?"

"It's not just that he was going to jack up my rent," Damon explained, since she'd obviously missed the main reason he'd been so ticked at During. "He was going to cut my space so I couldn't work on my boat. That was a bigger deal to me than the money."

"Thirty percent?"

"Keep going."

"I'm trying to be fair here, Damon. I don't know how much it costs to remodel a boat, but it's bound to cost…"

"Refit."

"What?"

"You remodel a house. You refit a boat."

People who understood nautical terminology apparently had little tolerance for those who didn't. Damon sounded as tutorish as Mr. Lindstrom had when she'd called Damon a boss instead of a skipper. "*Refit* a boat," she repeated, fighting exasperation. She was trying to make a point here. She was also trying to be fair. He wasn't making either very easy. "As I was saying, it's bound to cost you a bundle. This area was just going to sit here empty, so I really think adding thirty percent is fine."

"How did you ever survive in the city? Or manage to run a business, for that matter?"

"I beg your pardon?"

"I'm really curious to know," he added, though he sounded more critical than anything else. "You're not supposed to negotiate a price down when you're the one with the property."

"I wouldn't criticize my business practices if I were you. You're the one trying to negotiate the rent *up*. So," she continued before their disagreement could get any more ridiculous, "do we have a deal, or not?"

His eyes narrowed, his exasperation with her as vivid as the bruises on his face.

"Is that a yes or a no?"

"Do you always get your way?"

"Rarely."

"Why don't I believe that?"

She smiled sweetly. "Maybe you're not the trusting sort."

"You got that right," he muttered. He wanted no favors from her. If she'd let him pay what the space was worth, then he wouldn't feel like she was doing him one.

"Do we have a deal?" she asked, holding out her hand.

He should have been pleased to find the space, but Hannah saw little beyond resignation in Damon's bruised and brooding features before he finally reached out and engulfed her hand in his. Had he not needed the space so badly, she'd have thought he was weighing whether or not to take it in the moments before he caved in. But she knew he had little choice.

It occurred to her that the lack of choice itself could well be what bothered him. But it was also entirely possible that he simply didn't like the idea of renting from her. The thought would have had her pulling back had Damon not just tightened his grip. She could feel the calluses below his fingers, the roughness of his skin. She could feel his heat seeping into her skin, her blood.

The sensations tightened her stomach and drew her glance to his scraped knuckles. A small white scar curved like a frown over his thumb. Another, fainter and silvery against his weather-tanned skin, angled the tip of his index finger. Both were old, evidence of dangerous work, or dangerous play. His hands defined him, she thought. Strong, callused and scarred. Yet, she felt a compelling sort of security in that strength— and unbelievable sensuality in the way his thumb slowly slipped over the delicate veins in her wrist.

Her pulse leapt at the contact. His touch was featherlight, as if he knew the nerves were sensitive there, though she'd never been aware that her wrist was sensitive at all. He moved his thumb slowly as he turned her hand, creating a sensation that was more warmth than heat, more promise than actual caress. The thought of what he might do if he ever got serious about touching her doubled her heart rate. But the tantalizing movement suddenly stopped, and she realized he was only turning her hand over so he could check the abrasions at the base of her hand.

The rashlike strip where the board had raked her skin was nearly gone. But he said nothing. Looking as if he hadn't meant to care whether the thing was better or not, he slipped his hand from hers.

"I won't move the boat in for another week," he said, his voice harder than it had been moments ago, "but I'll pay you now to hold the shop for me."

"You don't have to—"

The look in his eyes cut her off even before he spoke. "I'll give you the first month's rent now. If you want any other deposits or the last month's rent, too, I'll have to bring the money by tomorrow. I don't have that much on me."

She nodded, hating that he probably knew her heart was beating like a hummingbird's. "How long do you think you'll need it?"

"Four, maybe five months."

"Then one month in advance will be fine."

He pulled his wallet from his back pocket. Taking out several bills, he handed them over.

Quietly thanking him, she folded the money into her palm and crossed her arms. The motion was clearly protective. She told herself it was only because she was cold. "There's no hurry for the rest. Just bring me a check when you move your things in. You can start bringing your tools or whatever over anytime. I'll leave you a key for that door." She nodded behind her to indicate the door she'd come through earlier. "That's an interior stairway that leads to the café and on up to my apartment." She smiled, wanting badly to ease the strain filling the cavernous space. "Once the snow and ice settle in, it would be better if you'd use that instead of the backstairs if you need me for anything. I'd just as soon you didn't slip and bruise anything else.''

She'd meant her last comment to be teasing. But the moment the words were out her mouth, Hannah wished she could call them back. She'd been thinking only of his painful-looking bruises, but her veiled reference to his trip down a tavern's staircase apparently reminded Damon only of the fight preceding his descent. The sudden coolness in his expression as he replaced his wallet told her he neither needed nor appreciated the reminder.

He'd probably had his misdeeds thrown in his face all his life.

"Damon, I'm—"

"Do you want this back, or is it mine?"

His features were a study in stone when he held up the key for the outer door she'd given him earlier.

"It's yours. Listen—"

"Is there anything else I need to know before I move in?"

She truly hadn't meant to imply criticism, but he wasn't interested in letting her explain that. As he stepped back, stretching the gap of physical distance between them, it seemed that all he wanted was to leave.

"I think that about covers it."

His nod was as tight as his voice. "Then I'll get out of here and let you get back to what you were doing." He held up the key again. "Thanks."

He gave the key a little toss, caught it in a quick swipe and stuffed it in his pocket as he turned away. The thud of his boots echoed with each determined step, making the sudden silence when he stopped that much more profound.

He had his hand on the knob, his broad back to her when she realized that something wasn't letting him leave. For several seconds, he simply stood there, still and immovable as a mountain.

"The old man," he finally said. "Did they find him?"

He still faced the door, but he'd turned his head slightly to hear her response. Aware of the tension in his strong profile, wondering at the grudging concern in his voice, she murmured a quiet ''Yes, they did.''

''Was he all right?''

She told him he was. She would also have told him where the old gentleman had been, but Damon wasn't interested in the details. The moment his question was answered, he gave a taut nod, opened the door and walked out.

''What in heaven's name was that?''

Brenda spun around by the kitchen's swinging door, her widened eyes darting from the ceiling fixtures to the copper pans swaying on their hooks. The noise that had vibrated the walls and rattled the shelves in the pantry sounded like a sonic boom. Or a bomb blast.

Hannah spun toward the ovens. ''My cake,'' she moaned. The thing was going to fall like a rock. ''I'm going to strangle that man.''

''What man?''

''The one downstairs. He must be moving in.'' Tossing her oven mitts onto the counter, she yanked open the door by the pantry. That boom had to have been one of the big doors below banging open. ''I'll be right back.''

She was vaguely aware of Brenda gaping at her just before she fairly flew down the narrow stairwell. She'd just have to explain later. If by some miracle her cake survived the crash of the first door, she wanted to get to Damon before he could ruin it for sure with the second.

The big outer doors of the welding shop locked with metal rods that slipped into holes in the cement. Hannah burst into the shop's nearly empty space to see Damon's big frame silhouetted against a backdrop of gray sky and the hulking hull of his boat parked in the gravel lot. He had the rod on the second door lifted and had just put his shoulder to the frame.

In another second, he'd be swinging out the huge, heavy mass.

It vaguely occurred to her that his shoulder must be better, just before she cried, "Wait!"

His dark head snapped up, his whole body coming around so fast that she was the one who froze. She'd never seen anyone move so quickly, or look so murderous.

"Damn it, woman. You scared the hell out of me."

"I have a cake in the oven."

Confusion joined irritation. "So?"

"I bake from scratch," she explained, glaring at his fading bruises. Not one of them was as dark as his expression. "Scratch cakes aren't stable. You can't jar them like that."

"Like what?"

"Like you just did. When you opened that door," she said, arcing her hand toward the large gap where the other door had been, "it felt like an explosion upstairs."

It had been a week since she'd seen him. She wished she could say it had been that long since he'd entered her thoughts. Unfortunately, not a day had gone by that she hadn't found herself listening for him, and wondering if it was relief or disappointment she'd felt when another day had passed and he hadn't arrived. It wasn't as if she wanted a relationship with him. He wasn't the sort of man any sane woman would have a relationship with. She just wanted...

She didn't know what she wanted. When it came to Damon Jackson, she had no answers at all.

She shivered as the easterly breeze filled the shop with frosty air. Intent on saving her cake, she hadn't stopped to grab the jacket she usually threw on when she came down there.

"What happens when they're jarred?"

His deep voice lost some of its edge as he moved closer,

his expression more guarded than antagonistic now that he'd recovered from the start she'd given him.

The cut above his eyebrow was healing nicely and the rainbow shades around his eye had muted, for the most part, to a sickly shade of green. But his cheekbones seemed more prominent to her, the rigid angle of his jaw more defined, the sculpted shape of his lips more sensual. She couldn't imagine what could have caused such changes in such a short time, until it occurred to her that this was the first time she'd seen him freshly shaven. That was also about the time she realized she was searching his face with the same guarded intensity she could have sworn she saw in his.

Steeling herself against the tug in her midsection when he stepped closer, she murmured, "They fall."

"Did yours?"

"I don't know yet. But if it does, I won't be able to serve it. Since it was your fault, you'll have to eat it."

His eyebrows kicked up over the flecks of quicksilver in his eyes. "That's a threat?"

"I'd say that depends on whether or not you like spice cake."

He'd missed her. The thought hit Damon before he could deny it, before he could even try. He'd missed her spirit, her sass. He missed the way she smelled. It had never occurred to him before that the combination of soap and vanilla could be so erotic. But the scents evoked other images, too. Images of comfort and warmth, and those seemed far more dangerous and elusive than the sensual fantasies weaving through his mind. Sex he understood. The rest of it made him feel like a kid being teased with a toy he couldn't have.

Knowing he wouldn't let himself touch her made him edgier than he'd felt all morning.

"Is there anything else I shouldn't do?" he asked, absolutely determined to keep from screwing up this arrangement.

His biggest fear was that she'd change her mind about renting to him. When she'd nearly stopped his heart hollering at him to wait, he could have sworn she'd done just that. "Other than not bang things around?"

He tried to keep the challenge from his tone. Changing what came naturally wasn't all that easy. With his hands planted on his hips, it apparently showed up in his stance. She was eyeing him a little uncertainly when she wrapped her arms over the bib of her burgundy apron.

"No, there isn't," she quietly replied, apology in her eyes. "And I'm sorry I yelled like that. I didn't mean to sound like a shrew."

She didn't wait to see if he'd forgiven her or not. Glancing past him, she nodded toward his boat. "Is your deckhand with you?"

"He left after we got the boat out. I'm through fishing for the season."

"Do you have someone else to help you?"

"I don't need any help."

He could take care of the boat alone. Hannah got the message. More than that, she had the feeling he wouldn't have wanted help even had any been available.

"Well, let me know if you need anything," she told him, extending the offer, anyway. "I'm right up there."

"I know where to find you. Thanks," he added, the word softening his abruptness. He lifted his chin toward his boat. "I better get back to work."

He had no intention of seeking her out. Hannah felt certain of that in the seconds before she noticed the scratches on the side of his neck. They hadn't been visible until he'd turned his head. Now she could clearly see three pink parallel lines disappearing below the edge of his heavy blue sweatshirt.

The scratches looked like fingernail marks. Marks made by

someone grabbing for him, perhaps—or by a woman in the throes of passion.

Hannah's glance met his. Had he been in another fight, there would surely be other indications, a bruise, an abrasion. But the only marks she could see were the healing ones she'd noted before. Searching again, feeling concern shift to something she didn't want to acknowledge at all, she saw distance entering his cool gray eyes, and the faint pinch of his beautifully carved mouth.

He knew what she'd seen. He said nothing, though. He simply held her glance long enough to make it apparent that he knew what she was thinking, and that he wasn't going to deny it.

An odd little knot had just formed in her stomach when she became aware of feet pounding behind her.

"Hannah? Come on. You have orders backing...up."

In her rush, Hannah had left the stairwell door hanging open. Brenda's voice had started echoing off the narrow walls even before she'd hit the bottom step. Now, having practically swallowed her last word, the petite brunette slammed to a halt. With her arms braced on either side of the entrance, she gaped at the man whose expression had closed like a breeze-blown door.

"You'd better go," Damon said, then left her standing there, his long, powerful strides adding to the distance he was so adept at creating.

"Why didn't you tell me you'd rented this to him?" Brenda whispered as she backed up the stairs ahead of Hannah moments later.

"Because I haven't seen you since last Saturday. Eden worked your shift for you Sunday so you could go to Ron's parents for his dad's birthday, remember? By the way, you never did say how it went."

"It went the same way it always does at my in-laws. We

visited, we ate, we did dishes, we came home. And don't change the subject.'' Brenda's eyes narrowed as she kept backing up. ''Are you sure this is a good idea?''

''He needed a place to work on his boat, and I can use the money. It's a business arrangement, Brenda. That's all.''

The way her waitress's brows lowered spoke more of curiosity than condemnation. ''I didn't suggest it wasn't,'' she said mildly. ''I just asked if it was a good idea. Judging from the way you look right now, I don't think you're so sure it is. Neither one of you looked very happy with the other.''

Hannah didn't doubt Brenda's observation. What she questioned was why she should care what Damon did, or with whom.

''Everything's fine.'' She offered the assurance with a smile, determined to convince Brenda, if not herself, that she hadn't made a huge mistake. ''I just explained why he couldn't bang things around down here while I'm baking.''

''Nothing like starting off with a landlord-tenant dispute.''

''Please don't repeat that, Brenda. I know you're only joking, but you and I both know what someone else could make of a statement like that. There'd be a rumor going around that I was throwing him out before he even finished moving in.''

''There'll be rumors enough as it is,'' Brenda warned. Resignation swept her features. ''You might as well get used to that idea now.''

They had reached the door to the kitchen. Brenda had left it open and had already started in. Hannah let her go. She trusted Brenda, so her growing sense of unease had nothing to do with what the woman might say to anyone else. The sinking sensation in the pit of her stomach had to do strictly with the man downstairs.

Brenda was right. There would be talk. But Hannah hadn't let herself think about that uncomfortable fact because there was nothing she could do about it. When she'd made the offer to Damon, she'd been responding to needs she'd sensed in him, just as he'd done before with her. It made no sense that they should possess that sort of empathy, but because of it—and the fact that she hadn't been able to walk away when she could help—she now found herself in a rather unsettling position.

If there was anything positive to be found in the situation, it was the extra income—and the fact that she wouldn't have to worry about Brenda trying to fix her up with her new tenant. Playing cupid had become the woman's favorite pastime lately and no possible match had been overlooked.

"You're letting this place take over your life," Brenda had insisted just last week, oblivious to the fact that that was exactly what Hannah wanted. "It's not healthy. You're not interested in any of the customers. You won't let me fix you up with Ron's friend. And you haven't even noticed that Deacon Jim has the hots for you. What kind of a man do you want, anyway?"

The image of a scarred and battered man on a derelict boat had immediately come to mind, and Hannah had promptly banished it. She didn't want any man. For Brenda's sake, though, she'd simply smiled and said, "The right one." As for Deacon Jim, she was dead certain that her good-hearted friend had only made up the line about him. Hannah had met the mild, unassuming church deacon only twice. Both times had been at the fellowship hall when she'd dropped off meals, and neither time had she considered him anything other than...pleasant. Except for making it a point to compliment her kindness and her cooking, he hadn't paid any more attention to her than she had to him. She couldn't even remember what it had been like to shake his hand.

She had no trouble at all, however, recalling the unnerving sensations she'd experienced when her hand had slipped into Damon's the evening he'd rented the shop. With nothing more than the brush of his thumb, he'd had her nerves humming and her knees going weak. Yet, he'd shown no interest at all in capitalizing on her response. Not the way he obviously had with someone else.

Not that she wanted him to, she hurried to remind herself. She might have left Brenda to believe that she was just being picky, but where men were concerned, Hannah's self-confidence had been ground to dust.

Chapter Six

According to the radio, the storm blowing across Lake Superior the last week of October was "typical." As Hannah understood it, that meant she didn't have to drag out the shutters, but as she listened to the wind throw rain against the windows, she would almost have been grateful for the task.

She hadn't had a customer since lunch, and then only two truckers headed north. Had it not been for the thought of other travelers seeking a meal or a respite from the storm, she'd have closed the café and taken the envelopes she'd addressed for the senior center fund-raiser over to the fund-raiser chairman's house. She wouldn't close until it was time, though. She wanted people to know they could count on her to be there during her posted hours. Especially when they might really need her. So she packed up the envelopes, reminding herself to tell the chairman she'd be happy to stuff them with flyers when the flyers were ready, and proceeded to pace between the front windows and the kitchen, fiddling with nothing in particular, and growing more restless by the second.

She couldn't sit still to read. And she'd run out of pine-cones and dried statis to finish the huge, intricate grapevine wreath currently occupying her desk. She wanted the wreath to replace the moose head she'd taken down out front the day she'd taken over the restaurant. Until she could gather more pinecones, dry them and buy more of the strawlike purple flower from Hattie, the project would languish right where it was.

There had still been no sign of a customer when, having nearly paced the polish off the floor, she finally flipped the Open sign to Closed at exactly seven o'clock, turned off the grill and tried to pretend the distant rumbling she heard wasn't thunder. The last thing she needed was a dose of irrational apprehension on top of the restlessness dogging her every step. She hated not having something specific to do, but now that she didn't need to be available in case a customer showed up, she could tend to the few closing chores she hadn't already done, then go downstairs and water her herbs.

She couldn't imagine that Damon would still be down there. Not as late as it was. She'd heard him a few times in the past couple of days, but she hadn't seen him once since he'd moved in. She wasn't anxious to run into him now, either—which was precisely why she hesitated when she opened the door from the stairwell.

The shop lights were on. Considering that to be a fair indication that he hadn't yet left, she straightened her shoulders, wondering as she did why she felt a sudden empathy for Daniel when he'd stepped into the den.

Damon was nowhere to be seen.

Closing the door behind her, she cast a quick glance from the boxes of parts and equipment stacked against one wall, then over to his boat. It had been backed in and left on its trailer, its pointed prow inches from the bolted double doors. The pathetic old vessel looked even more derelict out of the water than it had in. The shells of bearded mussels clung like barnacles below the gray waterline on the bare, swollen wood. Below the stern, the blades of both propellers were pitted with rust.

A faint scraping sound had her looking back up, her glance drawn farther by the heavy chain and pulley looped over the steel bracing crisscrossing the ceiling. A second later, the dull thud of something metal hitting something wood preceded a truly inventive curse.

Damon was inside the boat. He was also now visible. The top half of his broad-shouldered frame appeared above the stern. If the thunderclouds in his expression were any indication, whatever he was doing didn't appear to be going well.

"Problems?" she quietly asked.

His head jerked toward her, his dark glance lasting a mere second before he returned his attention to whatever he was working on. "Nothing a stick of dynamite wouldn't cure."

"Interesting." Hannah caught a flash out the window and crossed her arms. "That was Mr. Lindstrom's solution to fixing a radio. Is that a standard remedy with fishermen?"

His annoyed scowl was directed at something she couldn't see. Turning that irritated expression on her, he muttered, "What?"

There was no mistaking his irritation, or his preoccupation. When it came to his boat, the combination seemed perfectly natural.

"Never mind," she murmured, since she didn't really have his attention, anyway.

"Hand me one of those rags over there, would you?"

He indicated a cardboard box full of torn and tangled cloth. Picking up what looked to be the back of an old flannel shirt, she stepped over a huge, decidedly barbaric-looking hook on the end of a chain and held the rag up to him. A moment later, with her head tipped back and her eyes squinting at the brightness of the overhead work lights, she watched the rag and his hand disappear from three feet above her.

"Can I get you anything else?" She directed the question to the mussels clinging to the wood in front of her. The little brown mollusks reminded her a lot of Damon. Stubborn, hard, the vulnerable places all hidden inside. As she gingerly touched one of the smooth shells, it occurred to her, vaguely, that the only way to get to the tender parts was to pry them out.

She dropped her hand, curling it into her palm as she stepped back.

"No, thanks," came his disembodied reply. "I can't start this until I finish bracing the boat. I just wanted to know if I could use a wrench on the engine bolts or if I was going to have to cut them off."

"I take it you have to cut them."

His silence implied hesitation. "Yeah," he finally muttered, sounding as if he wasn't sure how she'd known that. "That's exactly what I'll have to do."

Even as he spoke, another rag came sailing over the side. It landed with a soft plop on the scuffed concrete, its color indiscernible for all the thick, black grease on it. Seconds later, Damon appeared at the top of the ladder.

Swinging himself over the side, he made the trip down in two long steps, then walked over to where she'd backed up, still wiping grease from his hands with the faded rag she'd given him. "I wasn't disturbing you, was I?"

"No. No," she repeated, realizing he thought she'd shown up to complain about something. "I didn't even know you were still here. I came down to check the greenhouse." She offered him a smile that felt more strained than it should have and backed up another step. "But I can come back after you've gone."

"You don't have to do that."

"Come back?"

He gave her a level look. "Leave." The rag joined the

other. "If there's something you need to do down here, do it."

His glance dropped to her mouth, lingering long enough to make her heart jerk before he met her eyes once more. She couldn't tell if she'd been dismissed or devoured. Nothing in the masculine angles and planes of his features gave a clue to his thoughts. But, then, he was awfully good at giving nothing away. That was undoubtedly part of what made people so nervous about him. No one really ever knew what he was thinking.

That was obviously the way he wanted it, too. With the faint lift of his eyebrows, he turned away, leaving her to stare after him or tend to her task. The choice was hers.

Snagging her watering can from under the table supporting her greenhouse, she headed for the large utility sink at the back of the shop. Had her poor herbs not been gasping for a drink by now, she'd have bagged the chore and come back when she was sure he was gone. Hannah was edgy enough from the storm that had been building all afternoon. Now, between Damon and the threat of thunder, she felt downright anxious.

She turned on the water to fill the can, then grabbed a bottle of liquid fertilizer, all the while listening to the rain gush from the waterspout outside, and to the whistle of the wind through the cracks in the window frames. Behind her, a metal tool hit the cement floor. The sharp, ringing sound made her jump, causing her to slosh the fertilizer she was measuring over the side of her watering can where it swirled straight down the drain.

Irritated at herself for the waste, she took a deep breath, slowly let it out, then promptly tensed again when a flash of blue-white lightning lit the window behind the greenhouse.

"That's going to overflow."

The green watering can sat in the deep, stained sink, water shimmering at its brim. It had just occurred to Hannah that she wasn't entirely focused on her task when she felt Damon's arm brush hers. Jolted by the contact, she glanced around as he turned off the faucet and found herself eye level with the hollow of his throat.

"I didn't mean to startle you. I thought you knew I was behind you." He took a step back and held up his dirty hands. "I just need to wash up."

Telling herself to get a grip, wondering why she hadn't considered just how stormy it was around the lake before she'd moved there, she eased away from the sink with her can and watched him reach for a jar of something that looked like gray soap mixed with sand. The sleeves of his gray sweatshirt were pushed to his elbows, revealing the fine, dark hair covering the corded muscles of his forearms. Even now, long since Pine Point had seen much of the sun, his skin was still tanned from all the time he spent in the weather. She remembered the first day she met him, seeing him in the sleeveless black shirt that had revealed the thin tattoo circling his left bicep, and thinking that he looked as if he'd been hammered from bronze. Now she couldn't help wondering if he'd worked his boat without a shirt, and if his back and chest were that same shade of walnut.

She wanted to distract herself from the weather, but thoughts of Damon without a shirt didn't do a thing for the agitation she fought. Leaving him to work the soapy gray stuff around his nails, she turned off the artificial growing light attached to the greenhouse and tilted back a quarter section of the long lid.

"The radio says the storm should be peaking right about now," she said, needing to fill the silence with something other than the sounds coming from outside. As if to back her up, rain blew against the window glass, the ticking sounds of ice telling her it was mixed with hail. Wind whistled around the edges of the window, cold leaking into the room. "I don't remember what they said the wind gusts were supposed to be, but it didn't sound too threatening.''

"You should still have your storm windows up."

He didn't glance up, didn't stop scrubbing.

"I had to order new ones for down here," she told him, too busy anticipating the first loud crack of thunder to tell him she was well aware that everyone had put up their storm windows ages ago. "They were just delivered last week."

He reached for more of the abrasive-looking goop and went to work on his hands with a brush. "I'll put them up tomorrow."

"Thanks, but you don't have to do that. The building is my responsibility. I've already made arrangements with Brenda's husband to do it as soon as he gets a free afternoon."

"When will that be?"

"I don't know."

"Then I'll do it tomorrow. We don't need to be wasting heat."

She couldn't argue that, so she didn't try. She didn't get to thank him, either. He turned on the water, drowning out anything she might have said.

Taking his not-so-subtle hint, Hannah abandoned conversation and went to work with her hand trowel and watering can. She loosened soil, pinched some plants back for fullness and thinned the dill threatening to take over one end of the long tray, making it into a sheaf to dry. The pleasure she normally took in the motions was nowhere to be found. She simply did it because it had to be done, much as she'd found herself doing more and more lately.

The thought deepened the furrows in her brow. It had been the simple pleasures she'd come here to savor. If they lost their appeal, she'd have nothing left.

From the corner of his eye, Damon caught Hannah's pensive expression in the night-blacked window over the greenhouse. She was strung tighter than a bow tonight. When he'd come up beside her at the sink, she'd nearly jumped out of her skin. She'd done the same thing when he'd dropped a wrench putting his tools away.

Ten minutes ago, he'd been ready to call it a night. When Hannah had shown up, he'd known that was *exactly* what he should do. The more distance he kept between them, the better. But he'd seen her this way before, and like before, something about the brave front she put on made it impossible for him to grab his coat and go.

Thunder rumbled low in the distance, bringing her head up and magnifying her troubled expression. Her whole body had stiffened, but she diligently continued tying string around the stems of some long, weedy-looking plant, intent on ignoring what so clearly disturbed her. When she'd started talking about the weather, he'd thought she was just doing what she probably did with everyone by making polite conversation. Now he wondered if she hadn't been trying to talk herself out of her fear of the storm.

"Does thunder really frighten you, or does it just make you edgy?"

A stalk of the weed slipped through her grasp. "Edgy?"

Thinking an explanation was hardly necessary, he watched her swipe up the leafy stem. "You know, restless, jumpy."

"I'm not sure," she murmured. "I've never thought about it before."

"Think about it now," he suggested, since it was on her mind, anyway. "Think about something that scares you. Then think about something that makes you jumpy. Which feeling is closer to what you're feeling right now?"

The beat of the rain picked up again, hammering against the glass and the sturdy siding. Her delicate features strained, she quickly glanced toward the window, then returned her attention to making a hanging loop in the end of the string.

"What scares me is the thought of losing the café. As for edgy, I really can't thing of anything offhand."

He'd expected her to admit she was scared by fire or street thugs, or the thought of being lost in the dark at the edge of a cliff. Something that would put a person in physical danger. Losing some *thing* hadn't occurred to him.

"Try," he prodded.

You. You make me feel that way, Hannah thought, but there was nothing to be gained by that admission. "I don't know of anything else that makes me feel quite like this." It wasn't exactly a lie. The restiveness she felt wasn't completely due to his presence. "It's not like I was ever traumatized by a storm as a child. I was never left outside during a thunderstorm, or hit by lightning or anything so dramatic. The wind starts blowing and I start pacing." She gave her head a shake, shoving back the strands that had loosened from the restraining clip. "I told you once that it didn't make any sense."

Her annoyance with herself was as apparent to Damon as the apprehension robbing the light from her eyes. She believed it was her own fault she couldn't get past the distress she felt.

"It might make more sense than you realize." He grabbed a towel to dry his hands. When he glanced back up, her annoyance had turned to skepticism. "From what you describe, it sounds as if you're sensitive to changes in the atmosphere."

"You mean the way animals are? Like some can tell when a storm is coming?"

He shrugged. "Animals aren't the only ones who pick up atmospheric changes. I've known sailors who can sense when the weather's going to turn even before they check their instruments. In some cases it has to do with the effect of barometric pressure on the inner ear. I know one guy who claimed it was because his skin picked up the positive ions discharged during a storm. It's the negative ions that usually make people feel good. That's why some people like to walk in the rain, or stand by waterfalls.''

"Shouldn't that be the other way around? Which is positive and which is negative, I mean.''

He held her glance, absently rubbing the scratches fading from the side of his neck. His dark eyes grew intent, almost reproachful. "Not everything is as obvious as it would appear.''

Damon wasn't speaking only of the storm. He was talking about people's perceptions of him. And hers in particular. Hannah felt dead certain of that as the air in the shop became as charged as the air outside.

"I'd love to think there's a logical explanation for this,'' she told him, unable to understand why he would think she judged him the way everyone else did. She pulled her glance from his hand, not caring to consider the telltale marks under it. "But I doubt I'm anywhere near as sensitive to the atmosphere as the people you're talking about.''

The reproach had already disappeared. So had his interest in their conversation. Or so she thought as she watched him turn away to toss his towel over a sawhorse.

She'd turned away herself, thinking it best to just get her task finished and leave, when he came up behind her. Taking the trowel out of her hand, he stuffed it in the dirt.

"Push up your sleeve.''

Her glance skimmed from his chest to the shadowed angle of his jaw and collided with his enigmatic gray eyes. "My sleeve?''

"I want to show you something. Push it up and give me your arm.''

She didn't know what it said about her state of mind that she didn't question him any further. Doing as he'd more or less commanded, she held out her bare forearm. He lifted it, positioning it in an L between them as if she were about to exercise a karate maneuver.

She didn't know karate from a carburetor. She also had no idea what he was going to do.

"You don't think you're especially sensitive?"

More curious than wary, she murmured, "Not especially."

"What do you feel against your skin?"

She frowned over at him. "Nothing."

"How about now?"

He lifted his big hand, slowly skimming his blunt-tipped fingers a fraction of an inch above her smooth skin. He wasn't even touching her, yet the unnerving sensation had her immediately dropping her arm.

Shooting him a wary glance, she rubbed at the still tingling spot. "It tickles. What did you do?"

"Hold it back up here and I'll show you."

Between the banks of double fluorescent tubes above them and the work light over the long workbench a few feet down the wall, the spot where they stood was as bright as noon on a cloudless summer day. That strong light made it easy to see the gap between his fingers and her skin—and the fine, nearly invisible hairs covering her arm. He let his hand hover over one spot, lowering it until one finger scarcely brushed the end of just one of those tiny hairs.

The sensation unnerved her, making her feel jumpy. Edgy.

Her glance flew to his when she started to pull away, only to have him stop her short when his hand covered the spot he had sensitized.

"That sensation can be disturbing," he murmured, "if you're not in the mood for it." He moved closer, rubbing her lowered arm, and taking away the feeling he'd caused. "If the air in here was drier, I wouldn't have to get even that close. I could do the same thing with electricity on the tips of my fingers." The motion of his hand slowed. "That kind of subtle friction could be why you get so agitated when it storms. The physics are a little different, but the principle is the same. Especially when you're outside in the wind."

"Then why is it that the thunder bothers me when I'm inside?"

"Maybe you're like the guy who reacts to the positive charges and it doesn't matter if you're inside or out. Either way, the thunder is just the thing that makes you jump. If you're already feeling edgy, any loud noise would do it." Understanding settled in his smoky eyes. "You did it when I dropped a wrench a while ago."

He believed there was an explicable basis for something she had considered totally unreasonable. And while what he'd said actually made sense to her, she would have felt grateful to him even if it hadn't. He hadn't laughed at her fear, or teased her about it, or dismissed it as irrational or childish. He'd simply accepted it as something she felt, then helped her—made her—define it. It didn't matter that she'd still feel the same agitation when it stormed. It helped enormously just understanding why that agitation was there.

"What made you think the weather was the reason?"

His hand still moved against her arm, the slower motion seeming almost unconscious as he quietly studied her face. He said nothing for a moment, but the way he looked at her made her think he was wrestling more with whether or not he should admit how he'd reached his conclusion, than with the answer itself.

"There's a difference in you when the weather's bad," he finally said. "In the way you hold yourself. The way you move." He drew his fingers over her elbow, his eyes drifting to her mouth. "And I've noticed how sensitive you are to touch."

The sensitivity he spoke of now was only to *his* touch. But as vulnerable as that thought made Hannah feel, she couldn't admit it. She found the phenomenon threatening, alarming, fascinating. The latter, most of all.

The pressure of Damon's hand had slowly decreased, the firmness of his touch easing until his fingers barely whispered along her inner arm. The sensations that had made her so edgy before now elicited an entirely different set of reactions. Instead of wanting to pull away, she wanted to lean into him, to feel those strong fingers work over her shoulders, her back.

The scent of soap and warm, musky male filled her lungs. "I see," she whispered.

He'd said that the light, feathery sensation could be disturbing if a person wasn't in the mood for it. But he had altered that mood quite effectively with nothing more than his understanding, and his touch. She felt powerless against that combination. Powerless against him. He was far more perceptive than she could have imagined. Far more sensitive. And every glimpse he allowed her of the man behind the tough facade made it that much harder to deny how drawn she was to him.

Wind rattled the windows. Thunder rolled in the distance. She heard it. Felt it. But she didn't jump this time. It was as if, simply by touching her, Damon grounded her somehow.

The thought was as compelling as the feel of his skin brushing hers when he lifted his hand to cup her face. Without thinking, she turned her cheek toward his palm. The movement was barely perceptible, and completely instinctive. It was as if something inside her was seeking more of everything he offered and knew no other way to tell him how very much she needed whatever he would share. But the instant she moved, the dark slashes of his eyebrows jammed together like lightning bolts.

As if he'd only now realized what he'd been about to do, Damon dropped his hand and stepped back. A muscle in his jaw bunched when he pushed his fingers through his hair.

"I've got to go." His voice was tight, heavy with self-recrimination. "If I don't, I'm going to wind up doing something I'll regret."

Something far too vulnerable flashed in the depths of Hannah's eyes. An instant later, she'd lowered her head, but not before Damon saw the color drain from her face. He'd seen her react that way once before, the day he'd told her she didn't belong in Pine Point. Now, as then, she recovered so quickly he might have thought he'd only imagined how his words had affected her. But he knew exactly what he'd done. Once more, he'd protected himself at her expense.

She stepped back, her eyes avoiding his. "Thanks for the object lesson," she murmured, and turned to her greenhouse.

A hinge squeaked as she closed a section of lid. A moment later, she was checking the thermostat to make sure the temperature was still set correctly. Her motions were swift, efficient but not as rushed as they could have been. She wasn't wasting time getting out of there, but she wasn't going to let him see how deeply his rejection had wounded her, either.

He could see it, anyway, when she stuffed her pail under the table and headed for the stairwell door. Her quiet tone totally belied her guarded expression when she told him to have a good evening, offered him a smile that didn't quite work and closed the door behind her.

He'd already picked up his jacket. Now the soft leather bunched in his grip.

He hadn't meant to sound as terse as he had. He hadn't meant to voice his thoughts aloud at all. But the feel of her soft skin had elicited thoughts of how soft the rest of her body would be, of how that same silkiness would feel under him, wrapped around him, and his own body had grown tight as a fist. That tightness had worked its way into his voice, and the words had come out before he'd considered how they would sound.

He closed his eyes, clamping his hand over the back of his neck as he shook his head. He usually didn't give a damn if someone misunderstood him. People could think what they wanted. He even had Hannah thinking things that couldn't have been further from the truth. But he couldn't let this go. Not with her.

Dropping his hand to his pocket, he reached for his keys, picking out the one she'd left for him for the stairwell door. As he stuck it in the lock, he just hoped he wasn't about to make things worse.

She wasn't in the café. Or if she was, she wasn't answering his knock and neither of the keys he had fit the lock for the café's inner door. Damon knocked once more, on the possibility that she was on the other side silently wishing he'd drop dead, and called her name again.

"Hannah, come on," he coaxed, his deep voice echoing off the close white walls. "I need to talk to you."

"I'm up here."

He glanced up from where he stood on the landing. In the light of the single bulb illuminating the long stairwell, he saw her at the top of the second flight of stairs. A door stood open behind her.

"I need to explain something."

"There are some things a woman doesn't want to hear, Damon. And you don't need to tell me you have a girlfriend." Her glance darted toward the side of his neck. "I've already figured that out. It's just nice to know there are still men around who don't cheat."

Abject confusion washed over his face. "What?"

"Isn't that part of why you didn't…"

"Kiss you?" he suggested, since she couldn't seem to get it out.

He knew by her silence that was exactly what she meant, and he had no one to blame but himself for the conclusion she'd drawn. It was one he'd allowed, after all. It had served his purpose at the time, created the distance he wanted, needed.

With anyone else, he'd have let the impression stand. With her, he couldn't. She'd never judged him the way everyone else had.

"May I come up there?"

She didn't look terribly pleased by the request. Still, she held her hand palm out and motioned him in, then disappeared through the doorway herself. He followed, taking the steps one at a time, buying himself another minute to figure out how to say what he wasn't totally sure he could explain to himself.

She was on the opposite side of the room when he closed the door behind him.

This was different from walking into the café. The café was hers, but it wasn't personal. Not like this. This was private space, and it was filled with vibrancy, color and mementos of things she cared about. The end table and mantel held pictures of young people and old. Relatives and friends, he supposed. Every frame was different, as if it had been picked just for the person or people in the photograph. Pillows in lake-country shades of lupine and daffodil were scattered over a deeply cushioned navy blue couch. A yellow-and-white-striped overstuffed chair faced the end of the dark wood coffee table in front of it. Plants, a brass box and ornate vases were tucked among the books in the wide bookcase. Scraps of fabric filled a basket, some of the pieces fitted together in the beginnings of a quilt. It was as black as pitch outside, but the room seemed filled with sunshine.

Except for the faint chill coming from opposite him.

"What did you want to explain?"

"Can I sit down?"

"Go ahead."

"Will you?"

He motioned to the sofa. Hannah moved toward it, trying desperately to tell herself that what he said didn't matter. It was her own fault she felt hurt. For some insane reason, she hadn't tried all that hard to protect herself with Damon. Or maybe she had tried, but something about him dissolved her defenses before she could get them in place. She'd lived for twenty-eight years without a defensive bone in her body. Not until Greg had she needed one. She obviously needed more practice.

Maybe she should take lessons from Damon.

She thought he'd take the chair, but he sat beside her, much as he had the day on his boat. Resting his forearms on his spread knees, he hung his head, blew a breath that fluttered the dark hair falling over his forehead, then glanced over at her as if it were somehow her fault he'd found himself in this decidedly uncomfortable position.

"This isn't about any girlfriend," he said, his voice low. "I don't have one. And I haven't been with anyone," he added, touching the pink scratches on the side of his neck. "I know what you think these are, but they're not from a woman. They're from an animal."

For a moment, Hannah said nothing. She simply studied his profile, while he stared at his hands. He had no reason to lie to her.

Guilt stabbed at her heart. She'd jumped to conclusions about him, much as she'd suspected everyone else did. That he'd deliberately allowed the impression to stand didn't occur to her until she murmured, "What happened?"

"A raccoon moved into my back porch. He didn't like the idea of moving out." His voice dropped to a mutter. "I just wanted to explain that so we don't confuse the issue."

"I'm not sure what the issue is, but tell me something before we get into it. Do you do that a lot?" she asked, as confused as she was annoyed by what he'd done. "Let people get the wrong impression and just let it stand?"

He met her annoyance with challenge. "If it suits my purpose."

"What purpose could giving people the wrong idea possibly serve? That just makes things harder for you."

"We'll just have to agree to disagree on that. I happen to

think it makes things easier.'' The muscle in his jaw twitched as he looked back at his hands. "Except in this case."

He stared hard at the stains around his nails, stains all his scrubbing couldn't touch.

"I don't want to blow this, Hannah. This arrangement we've got," he clarified. "You said that the thought of losing the café scares you, so maybe you'll understand why restoring my boat is so important to me. If I don't get it fixed, I don't fish next year. That boat has been on Superior every year since my grandfather bought it. He and my dad worked it together, and I worked it with my dad until I left. He never could afford to do more to it than just keep it running, but it meant a lot to him."

Because it had meant a lot to his father, it meant a lot to Damon. The meaning was there, even if he hadn't put it in quite those words. She already knew his home was important to him, and she could see his unspoken need to preserve this part of his legacy in the determined set of his features when he met her eyes. But a man who pushed people away as readily as he did wasn't likely to verbalize such a sentiment. And pushing people away was exactly what he did when he allowed wrong impressions about him to stand.

As if he knew she saw more than he wanted, he glanced away once more.

"Like I said, if I don't get it fixed, I don't work. That's why I'm not willing to risk getting involved with you. All I'd need is for you to decide you don't want me around after we fall apart, then I'm stuck trying to find someplace else to work in the middle of winter. That's what I meant when I said I didn't want to do anything I'd regret."

He held up his hands, making a space that was scarcely visible between his fingers. "I came this close to kissing you a while ago, and I don't think you'd have stopped me. But I have a feeling you're the kind of woman who wants more than just sex from a man. I'm being as honest as I can by telling you that if we got started with anything, that's what I'd want and that's all it would be.'' His deep voice dropped like a rock in a well. "I'd rather we just keep things the way they are.''

Hannah blinked at his jaw, his arm, his hands, everywhere but his eyes. She didn't know which she found more revealing. The way he automatically assumed that any relationship they had wouldn't last, or the surprising sadness she felt because of it. Either way, she supposed a woman had to appreciate honesty like that. Most men would have taken the sex and kept their mouth shut about whether or not it meant anything to them. Not that she'd been offering it. Not that she'd been anywhere close. But he hadn't read her wrong. She wouldn't have pushed him away.

She tucked her stocking feet beneath her, trying to look as if she was making herself more comfortable when what she wanted to do was curl up inside herself. Maybe she would feel grateful to him later. At that particular moment, she simply couldn't. Something about knowing that a man wanted nothing of her except what she could offer physically tended to make her feel a little inadequate, not to mention a tad humiliated. The worst part was that the feelings were so horribly familiar.

"I knew I'd make it worse,'' he muttered, and slapped his hands on his knees to push himself up.

Hannah's hand shot out, catching his arm. Having stilled him, she immediately pulled back.

"No. You didn't... No,'' she concluded, forcing herself to separate what Damon was doing from what Greg had done. The man tensely watching her now was nothing like her ex-husband. Damon surrounded himself with a fortress of walls, but he was being as upfront as he could be. After all, knocking the wind out of a person's sails before she left the harbor was far kinder than ripping a hole in the bottom of the boat once she got to sea.

It took integrity for a man to say what Damon had—even if he hadn't been terribly sensitive about it.

"You don't need to worry about the shop. We made a deal and I'll stick to it. As for the other…" She cut herself off, hugging a blue throw pillow to herself. "Let's just say that I'm no more interested in a relationship than you are. I've sworn off for the duration."

"I'm trying to do something right here, Hannah."

"I know that. I'm just being as honest with you as you were with me."

Damon's glance narrowed. For a moment, he'd thought her declaration nothing more than tit for tat. *You don't want me, I don't want you.* But there was nothing in her expression to back up that conclusion. She hadn't even sounded defensive. If anything, curled up as she was and hugging that pillow like a shield, she looked almost defenseless.

He'd bet his boat she had no idea how vulnerable she looked.

"I take it that your ex got the restaurant."

He posed the premise flatly, more conclusion than question. It was that unerringly accurate insight that relaxed Hannah's unconscious stranglehold on the pillow and sharpened her glance.

"How did you know that?"

"I didn't until now. But it wasn't too hard to figure out. The day I helped you with your shutters, you told me you'd owned a restaurant with your ex. A little while ago, you said the thing that scares you most is losing this place. Now you're saying you've sworn off men." He shrugged, the muscles in his broad shoulders shifting beneath midnight blue fleece. "It just adds up."

The man seriously underestimated his powers of deduction. His perceptions where she was concerned were amazingly accurate—and more than a little unnerving.

"He got the restaurant," she confirmed. "And the house,"

she added, because Damon seemed to be waiting for her to go on. She'd worked so hard to make that house a home, and to make the restaurant a success. And she had. The home had been lovely. The restaurant had been four-star. "He bought out my interests in both."

"Why didn't you buy him out?"

She liked that he thought she could have done that. "Because it was all a lie." Her voice grew softer. Not with hurt. It felt more like bewilderment now. As if she couldn't believe she'd been so malleable. "When I look back on it, it's so easy to see it was all a facade. I didn't even realize how much of myself had ceased to exist. We did everything Greg's way. We used his ideas in the restaurant. His tastes in the house. We associated with his friends. His family.

"It wasn't as if he kept me from my family," she added, plucking at a thread. "Greg just always managed to be busy when it was time to celebrate an occasion at my parents' home, or when they came to visit. He couldn't be bothered."

"No wonder you divorced him."

"I didn't. He divorced me." She set the pillow aside, propping it against its yellow mate. "He left me a note one morning saying that he'd made a mistake. He didn't love me. He never had." She toyed with the thread, pulling it through her fingers, rolling it into a little ball. "When we talked later that day, he told me he'd married me on the rebound. It seemed his old girlfriend was back and that she wanted another chance with him. There was nothing for me to do but leave.

"I bought the café," she continued, knowing Damon would understand, "because I wanted something that was truly mine. A place I felt I belonged in, and that no one could take from me." A sardonic little smile tugged at her mouth. "So this is where I work and this is my home, and I like things the way they are just fine."

From the corner of her eye, she saw him glance toward her.

"Sounds good," he said, watching the nervous movements of her hands. "But which one of us are you trying to convince?"

Her hands went still. The mild question threw her, but not nearly as much as the sympathy in his tone.

"I don't know how we got onto this," she murmured, disconcerted by the notion that she might actually have more in common with him than she did with anyone else in town. She couldn't imagine that he was all that happy with the life he'd created for himself. Not as lonely as it seemed to be. "It's not what you came up here to discuss."

"No," he agreed. "It's not. But before you kick me out of here, you might as well know that I think your ex is a jerk."

The sentiment made her smile.

"So," he said, forcing his glance from her mouth, "I suppose I'd better get going." The muscles in his thighs bunched as he rose in one powerful move. As he towered over her, his glance grazed her upturned face before he stepped to the side and pointedly stuffed his hands into his pockets. "I want to pick up something to eat before the hamburger place on Fourth Street closes."

Hannah rose more slowly, aware of his size, and the way the subtle tension he radiated filled the room. The rain still drummed on the roof, louder here than anywhere else in the building. He'd said he didn't want to mess up their arrangement, and he was trying now to put their situation back on an even keel. She did her best to reciprocate.

"You don't have to go there."

"Sure, I do. There's nothing in my refrigerator but a six-pack and a bottle of ketchup, and I'm starving. I was thinking about getting takeout from you, but you're closed."

"Just because the café is closed doesn't mean I can't fix you dinner."

He gave her a look that clearly said he wanted no favors. "You don't have to do that."

She matched his expression perfectly. "You don't have to put up my storm windows, either."

"Sure I do. I'm paying for the heat down there."

"But the windows are my responsibility, not yours. I'll get someone else to put them up."

"Why do that when I'll do it for nothing?"

"Why drive to the other end of town for something to eat when I can fix you something here? I'll even fix it to go."

Damon went silent. He simply stared at her, his eyes narrowing as if he was either trying to figure her out, or wondering if he should even try.

"I think I know why you win most of your arguments," he finally said, his voice as flat as a griddle. "You just confuse the point so much that whoever you're arguing with finally gives up."

She thought her argument perfectly logical, in a roundabout sort of way. But she rather liked him confused. It softened his edges, lowered his wall. Since he confused the daylights out of her, she thought it only fair that he share the condition.

"So is clam chowder and sourdough all right?"

It was better than all right, but his sigh held pure frustration when he snagged his jacket from the end of the sofa and motioned her back to the kitchen.

Chapter Seven

It took longer than Hannah expected for the locals to realize that she had a tenant. Because there was nothing between the back of her building and the dock on the inlet, other than empty land, there hadn't been many people around to notice Damon moving in. Apparently, the only one who had was Dorothy Yont's son. Peter Yont had been on his way up the hill from the dock when he'd seen Damon back his boat into the shop, but he'd forgotten to mention it to his wife until just before they'd left to play cards at Millie and Gunnar Erikson's house a couple of nights later. At least, that was what Hannah was told by Hattie, the florist, who'd run into Millie at the beauty salon the morning after the card party.

Where the sheriff had heard it, Hannah had no idea. But Pine Point's highest ranking law officer was in the café's kitchen and looking none too pleased with his reason for being there.

Sheriff Jansson's rangy frame filled the doorway of Hannah's tiny office. His broad-brimmed uniform hat had left a hat-dent in his hair, and the strands at his crown stood on end, despite his attempt to flatten them with his palm. His sharp, angular features were grim. His manner, almost patronizing.

"I don't think you realize what you've done here," he informed her, keeping his voice low so their conversation wouldn't be overheard by the customers Brenda waited on out front. "I understand why you'd want to rent that space down there. It just makes good economic sense. I kept telling Lilly that she ought to get someone in there after Olaf retired," he added, speaking of the café's previous owner and the welder who'd last occupied the space. "But Jackson's not the sort of person you want for a tenant. He's not the sort you want around at all. I advised you of that myself."

Hannah stood by the elaborate wreath-in-the-making on her desk. Her expression was far more cordial than she felt. "I understand he has a reputation," she conceded, aware that the sheriff was not at all happy with the way she'd ignored his dogmatic "advice," "but he's paid his rent and he's quiet. I don't judge my tenant any more than I do any of my customers."

"There's a difference between judging people and thumbing your nose at the advice of your friends, Hannah. You've got a reputation for being a soft touch. That's not a bad thing in itself," he hurried to add, clearly willing to allow for compassion. "Everybody knows they can count on you to help out if you possibly can. And I suppose a nature like that makes you sympathetic to the underdog," he surmised, clearly figuring she didn't have the brains to avoid being taken advantage of. "But that kind of thinking blinds you to a person's flaws. In this case, you've allowed a man of questionable intent…a man no one wants around, mind you…to come right into the middle of us."

Hannah's stomach knotted, but she didn't even blink. "I've

rented a man space to work on his boat," she calmly explained, irritation fighting dismay. She'd expected talk, but she'd thought it would simply be more of the same. The same stories of Damon's transgressions. The same warnings. The last thing she wanted to do was create enemies. She especially didn't want to make an enemy of someone as influential as the sheriff. "From what I understand of Damon, he wants even less to do with the people here than they do with him. I can't imagine that his being in that shop is going to cause any trouble for anyone."

The man's hazel eyes turned sharp, assessing. "From what you understand of him, huh?" He tipped his head to study her closer. "What about you?" he asked, his voice a little too mild. "Aren't you nervous having him around?"

As loaded questions went, that particular one packed the potential of a small nuclear bomb. The sheriff was clearly measuring her reaction. But his question had Hannah considering something she hadn't realized before. It had never occurred to her to fear Damon. Even as rude as he'd been at first, as rough as he'd looked—still did, for that matter—she'd never been afraid of him.

Growing more cautious by the second, she chose her words carefully. "No more so than I would be with anyone else. He's been an excellent tenant." So far.

"You'd better be more nervous than that," he admonished, pointedly overlooking the commendation. "Having him here could be dangerous for you, Hannah. If you're as smart as I think you are, you'll break your lease or rental agreement or whatever it is you've got with him and get him out of there before you find out for yourself just how much grief he can cause a person."

He was undoubtedly thinking of the grief Damon had personally caused him, as well as whatever he'd caused the town. But no matter how self-serving or well-intentioned his warnings, the threat behind them made her throat feel tight. The sensation was disconcerting, a little like she imagined a noose might feel being drawn around a person's neck.

"I can't do that," she replied, hoping desperately that she wasn't hanging herself. The sheriff was forcing her to choose, and her choices were between Damon and her integrity, and the town.

It occurred to her, vaguely, that even though Damon would never offer himself as a choice, he would never put her in such a position.

"I told him he could rent the space until spring, and I'm not in the habit of going back on my agreements." Consternation shadowed her features. "I can't imagine that you are, either, Sheriff."

The skin above the tight collar of his khaki shirt and necktie turned a pale shade of fuchsia. "I'm trying to help you here, girl. You've got yourself and us into a situation that no one else in this town would have even considered."

"It's only a situation if people let it become one. For heaven's sake," she said, irritation leaking through her composure, "he keeps to himself so much I don't even know when he's there."

That was the truth. She hadn't heard or seen Damon since she'd prepared takeout for him a few nights ago. He'd watched her fill a carton with chowder and box up sourdough rolls and a generous slice of pie. Then he'd thanked her and left before the tension snaking between them had them arguing about something stupid again. She'd gone downstairs twice since to thank him for putting up the storm windows. He hadn't been there either time.

"*I* know he's there. And I'll be keeping my eye on him," the sheriff added, sounding as if he were warning her rather than keeping her informed. "You can count on it."

He pushed his hat down over his cowlick and was gone seconds later, the kitchen door swinging behind him. It was as clear as the consommé simmering on the stove's back

burner that he'd expected her to be more cooperative, and
that he wasn't at all pleased by her refusal to back down to
his authority. She wasn't terribly pleased, either. She had
started out defending a principle. Now it seemed she was
defending herself.

In the process, she was standing up for Damon, and *that,*
she felt certain, was why the sheriff had looked as if he was
about to pop a vein when he'd walked out.

Hannah heard nothing more from Sheriff Jansson that
week. He didn't come in for lunch. Nor did he stop for coffee
and pie to catch up on gossip as he often had when he hadn't
been able to make it in for a while. Hannah noticed the absence of a few of her other regulars, too. Mostly friends of
the sheriff. But the weather had been pretty nasty lately, and
she wanted to believe the miserable wind and rain was what
kept those particular customers from venturing out. Neil Lindstrom and his cronies from the Snow Daze committee had
been in a couple of times, pushing the tables by the front
window together for their meetings, and she still had her
truckers and travelers, people who couldn't have cared less
what she did so long as she kept her coffee hot, fresh and
strong and she got their orders right.

Dinner business, already slow, dropped off even further.

Hannah continued blaming the weather, and even though
she wanted customers, she almost began to dread the tinkle
of the bell over the café's front door. She couldn't count the
number of times she'd been asked if the rumor about her
renting to Damon was true, but it was equal to the number
of times she'd pasted on a smile, said "As a matter of fact,
it is" and promptly, politely changed the subject.

Brenda said she was the only person she knew who could
grit her teeth without clenching her jaw. Her wonderfully sup-
portive waitress also told her not to worry about the people
who hadn't been in that week. Before long, they would see

that Damon wasn't doing anything but working and they'd be back. It was just a change having Damon literally right under their feet, and people were wary of change in Pine Point. As for herself, Brenda said that if Hannah didn't have a problem having him around, then she didn't, either.

Damon, too, had once mentioned how reluctant the locals were to accept change. Only he'd been a lot more cynical about it. Hannah didn't mention that, though. She told Brenda only that she hoped she was right about people getting used to him being there, and tried to put thoughts of Damon from her mind.

She was engaged in that same effort when she flipped the sign on the door to Closed the following Thursday night and headed back to the kitchen to finish cleaning up.

She had no more luck banishing Damon from her thoughts than she usually did. It had now been a week since she'd seen him, and as far as she knew, he'd done nothing but mind his own business. She knew he wouldn't seek her out. He was keeping his distance from her the same way he did with everyone else. Which was exactly what she wanted, she reminded herself. Even if they hadn't made it clear to each other that neither was interested in a relationship, he was a definite threat to her acceptance in the community.

So why did she keep listening for him, waiting for his knock on her door? Why did she worry about him working alone with all that barbaric-looking equipment? What if he got hurt?

With a sigh of disgust, she gave the stove one last swipe and tossed her sponge toward the sink. The sponge had no sooner hit its mark than she turned to see Damon in the open door of the stairwell.

Her heart slammed against her ribs, as much from the start he gave her as the way he looked standing there.

His broad-shouldered frame filled the doorway. A long-sleeved black T-shirt hugged his wide chest. Jeans, worn soft and streaked with grease on one powerful thigh, molded his lean hips. He stood still as stone, one hand on the doorknob and a day-old growth of beard as dark as his sable hair shadowing the stubborn line of his jaw.

His narrowed eyes darted to the darkened service window, then swept dispassionately over her pale features. "Are you all right?"

Willing her heartbeat to slow, determined to look as unaffected as he did, she dropped her hand from her throat. "I didn't realize you where there."

"I knocked, but I guess you didn't hear me. The door was unlocked."

She'd left it that way. In case he'd needed something.

"The dishwasher." She motioned toward the chugging machine that had masked the sounds of his heavy boots in the stairwell. "It's pretty noisy," she explained, quite unnecessarily since he could hear it himself.

"You're closed, aren't you?"

The dark rumble of his voice skimmed along her nerves. Disquieted by the effect, by him, she looked away before she could search his guarded features too closely, or give away too much of the ambivalence she felt at his presence. She didn't want to be affected by him at all—or to care that he looked so tired.

"I closed about ten minutes ago. I'm just cleaning up. But I can still get you something to eat, if that's what you want."

Damon watched her uneasy glance stray back to him as he stepped inside and closed the door. The overhead lights exposed the strain behind her smile and caught the strands of ruby and topaz in her deep auburn hair. The lovely contours of her face were more pronounced with her hair pulled back as it was, but the severity of the style also made it easy for him to see the faint lines of worry in her fragile features.

Those delicate lines weren't new, but they were deeper, as

if she harbored some concern that was beginning to weigh on her.

"I'll get something at home. But thanks," he added, surprised by the desire he felt to soothe the faint lines from her brow. It wasn't like him to offer comfort. He wasn't even sure he knew how. He did know, however, that touching her was not in his best interests. If he did, he'd want to ease his hands into her hair, take it down so he could see it tumbling around her shoulders the way it had that first day on the dock. He already knew its softness. That silken mass would feel like heaven in his hands.

He shoved his hands into his pockets, intent on blocking the next scenario unfolding in his thoughts. "I just came up to see if you have any spare fluorescent tubes. A couple were burned out when I moved in and another one went just a few minutes ago. I need the light."

"There might be a box in the storage area behind the water heaters."

"I already looked there. All I found was an old neon sign and a moose head."

She needed to get rid of that thing. Heading for the utility closet, knowing she had a box there, she glanced back over her shoulder. "Do you want it? The moose head, I mean."

"No, thanks."

"You're not into antlers?" she asked, trying for a lightness she definitely didn't feel.

"Only if they're on something that's walking around. I just need the tubes so I can finish what I'm doing."

All he wanted was to get what he'd come for so he could leave. No small talk. No polite conversation. Taking his not-so-subtle hint, she opened the door to the shelf-lined space and snagged the step stool with her foot. Just as she did, the telephone rang.

"Hang on," she murmured to him, and grabbed the portable phone off its station in her office next door. Thinking to take the call while she searched for light tubes, Hannah answered with a vaguely distracted "Pine Café" and started for the utility closet again.

Her foot had hit the first step on the step stool when she smiled. Her caller was Carin Holmes, Eden and Erica's mom. But she'd no sooner lifted the narrow three-foot-long box from the shelf behind the window and floor cleaners, and climbed down to see how many were inside when the last traces of her smile vanished like smoke in a stiff breeze.

"You want them to quit? Of course, I understand," she insisted, when Carin paused to let the dust settle from the little bomb she'd dropped. "I'm just really sorry to lose them. They're terrific with the customers.

"Absolutely," she replied after Carin hesitantly asked if the girls could still use her as a reference. "And if they want a job this summer before taking off for college, I'd love to have them back."

Hannah meant what she said. As long as she could afford them on the payroll, either or both of the girls were welcome back anytime. But as Carin thanked her, then hurried to add yet another excuse for why the girls had to quit so suddenly, Hannah began to suspect that there was far more than what Carin was saying about why she no longer wanted her daughters to work at the café.

By the time she switched the phone off a few moments later, the same sick feeling she'd had the day the sheriff showed up had settled like a hot rock in the pit of her stomach.

She looked at the box in her hand, then held it out to Damon.

"There's only one in here."

"It'll do for now."

"I'll get you the other two as soon as I can."

He tipped his head, something suspiciously like concern encroaching on his hard features. "What's going on?"

She couldn't quite meet his eyes. Skimming a quick glance past the strong cords in his neck, she made it as far as the masculine cleft above his upper lip before she turned to set down the phone.

"Two of my waitresses won't be working here anymore."

"Two quit at once?"

"They're twins," she explained, wanting to play down their defection. She had the feeling this wasn't the girls' choice, anyway. She could be wrong. Maybe they *had* suddenly found themselves so busy with their other commitments that they really couldn't handle working weekends. But why wouldn't they have told her that? "It's their last year of high school and they've got tons of homework and activities. Their mom said working here was just taking too much time away from everything else."

She started to mention that the holidays would be especially busy for them, too, since Carin had tossed that excuse in with the rest, but that rationale would undoubtedly sound as lame to Damon as it had to her. Thanksgiving was more than two weeks away. Aside from that, the girls had been looking forward to having extra money for Christmas. And the day before Damon had moved his boat in, in fact, Carin had been going on about how good it was for the girls to work for her, and how much she appreciated Hannah sticking by them when Inga's patience had run short because they were so young. They'd been busy with school then, too. The only factor in the equation to change since then was Damon's presence.

"What about your other waitress?" Damon's tone was mild, his expression deceptively casual when he set the box on the empty work island behind him. "The little one with all the hair."

Brenda would love that description, Hannah thought, but she was too unsettled to muster a smile. "I still have her."

Brenda was a friend. But, then, she'd thought Carin was becoming one, too.

"Do you want to tell me what else has happened lately?"

Between her conversation with the sheriff, her dwindling receipts and the fact that he'd been the topic *du jour* all week, she wouldn't have known where to start. But it wasn't the question, so much as the oddly offhand way he posed it that made the rock burn a little hotter.

"Nothing," she assured him, having no intention of burdening him, anyway. "Nothing's happened. It's actually been rather—"

"Slow?"

He offered the possibility in the same too-quiet tone, and deliberately stepped closer.

"It's been a little slow," she conceded, stepping back. The movement was automatic, instinctive. Like stepping out of the way of a big truck. "But the weather's been terrible. No one wants to be out in a downpour."

Frowning faintly at what she'd done, he stayed where he was, studying her over a five-foot stretch of beige linoleum. "People don't let weather stop them around here. If they did, they'd be in hibernation until summer."

He watched her cross her arms over her stomach, the frown increasing a degree before he refocused on her face. "Is it slower than it was before I moved in downstairs?"

She didn't trust the casualness of the question. His whole manner was too certain, too controlled. She had the feeling he already knew the answers to everything he asked. He just wanted to hear her say the words.

She had no idea why he would want that. But he would push until he got what he wanted, and given the week she'd had, she didn't feel up to pushing back. "Maybe a little."

It was easier to focus on anything but the gray eyes that slowly turned hard as tempered steel. The utility room door was still open. Turning her attention to it, she closed it with a quiet click, acutely aware of the silence across from her.

Five seconds passed. Then five more. Damon hadn't moved.

"Are you going to tell me what the sheriff said? I know he talked to you," he informed her when her surprised glance flew to his. "He paid a little visit to the shop last week to make sure I knew he was keeping an eye on me. He mentioned that he told you the same thing." His eyes shifted over her face, searching, assessing. "I want to know what else he said."

Damon's tone remained deceptively even, his outward calm remarkable for the resentment he must have felt at the sheriff's uncalled-for intrusion. Anyone else might have believed the incident had no effect on him at all. But, to Hannah, the tension slowly creeping into his body was unmistakable. It was in the subtle tightening of his jaw, the rigid set of his broad shoulders, the faint flare of his nostrils.

He'd suggested that she was sensitive to the electrical charges in the atmosphere. She was also exquisitely sensitive to him. He affected every nerve and cell in her body, and, at the moment, his tension was definitely feeding hers.

"He just wanted to know if it was true that I'd rented the shop to you. And to be sure I understood what I was doing," she added, considerably understating the man's warnings. She didn't want Damon angry over what the sheriff had said to her. That would only make her problems worse. Not that he would get himself involved, she thought, which made her wonder why he was even asking. "That was about it."

"You mean, he made sure you know what I can do to a woman's reputation."

An edge finally entered his tone with that blunt statement. It was matched by the flintlike hardness in his eyes.

"He didn't get specific, but I imagine that's what he was getting at."

"He won't get that detailed. The last thing he'd want is to remind people that his daughter used to sneak out of her room at night to meet me."

"Is that why he has it in for you?" she asked, voicing the suspicion she'd harbored ever since Brenda mentioned his involvement with the beautiful Maryanne. "Because you had an affair with his daughter?"

"That," he tightly agreed, "and the fact that he can't control me the way he does everyone else. And by the way, it was his underage daughter," he clarified, wanting to make sure she had the whole picture. "Only I didn't know she was his daughter when I saw her hanging around the docks, and I sure as hell didn't know she was only seventeen. She told me she was older."

"Did the sheriff know that?"

"Do you actually think it would have mattered?"

He didn't wait for an answer. Before Hannah could do much more than open her mouth to ask if he'd even tried to defend himself, Damon had dismissed the question.

"She was just using me to rebel against her old man," he muttered, sounding as if being used was of no consequence at all. "I was twenty-two, nowhere near good enough for that family and she knew it. Her daddy was scared to death that I'd gotten her pregnant and ruined her chances with a decent man.

"I didn't give a damn about much of anything back then," he admitted, his eyes locking on hers, "but the one thing I made sure of was that I didn't get anyone pregnant. There was no way I could support a kid. I was barely making a living as it was."

Damon didn't pull any punches with her. He never had. When he looked at her as he did now, his steady glance full of heat and challenge, it was hard for Hannah to tell if he was recounting his sins to her to push her away, or if it was because, in some indefinable way, he trusted her.

The latter possibility would have been laughable, had she not realized that she might very well trust him, too.

"That was what?" she asked, less stunned by that realization than she probably should have been. "Ten years ago?"

"About that. But it might as well have been ten minutes. Nobody forgets anything around here. Ever. When Jansson sees me now, all he sees is a giant black spot on his family's reputation. I don't give a damn about him or his family. I just wish to hell he'd forget about me." His voice fell, his words becoming barely audible. "And leave you alone."

He turned away from her, too agitated to stand still any longer. He faced the shiny surface where he'd left what he'd come for, but he didn't pick up the box. His back to her, he jammed his hands on his hips, pulled a breath that expanded his shoulders and slowly released it.

The dishwasher gave a metallic thunk as it switched from the drain cycle to dry. In the sudden silence, Hannah could hear the gentle patter of rain outside the back door. Without the wind, the sound should have been soothing. Had her thoughts not been so chaotic, it would have been.

She couldn't believe how easily he'd dismissed what the sheriff's daughter had done to him. Maryanne had settled down, grown up and gone on to catch her prize in Cleveland—the prosperous lawyer in the pictures the sheriff so proudly shared. But she had used Damon to taunt her father. She didn't know if Maryanne's rebellion had been prompted by a desperate need to escape the controlling thumb of her parent or if the girl had just been a spoiled brat. Either way, it didn't sound as if the sheriff's parenting or Maryanne's behavior had come under near as much fire as Damon's actions. But, then, he had come from the wrong side of the tracks, and while hardly an innocent, he was the one who'd been held accountable.

How many other times had he been judged more harshly than he might have been had his family name been different?

And when had he first started thinking of himself as not being good enough?

"If you want me to leave, I'd just as soon you tell me before the snows start. It's easier towing a boat on wet pavement than slick."

She stared at him in disbelief. He thought she was going to kick him out. It didn't matter that he was only expecting her do to what she suspected people routinely did to him. That he thought she was like them was an insult.

"Just because the sheriff talked to me doesn't make any difference, Damon. I knew about your reputation...about you," she added, because there were things about him no one else acknowledged, "when I rented the shop to you."

"You don't know as much as you think you do."

"Do you want me to ask you to leave?"

He whirled around, his hard features set in an impenetrable mask. "Of course I don't. You know I don't have anyplace else to take that boat."

"Then, don't treat me that way. I don't care about what happened when you were here before."

"You should."

"Why are you doing this?"

Seeing the naked plea in her eyes, Damon felt the muscles in his stomach tighten. Years ago, he'd felt the same undirected anger simmering inside and had no idea what drove his need to lash out. That wasn't the case now. Right now, he knew exactly what was driving him.

He was accustomed to being treated unfairly. But Hannah wasn't, and she didn't seem to appreciate at all what kind of trouble she'd just borrowed for herself. She actually seemed to believe what she'd done for him wasn't that big a deal. To him, it was huge. What she'd failed to realize was the sort of impact her decision to rent to him would have on the locals' opinion of her. And he knew how badly she wanted to be part of those who would have no part of him.

He just didn't want it to matter.

He didn't want *her* to matter.

"I need to go," he muttered, hating the ambivalence clawing inside his chest.

He turned away, reaching for the box behind him. Hannah reached for it, too. Before he could pick it up, her hand came down on the nearest end.

"You're not going to do that to me," she insisted, refusing to let him slam that invisible door in her face. "This is my home, Damon. All of this." She motioned around her, including upstairs and down. "And I'm not going to spend the next however many months bumping into that chip on your shoulder.

"You say I don't know all that much about you? Well, you wouldn't be here if I didn't think I knew you better than the gossips in town. I'd already heard about you and Maryanne getting caught in the woods, and about how you ran the Olmstead boys off the road just before you hit a tree, and about the row of mailboxes you wiped out, and about how you used to steal fuel when you were a kid." It hadn't been right of him to do that, but given how meager his existence had been, she thought she might understand why he'd done it. It was a little like stealing bread. Without fuel, he and his dad couldn't fish, and if they didn't fish they didn't eat. "I'm sure the details aren't entirely accurate, because people tend to get their facts and their fantasies a little confused around here, but if there's something else you think I should know, or if any of that isn't true, then tell me."

There was more she knew about him. She knew his compassion and his quiet understanding. But he didn't give her a chance to get to that. As she'd recounted his transgressions, he'd gone quietly still.

"Did you know my father was a drunk?" he asked, his voice the deadly calm of the air before a storm. "Or that my mother ran off with some tourist when I was nine years old and never bothered to call or write or come back?

"Did you know I barely made it through school? That I'd be up all night, patching nets, then fall asleep in class and get sent to the principal's office for not paying attention and causing a 'disturbance?' They kept suspending me, then they'd tell me I didn't have enough class days so they'd hold me back. By the time I was fifteen, I'd spent so much time on suspension and in detention that the principal called in a social worker to take me from my dad. Did you know that?"

He stepped closer to her with each angry question, crowding her, making her back away. "Did you know that the social worker took one look at me, said there was nothing she could do and walked out." Damon had been fifteen by then, but he'd already been six feet tall and pushing two hundred pounds. The caseworker had blanched at his size and the surly glare he'd aimed at her and promptly counted him a lost cause.

"That's what I came from, Hannah. And around here, that's just not acceptable." He backed her up another step. "Neither is associating with someone like me."

She heard the warning in his harsh voice, saw it in his turbulent eyes. He was as bitter as a northern winter, but all she could think about was what she'd glimpsed seconds ago. She recognized the ache of betrayal when she saw it.

"Your mom left when you were nine?"

He clearly didn't expect her question, and Hannah didn't expect the pain that shot through his bridled hostility. For an instant, he was totally unguarded, the look in his eyes as bleak as winter. He'd been counted as unsalvageable. And he was still being made to pay for a past people wouldn't let him forget. He'd learned to live with the animosity he usually managed to keep in check. But having to acknowledge being abandoned by the woman who'd given him birth struck at something that festered far more deeply than all the other slights and insults combined.

"Now you're getting the idea," he muttered, jerking his defenses back into place. "I wasn't worth sticking around for even then."

He started to turn away. Appalled by the thought of a nine-year-old questioning his own worth, Hannah grabbed for his arm. It was like grabbing rock. Nothing yielded.

"You were a *child,*" she insisted, trying to imagine the man before her being that young. She couldn't. It was as if he'd been born with the scars he bore. "The problems were with her. Not you."

His glance moved to where her hand curved over his forearm, then slowly lifted to her face. The compassion in her eyes nearly undid him. "I don't blame anyone else for who I am, Hannah. I've always known right from wrong. I didn't always know why I did something. If it was lashing out, getting attention or getting even. But I knew whether it was right or wrong to do whatever it was that I did. There's plenty that was my fault. I just didn't care. I still don't. Got it?"

He wanted to intimidate her, to impress upon her that he wouldn't tolerate her excusing the man he had become. He was what he chose to be. The scar slashing his eyebrow was a stark reminder that he was no stranger to violence. The distance in his cool gray eyes spoke of a soul that refused to be reached. Only a fool would ignore what he so obviously wanted her to see.

Hannah was no fool. She wasn't fooled, either. "I got it," she quietly replied, refusing to count him as irredeemable simply because he wanted her to. "I just don't believe you're as tough as you think you are."

She had done an amazing job of keeping the tremor from her voice. She just couldn't stop it from shuddering through her when he took the step that backed her against the utility room door.

Flattening his hands on either side of her head, he leaned closer, his eyes glittering hard on her face. "I need you to believe it."

Hannah could feel the tension in his body snake through hers. He was so near she could feel the heat radiating from his chest. Feeling singed by that heat, she practically swallowed her quiet "Why?"

Damon could think of a half a dozen reasons why he needed to back away. Two seconds ago, he could have counted them off with no trouble at all and thrown in a couple extra just for good measure. He just couldn't think of a single one of those reasons now. The way she looked at him, her liquid blue eyes pleading to understand, made him feel raw inside. He didn't want to feel that exposed. Breathing in her scent, he didn't want to remember why he shouldn't touch her, either.

Need knotted in his gut when he cupped the back of her neck and drew her toward him. He didn't want her getting inside his head. He didn't want her understanding or her compassion. Yet he craved the sense of absolution she offered, and the sweet, mind-numbing pleasures of her body.

His mouth came down on hers and he pulled her against him, molding her curves to the hard ridges of his body, encouraging a delicate shiver from her when his tongue touched hers. He didn't expect to shudder himself at the incredible softness of her hands when she slowly slid them along his neck and into his hair—or the wildfire that strafed his gut when she opened to him. He didn't expect her to kiss him back. But she did. And the knowledge that she wanted his kiss tore a groan from deep within his chest.

Hannah felt that deep rumble radiate from her mouth to her toes. Exquisite sensations bloomed everywhere in her body, filling her breasts, pooling heat low in her abdomen. Damon crushed her to him, imprinting himself on her body, shaping her curves with his hands to lift her against him. The shock of his arousal shimmered through her as he skimmed his hands to her shoulders, then up into her hair.

His big hands cradled her head on either side when, scattered moments later, he slowly eased himself away, his lips clinging to hers until physical distance forced contact to break. His breathing was as erratic as her own.

Closing his eyes, Damon leaned his forehead against hers. "That shouldn't have happened."

There was no absolution. And the pleasures of her body were off-limits to him. All he wanted was sex. Honest, straightforward, no-regrets-in-the-morning sex. Even if he hadn't wanted to avoid lousing up their arrangement, he couldn't take advantage of her. She was a good woman, compassionate, generous and possessing of a trusting heart that had already been badly bruised. He wasn't what she needed. Not when being involved with him jeopardized everything she'd come there to find.

He let her go, refusing to torture himself with whatever he would see in her eyes.

"I'll pick up some more of these in Duluth," he said, grabbing what he'd come for. "I'm going in the morning, anyway."

He headed for the stairwell, closing the door quietly behind him. He'd have been far better off if he'd had no idea how she would respond to him. Now that he knew, his nights would be pure agony.

Chapter Eight

The rain had turned to snow by morning. The light, crystalline flakes fell steadily, slowly blanketing Pine Point in white, and lightening moods as surely as sunshine. Within two days, the merchants along Main began putting up their holiday decorations, and displays of pilgrims and turkeys graced windows surrounded by twinkling Christmas lights. Rain was wet and miserable. Snow was cleaner, brighter, drier.

It also had to be shoveled.

On the upside, Hannah considered being outside straining muscles in the frozen air infinitely preferable to being inside with nothing to keep her mind off the man who so clearly regretted having touched her. Thinking about those explosive moments in Damon's arms and the shuttered look on his face when he'd pulled away was something she avoided as much as Damon now avoided her.

The downside to the welcome physical activity was that

nearly every time she'd get herself bundled up to tackle the task, a customer would stray into the café and she'd have to hurry back in, unbundle and start all over again a half an hour later.

It had taken two attempts that afternoon to clear the sidewalk in front of the café. When she turned the corner to start on the hillside, wondering if she should even bother because hardly anyone used it this time of year, her progress was interrupted once more.

A single set of footprints trailed through the eight inches of snow covering the narrow sidewalk. Those large, heavily treaded steps ended where Mr. Lindstrom leaned against the café's sea green siding. The short brim of his plaid flannel hat hid his thinning gray hair, and a heavy tan canvas hunting jacket hung on his lanky frame. His shoulders were hunched, his head down and his wrinkled, liver-spotted hands covered his face.

Hannah's heart lurched an instant before she propped her snow shovel against the side window and started crunching her way toward him. "Mr. Lindstrom?" she called, hoping he wasn't having a stroke or something, "are you all right?"

He'd stopped at the far end of the building. From the pattern of his footsteps, he'd been heading downhill when he'd turned to lean against the siding for support.

"Mr. Lindstrom?"

The earflaps of his flannel hat resembled drooping bird's wings when his head came up. The first thing Hannah noticed was that he had a lighter in one hand and a pipe clamped between his teeth. The next thing she registered was the ruddy glow of his cheeks.

Removing the pipe, he peered at her through the top half of his clear-rimmed bifocals. "Yah. Sure, I'm all right," he replied, sounding genuinely puzzled by the panic in her tone. His pale blue eyes narrowed in curiosity. "Who are you?"

He truly did look fine—which was more than she could

say for herself just then. The moment she'd thought there was something wrong, her own heart had kicked into double time. It was still knocking hard against her ribs when relief made her smile.

"My name's Hannah." She drew a calming breath, exhaled it in a thready cloud. "We met once before. On the docks," she reminded him. "I own the café."

"Ah, yes. I remember hearing that Lilly had sold it."

The elderly man obviously had no recollection of having heard that particular piece of information from her. Hannah didn't consider that especially peculiar, though. Not when she considered the shape he'd been in that day.

Biting down again on his pipe, he gave his lighter a few quick flicks.

"Can't get the dang thing to flame." He held the lighter up, disgust written in his wrinkles. "Flint's shot." With a frown that caused his fleshy lower lip to protrude even farther, he opened his coat to unsnap a pocket on his fishing vest. "I think I've got a spare here, somewhere."

He hadn't been using the building for support, after all. He'd only been blocking the breeze blowing up from the lake so he could light his pipe. Realizing that, Hannah's concerns faded a little more—until she considered where he'd seemed to be going.

"There isn't much down this direction," she told him, trying to sound conversational rather than nosy. "Where are you headed?"

"Forgot." He mumbled the word, frowning at his pipe as if it were the cause of this afternoon's forgetfulness. "Got to the corner. Turned it and flat couldn't remember where I was headed. Young as you are, I don't suppose that's ever happened to you."

"Sure it has," she murmured, smiling. "I can't count the number of times I've put the sugar in the fridge or walked into a room and forgotten what I'd gone in there for. Where were you coming from?'' she asked, thinking he looked more annoyed than bewildered by his forgetfulness. ''Maybe if you retraced your steps, you'd remember.''

He pondered her question, then shook his head. ''Just came from home.''

He'd been heading in the direction of the docks. If that had been his destination, though, she didn't particularly want to remind him by mentioning it. With the boats all dry-docked now, no one went down there this time of year. There weren't even any other tracks, human or automobile, marring the snow-covered hill. At least there weren't any beyond the point where Damon's truck had pulled in behind the building— hours ago, judging from how the single set of tire tracks had refilled with the constant flurries. Even the surefooted could slip on the ice and snow. An elderly man could lose his footing all too easily, and with the severest of consequences. Bones broke more easily when a person was old, and healed slower. A broken hip could be disaster. Being bedridden for months could lead to complications like pneumonia and infections.

''Do you want me to call Neil?''

''What for? He'd just dump me at home, and there sure as blazes isn't anything there to do. I don't like driving in the snow, so I'd just have to walk all the way back here.'' He reached inside his open jacket and, giving up on finding the flint, pulled a book of matches from one of the fishing vest pockets. ''I can't garden,'' he continued, enumerating the pleasures being deprived him at the moment. ''The ice is too thick for boat fishing, and it's nowhere near thick enough to fish *on* yet.''

In other words, Hannah thought, noticing the faint trembling of his hands when he struck a match and cupped it to the bowl of his pipe, he didn't know what to do with himself.

''Why don't you call a friend?'' she suggested, suspecting his shaking had as much to do with cold as age. He should button his coat back up, she thought. And put on gloves. "You can come into the café and use my phone. Maybe you could go visit."

"Could," he returned, satisfaction moving into his eyes now that he was finally puffing smoke. "But they're dead. Except Sven," he amended, "but he doesn't know who I am anymore. His daughter's taking care of him, and I talk with her some when I go to visit, but it gets kind of depressing sitting there watching him drool, and I don't want to take up her time. You know, once a fella's seen the sunny side of eighty, even some of his friend's children aren't around anymore."

His expression, like his tone, was absolutely matter-of-fact. But the fact of the matter was that Hannah had never considered how alone an elderly person could be. She remembered her grandmother once saying that the best thing about being older was not worrying about what others thought of you; the worst was slowly losing the people who'd once filled her life. Others came in, filled some of the gaps, but friendships that spanned decades were impossible to replace.

"Why don't you go over to the senior center?" she suggested, thinking of the activities going on over there.

His jowls folded into his sagging chin as he eyed her through the top of his bifocals. "What would I want to do that for? There's nothing but a bunch of old people over there. Old women, mostly. A fella doesn't stand a chance in that place. I'll just go down and watch the lakers. Now that I think about it, that's where I was headed, anyway."

Clamping his pipe between his teeth, he tipped the short brim of his hat to her and turned into the breeze coming up from the frigid water. The lakers were the huge cargo ships that hauled ore, grain and materials along Superior's horizon and through the locks at the Soo, nearly four hundred miles away. Sitting on a bench watching them go by sounded harmless enough. But Hannah had a bad feeling about him going to the dock. She didn't like the feeling she had about him being so alone, either.

The faint chime of the bell over the café's door drifted toward her, indicating that she had customers. As she took a step backward toward her door, her eyes on the slope of the old man's shoulders as he slowly moved on, that bad feeling about the dock doubled.

"Mr. Lindstrom," she suddenly called, hoping she wasn't overstepping herself. "Would you like to come in and have a cup of coffee with me before you go?"

He didn't even turn. From ten feet away, still going, he lifted his hand in a little wave. "That's very kind of you to offer," he called back, "but I think I'll be getting along now. You have a nice day."

She had customers, and there was no one in the café. Since she was hardly in a position to let business walk away, that meant she needed to go. It was entirely possible that Mr. Lindstrom would be fine—if he didn't slip and break something. Or drown. After all, he had managed to survive more than eight decades without her help or interference, and she truly didn't want to meddle in the man's life. There was no one around to help her stop him, anyway.

Except Damon.

The older man probably thought she was missing a few vital brain cells when she hollered at him to wait. Though she added a pleading "Please?" there was no mistaking his puzzlement when she asked him to stay right where he was, then, walking backward to make sure he didn't move, told him she'd be right back.

The bell over the café's front door chimed again when she poked her head inside. A young family of three stood by the counter looking around. Apologizing, she told them to make themselves comfortable and that she'd be right back. Moments later, relieved to see that Mr. Lindstrom hadn't moved, she crunched back through the snow to his side and asked if he remembered the man he'd met on the docks last summer, the one who'd taken him home in the black truck parked a few yards away.

Mr. Lindstrom wasn't sure if he did or not. But as soon as she told him what Damon was doing to his boat, he forgot to balk. Taking advantage of his interest, she promptly steered him toward the shop.

"He's refitting his boat, you say?"

That was exactly what she'd said. And something about the fact that Damon was working on a boat definitely had him curious.

Curious was not exactly how she would describe Damon, however. When she opened the entry door to the shop and ushered Mr. Lindstrom inside, Damon just looked irritated.

But not at her. Not yet, anyway.

He jerked his scowl from the piece of metal on the workbench. She couldn't begin to identify the oil-and-grease-blackened object that had earned his current displeasure. Mr. Lindstrom apparently could, though. Hannah had no sooner escorted him over to where Damon dubiously eyed their approach, than the elderly man began shaking his head.

There were advantages to being rushed. For one thing, she had no time to dwell on the decidedly guarded look Damon gave her when she moved beside him. Keeping her back to their guest, she tugged his sleeve to get him to bend his head toward her.

With her mouth two inches from his ear, she felt his arm brush her breast. Not sure which of them tensed first, she edged back ever so slightly. "He was going to the docks," she whispered, ignoring the knots his nearness put in her stomach. "You know how dangerous it would be for him to go down there. Keep him here with you until I can figure out something else for him to do, will you?"

He lifted his head, his glance darting to the man studying the mess on the workbench. "No way."

It was bad enough that she was whispering about someone when that someone was standing right there. Hoping the elderly man would forgive her, she gave Damon's arm another tug. "Come on," she insisted, feeling a painful wrench in her chest when he tensed at her touch. "I have customers I need to take care of, and I couldn't get him to come with me. There isn't anyone else to watch out for him."

"I don't care if there isn't anyone else," he shot back, whispering, too. "You found him, you baby-sit him. I'm not getting involved with any—"

"I'm sure you don't want to get involved, Damon. But I don't think you want him to get hurt, either. Just talk to him. About boats," she added, hating the way he insisted on isolating himself. He could shut her and the old guy out later. Right now, she was in a hurry. "Just do it like you did the last time."

"You're making a lot of work for yourself there, you know?" Mr. Lindstrom said.

The flatly delivered statement drew Damon's cool expression from her to the man at the end of the workbench.

"I know what I'm doing," he muttered.

"Suit yourself." Mr. Lindstrom blew a puff of smoke that smelled like cherries and old leather, then gave a shrug. It clearly made no difference to him which way Damon did whatever he was doing. "But it'd be easier to break those seals if you'd run some fishing leader between them instead of trying to pry them apart. Got some here, if you'd like."

Hannah couldn't tell if Damon was gearing up to refuse her request, or if he was actually considering the unexpected tip. But Mr. Lindstrom was extracting a small disk from the plethora of pockets on the fishing vest under his coat, and she knew an opportune moment when she saw one.

With Damon's attention diverted, she headed for the stairwell door, hoping with every hurried step that he wouldn't let the old man leave. He could help or he could refuse. She'd known him to do both. But if he was truly the man she suspected he was beneath that tough-as-titanium exterior of his, he'd keep Mr. Lindstrom with him until she got back. He might not like it, but he'd do it.

Hannah truly tried to hurry. Her intentions, however, hadn't seemed to count for much lately. She'd just finished serving the young family who'd come into town to buy snow tires, when a couple of kids from the high school stopped by selling calendars to raise money for sports equipment. Hannah bought one for herself, then had the two boys leave a few with a sign and money jar by her cash register in case any of her customers were interested. It was something she did for several of the organizations in town. Last month's project had been selling candy bars to raise money for new band uniforms. The month before, a local garden club had collected donations for the bulbs it planted every fall around the Welcome to Pine Point signs at either end of town.

By the time the kids left, the couple at the table wanted more corn bread to go with their turkey chili, and their toddler had dumped her milk over her grilled cheese sandwich, which meant Hannah had to make another one since the little girl's was soaked. Then three more customers walked in, including a chatty pharmaceutical sales rep who'd just made calls on the local doctors and Petersen's Drug Store. He wanted a rundown on the nearby cross-country ski trails and the bed-and-breakfasts in town.

It was obviously going to be a while before she could rescue Damon, but she couldn't stand not knowing if he'd managed to keep Mr. Lindstrom from going to the docks. Afraid to consider what either man thought of her latent mother-hen tendencies, she got the new orders started, then dared a quick, quiet dash down the stairwell.

What she saw when she cracked open the door to the shop

and peeked inside eased her mind considerably. It also caught her completely off guard.

Mr. Lindstrom had shed his coat and hat and sat with his feet planted on the rungs of a tall stool by the workbench. The bright overhead light turned his steel gray hair a shiny silver and illuminated the pink skin visible through the thinning patch at his crown. An ice scraper had replaced the trowel that had once hung from a side loop on his fishing vest.

His pipe must have gone out again. Either that, or he'd put it out because of the cleaning solvents Damon was using. He had the cherrywood bowl in his fist and was using the black stem end to point at the oily chunk of metal Damon was working on. She couldn't hear what they were saying, but the thoughtful way Damon considered the older man made her think he was either asking his advice or following his instructions.

Holding her breath, she slowly closed the door, praying the thing wouldn't squeak and interrupt them, and hurried back up the stairs. She could stop worrying about Mr. Lindstrom for the moment. He was inside, warm, safe and looking as content as a kid with his favorite toy.

Both men were still there when she made the same trip an hour later.

It became immediately apparent when she opened the door from the stairwell that her presence wasn't required. Or wanted. They both turned at the same time, and both wore the same expression her father and her brother-in-law got when they had their heads together on a woodworking project. It was a rather blank look that somehow managed to say, "We're doing something important here, so what do you want?"

More than happy to let them get back to their grease, she just smiled at Mr. Lindstrom, felt that smile fade when Damon glanced at her, then headed back to the café to add mushrooms to the large roast in the oven she was preparing for the dinner special. By the time she found a break from serving the dozen customers that constituted the supper rush and made it back down the stairs to see if Mr. Lindstrom would be interested in supper himself, Damon was alone.

He glanced up from the workbench the instant he heard the door open.

"I wondered when you'd show up," he murmured, skimming a quick glance over the hesitation in her face. "He's not here."

Holding two metal cylinders in his hands, he crossed the length of the long workbench and hunkered down by three galvanized metal buckets. "Don't worry," he added, resigned to her concern, "he didn't go to the dock."

"When did he leave?"

"I took him to his house about an hour ago. He wouldn't call his nephew, and it was too dark for him to walk."

Had Damon not sounded so grudging about his thoughtfulness, Hannah would have felt relieved to know the old gentleman was safely back home. All she felt was caution.

Leaving the door open so she'd be able to hear the front bell, she ventured inside the shop. There were boat parts everywhere. All were unidentifiable to her, and all seemed to belong to the inner workings of the vessel. The large trawler taking up the middle of the space looked the same as it always had on the outside, as battered and crusty as its owner.

"I hope he didn't give you a hard time about going home."

"It was his idea. There was a game show on that he never misses. He said coming up with the answers helps keep his mind from turning to mush."

He'd lowered the two lead-colored cylinders he'd held into the cleaning solvent. Reaching for an old paint stick, the muscles of his broad shoulders shifting beneath dark flannel, he fished a piece just like the others out of the last bucket.

"I know you weren't happy about me bringing him here,"

she admitted, thinking he looked every bit as preoccupied as he sounded, "but I didn't know what else to do. Then, when I saw that he was helping you, I didn't think you wanted me to interrupt."

"Don't worry about it." He let the cylinder he'd fished out sink back into the murky liquid, then rose with the powerful surge of his thighs to grab a rag from the workbench. "He's pretty set in his ways, but he actually helped me quite a bit."

"He did?"

Hannah couldn't hide her quiet surprise. Not just that Mr. Lindstrom had been of real help to Damon, but that Damon had so easily admitted it. As insular as he was, taking anything from anyone, even advice, seemed extraordinary.

Almost as extraordinary, she thought, as the fact that he continued to let her see far more deeply inside him than he did anyone else.

He'd taken Mr. Lindstrom home because he couldn't let the old man walk home alone in the dark. She was certain Damon hadn't wanted to go there. He seemed to have a comfort zone—his home, the lake, the shop. She had the distinct feeling that he seldom strayed beyond those borders.

"You know what I can't figure out?" Wiping his hands, he glanced toward her. "I can't figure out how he could have been so confused the day we found him on the dock, and so clear about everything now.

"This engine I'm tearing down..." he continued, indicating the loveseat-size, black iron object he'd hoisted from the bowels of his boat, "he took one look at some of the parts I thought I'd have to replace and told me how to retool them and save a couple hundred bucks. He was a mechanic for years."

Moving around the engine under discussion, Hannah stepped over a long rod and came to a halt a few feet from where Damon stood. It was apparent that he was confused by discrepancies in Mr. Lindstrom's mental acuity. She, on the other hand, was simply confused. "I thought he'd been a fisherman."

"He's done that, too. And he carved bow struts, and spent a few years hauling potash on a freighter. He said that over the years he did whatever he had to do to make sure he could always set a little aside for a rainy day." Damon shook his head, looking as if he wanted to smile but had forgotten how. "He told me he still saves part of his pension checks because a man needs to think about his future. The guy's older than Neptune *now* and he's still thinking ahead. Does that sound like the same man we ran into before?"

It definitely did not. What it sounded like to her was a man who'd worked hard all his life, always made his own way and who intended never to be a burden to anyone. She told Damon that, too. Then she mentioned that while Mr. Lindstrom had seemed a little light on a few details when she'd talked to him earlier, he'd exhibited none of the anxiety or deep-seated confusion he had that first time.

"He mostly just seemed at loose ends to me," she also told him. "I get the feeling he doesn't have much to do with his time."

She tipped her head, watching Damon's brow furrow in the daylight-bright lights. With his jaw shadowed by the day's growth of beard, his dark eyebrows drawn in concentration, he was a truly formidable-looking man. Hard, handsome, unapproachable. That was the image he wanted, too. The hard, unapproachable part, anyway. And, for the most part, people saw exactly what Damon allowed them to see.

His eyebrows knitted tighter. "I just thought it was kind of strange, is all. He didn't act anything like he did before." He nodded toward the open stairwell door, his preoccupation fading. "I didn't mean to keep you. It sounds like you've got customers up there."

The muffled clatter of silverware on plates drifted down the stairwell. She'd already been gone longer than she thought she'd be, and Damon clearly wanted to get back to work himself. Thinking to offer a quick thanks for his help, she took a step back to get out of his way.

The words never came out. Her heel caught the edge of the long metal rod, throwing her balance completely.

The thought that there was nothing behind her but hard concrete and harder-looking engine parts registered the instant she sucked in a startled gasp. That breath had barely locked in her lungs when Damon shot forward.

It was incredible to her that a man his size could move so fast. He'd been six feet away, but before she could turn to break her fall, his strong fingers clamped around her upper arm and she was jerked back from the rod. A frantic heartbeat later, he'd swung himself in front of her, snagged her other arm, and she grabbed his stone-solid biceps to keep from bumping into the wall of his chest.

She'd more or less caught her balance when his eyes locked on hers.

The oxygen seemed to vanish from the room. It suddenly seemed hard for her to breathe, to think. Damon's glance dropped to her mouth, the chiseled shape of his own parting slightly as memories rushed in to taunt them both.

''Are you all right?'' he asked, his voice oddly husky.

She hadn't been all right since the moment she'd met him. ''I'm fine,'' she replied, since the truth felt too threatening. ''I just wasn't paying attention.''

''You have to be careful down here.''

She gave a little nod, but he didn't notice. His attention had shifted to where his hand curved around her slender arm.

As if he'd only now realized that he didn't want to touch her, he let her go and stepped away.

Her heart already hammered her rib cage. Each beat now just made it feel a little bruised. Ducking her head to hide the unexpected hurt, hoping it only looked like she was watching where she stepped, she started for the door.

"Hannah. Wait a minute."

She was the one who didn't want any strain between them. That was why she'd told him she didn't want to keep bumping into the chip on his shoulder. Their situation was difficult enough without feeling constantly anxious about running into him. If she kept walking now, she'd only be contributing to the tension that popped to the surface like some undersea monster every time they came within sight of each other.

Determined to keep from tripping over her own pride, she glanced back as if he hadn't touched her at all.

The instant she did, he looked down at his hands, then to each sleeve of her white blouse. "I ruined your shirt."

Following the path of his glance, she saw the black smudges where his fingers had closed around her upper arms. "That's why I let go."

It wasn't the only reason. They both knew that. But it seemed he was trying to help ease the strain, too, and that made far more difference to her at the moment than a little dirt—or what someone else might think of the obvious handprints on her arms.

"You kept me from breaking my neck. Don't worry about it," she said, deliberately using his words from minutes ago, and gave him a soft smile before she hurried away.

No one saw the handprints. Hannah pulled on a sweater before she headed into the café to refill coffee cups that evening. And the next morning, just to be on the safe side, she had on a black cotton turtleneck and black slacks under her apron. She certainly didn't anticipate a repeat of what had happened last night, but she was beginning to develop a healthy appreciation for unexpected situations—and how they could be misconstrued. The way she saw it, an ounce of prevention was worth a ton of damage control.

She was enjoying the fact that there wasn't any particular damage to be contained that morning when one of those situations walked by the window. Having just served plates of omelettes and Swedish pancakes to two of her truckers, she looked up from the counter to see Mr. Lindstrom strolling through the falling snow.

Like yesterday, he was wearing the flannel hat with the bird-wing earflaps and the brown canvas hunting jacket that hung on him like an old blanket. She couldn't tell if it was his pipe or his breath that made him look like the smokestack on a locomotive as feathery puffs trailed behind him, but his steps were full of purpose as he rounded the corner and passed the side window, the one facing the hill leading to the lake.

The man had a real thing about the dock, and Hannah just knew that was where he was going.

Leaving her coffeepot on the counter and her customers gaping at her back, she bolted out the door in her apron, nearly slipping on the four inches of new snow that had fallen last night, and swung around the corner herself. She'd barely opened her mouth to call out to him when she promptly gagged on the cold. The weather had been the main topic of conversation among her customers all morning. The mercury had finally hit zero. She just hadn't been out in it herself yet.

It was so cold that the breeze burned her eyes and her fingers were already growing numb. Freezing or not, she still needed to stop the man ambling down the sloping sidewalk in his tire-tread boots. He'd just passed the long window that occupied the wall between Hannah's greenhouse and the long, cluttered workbench.

Inside, Damon happened to be facing the window, and he caught the motion of someone passing by, but he didn't notice who it was. He wouldn't have cared, anyway. Standing in the middle of the cluttered shop, nursing coffee from his thermos, he focused on figuring out where to start that morning. The decision would have been infinitely easier had he not still been half-asleep.

He'd gone to bed early enough, but sleep hadn't come. He'd wrestled the blankets, willing rest for his body and his mind, but his mind had locked on one track and his body had ached with a need that had become all too familiar. Try as he might, he couldn't escape the memory of how Hannah's slender body had molded to his when he'd kissed her. He remembered exactly how she tasted, how she moved, the small, surrendering sounds she'd made. Just the feel of her body brushing his when he'd caught her from tripping had made him so hard he hurt. But he could get that way just looking at her. Just *thinking* about her.

That had been the problem last night.

He drew his hand down his face, staring at the snow falling softly outside the window. He'd tried to put her from his mind, forced himself to concentrate on anything other than her. He'd tried thinking about everything from re-siding his house next spring, to how he'd have to start stripping wood on the *Naiad* after he got the engine put back together—only to find himself wondering how long he could go without caving in to his need to touch her again. But touching wasn't all he wanted. And what he wanted had finally driven him out of bed, where he'd stood half-naked in front of his bedroom window watching the snow drift down, much as he was doing now. The room had been chilly. Downright cold, actually. And the air had finally cooled him enough to calm him down. But the desire he felt for her hadn't gone away.

It still hadn't.

The breeze blowing up from the lake put a sideways slant on the snowflakes falling outside. It was because of that breeze that the woman scooting past his window had her head down. Damon didn't need to see Hannah's face to recognize her, though. He was wondering only what she was doing out there without a coat when he set down his mug and three sharp raps sounded on the shop's entry door.

Louie Lindstrom smiled around his unlit pipe. "Morning,"

he said, mindless of the flakes swirling in over the concrete. "Did you get started on those fuel injectors yet?"

Damon's glance darted past the man's shoulder. Huddled into herself, Hannah turned the corner of the building, coming up behind Mr. Lindstrom as fast as she could without slipping in the snow.

He told the old man that he hadn't been there long enough to do anything yet, motioning him inside as he did, then aimed a frown at Hannah's snow-covered head when she rushed in, too.

Closing the door to conserve heat, he turned to ask her what she was up to now. The first question out of his mouth, however, was "What are you doing out there without a coat?"

"Freezing," she muttered, stamping snow from her loafers and batting snowflakes from her arms.

Realizing he was about to start brushing at the flakes himself, he immediately shoved both hands into his pockets, and turned a suspicious glance toward his other unexpected intruder.

Mr. Lindstrom's bifocals had fogged up the instant he'd stepped inside. Taking them off, he started wiping them on a handkerchief he'd pulled from a pocket somewhere and headed for the small space heater at the back of the shop like a homing pigeon heading for his roost.

"Watch where you step," Damon called, wondering how well the guy could see without his glasses. "There are parts everywhere."

"I know that," Mr. Lindstrom called back. "I'm not blind."

At the matter-of-fact reply, Damon's frown returned to the amazingly innocent-looking woman at his side.

"I didn't bring him this time," she whispered, clearly reading his thoughts. "I thought Mr. Lindstrom was headed for the docks. If I'd known he was coming here, I'd have stayed upstairs.''

''I'm not deaf, either.''

Whatever else she'd been about to say was immediately silenced by that bit of casually delivered advice. Damon figured he knew what he'd have heard from her, anyway. Something along the lines of how he would have done the same thing himself, and a challenge to deny it.

He didn't care to acknowledge whether or not she'd have been right.

''I'm sorry,'' she said to the old guy, looking chagrined, curious and cold. Still brushing at flakes, she headed toward him. ''That was rude of me. Would you like some coffee to warm you up, Mr. Lindstrom?''

''Yah, sure.'' He'd slipped his bifocals back on and now stood by the heater warming his hands. ''Coffee would be good. I was anxious to get here, so I didn't take time for breakfast.''

''Then, I'll get you some. Would you prefer hot oatmeal or eggs and pancakes?

''Whatever's the least bother.''

''Give me five minutes.'' She glanced toward Damon, the delicate arch of one eyebrow rising. ''Would you mind coming up to get it? Brenda couldn't come in this morning and things are pretty busy right now.''

It occurred to Hannah as she watched Damon's eyes narrow on her that he must have showered and shaved last night before he went to bed. His jaw was definitely smoother than it had been when she'd seen him last, but the faintest hint of stubble was already starting to shadow his face.

The thought of him standing in front of a steamy mirror, lathered and wearing nothing but a towel, did a fair job of chasing off her chill.

''Why didn't your waitress come in?''

"She has a cold. Honest," she said, when his expression turned skeptical. "I *told* her to stay home."

He was clearly remembering the last time she'd found herself short-staffed, but she didn't know if he believed her about Brenda or not. As disgruntled as he looked, it was hard to tell what he was thinking. Especially with Mr. Lindstrom peeling off his coat and preparing to make himself at home.

Still rubbing her arms, she edged toward the door. "Do you want breakfast?"

"No, thanks," he muttered, frowning at the old man's back. "But I'll come get his."

Five minutes later, Damon stood brooding in the kitchen doorway. He didn't go in. He just pushed the door open and, seeing Hannah through the service window, stepped back to wait until she returned from serving the men at the counter. It was better for both of them if he didn't remind anyone that he was there. Out of sight, out of mind. He hoped.

She was smiling when she came through the swinging doors, but that soft expression faded from her delicate features the instant she realized he was there.

He didn't like the wariness he caused her to feel. He was coming to hate it, in fact. But it served a purpose, created the distance he needed. He had other things on his mind, anyway, as he watched her snag the top bowl from a stack and deftly ladle cereal into it from a steaming pot on the stove. Within seconds, she'd cut a graceful arc to the work island and set the bowl on a tray that held sweet rolls and cream, and a lidded foam cup.

"It really wasn't your idea for him to show up this morning?" he asked, sounding more confused than accusing.

Hannah gave her head a shake. "What about you?" she asked, carrying what she'd prepared to where he waited. "Didn't you have any idea he was coming?"

The scents of warm cinnamon, brown sugar and rich coffee rose from the tray to tease his nostrils. But it was Hannah herself who made his stomach tighten. She'd smoothed her breeze-blown hair back into its restraining clip, and the heat of the kitchen and having to hustle had turned her cheeks pink from warmth rather than from cold. The fine grain of her skin fairly begged to be touched.

"None."

"I didn't think so. That's what I told Bill, anyway."

"Bill?"

"The man who owns the appliance store across the street. He's out there having pancakes. He has the same thing every morning after he turns the heat up at the store and before he opens for the day."

Damon couldn't have cared less about the man's routine. All he cared about was that Hannah didn't seem to get the importance of keeping quiet about his being there. He was doing everything short of coming and going from the shop at midnight to be discreet, and she still acted as if his presence was nothing to concern herself about.

"Why did you tell him that? Why say anything at all?"

She mimicked his disapproving expression, along with his low, faintly exasperated tone. "Because people wanted to know why I went tearing out the door like my apron strings were on fire. When I told them where I'd thought Mr. Lindstrom was going, they understood. The ones who know him, anyway." Which was everyone but the truckers and a couple she'd never seen before. Now even they knew about the elderly man's tendency to get confused and wander off. "Since I'd come back in alone, Bill was concerned about where he had gone, so I had to tell him he was with you."

"Had to?"

"What was I supposed to say? That I'd chained him to my drainpipe?" With a look of supreme indulgence, she nudged the tray toward him. "Did Mr. Lindstrom say why he came to see you?"

Damon's exasperation downshifted to puzzlement.

"Not specifically. But I think he wants to help." Directing his faint scowl to the tray, he took it from her. "Why would he want to do that?"

Hannah watched the question settle in his eyes. Why would he want to help *me* was what he meant.

"What did you do yesterday after he said you were going about that repair wrong?"

Damon shrugged, clearly not seeing what that had to do with anything. "I handed him the part and told him to go for it."

"What did he do?"

Again, the shrug. "Broke the seal for me."

"Did you have him do anything else?"

"His hands are kind of arthritic so he can't handle tools very well anymore, but he cleaned and oiled some parts. And he had plenty of advice. And stories. Man, when he finally gets going, he can really talk."

A gentle smile curved her lips. "Then, that's why he wants to help you. You listened. And you made him feel useful."

Four months ago, Damon wouldn't have had a clue what she was talking about. Now, because of Hannah, because of how she had treated him, he knew exactly what she meant.

His first reaction was to deny what he'd done, and how it made him feel. But with her eyes smiling into his, he couldn't resist the feeling any more than he could resist his next breath.

The knowledge of what she'd helped him do made his heart feel a little tight in his chest. It also humbled him. He'd made an old man feel useful. And feeling useful made a person feel good about himself—the way Hannah had made him feel good about himself when she'd turned to him for help with the old guy that day on the dock, and when she'd told him he was kind.

The little service bell she kept on the front counter chimed with a syncopated, five-count ring.

"That'll be one of my truckers wanting more coffee or to

pay his bill. I'll come get that later," she said, indicating the tray, then turned to take care of the men who returned her smiles, appreciated her hospitality and didn't give her anywhere near the grief he did.

Chapter Nine

The snow continued to fall, and the holidays, which Hannah knew were taken seriously in Pine Point, were suddenly upon the little town. Thanksgiving was followed by the St. Lucia festival where the fire chief's granddaughter was elected Queen of Lights. Julafton, the Swedish Christmas Eve celebration, came next. Then Christmas and St. Stephen's Day, for the animals. Finally, New Year's and St. Knut's Day on January 13, the official end of it all. During that time live reindeer were brought in by the Moose Lodge, the Lutheran church hosted the annual *lutefisk* dinner, complete with crepe-like *lefse* and pickled herring. Finally, the Santa Claus dog pull, round one of the competition to be completed with February's Snow Daze, took place down the middle of Main Street.

With so many people in town for shopping and celebrations, business in the cheerfully decorated café was better than usual. Hannah was grateful for the increase, but mostly she was just happy that the holiday bustle took people's minds off the man going quietly about his business in the shop below. The seasonal spirit didn't provide that distraction for her, however. She was always aware of him. Even when she closed down for two days each at Thanksgiving and Christmas to spend them with her family, she spent the entire time wondering if Damon had meant it when he said the holidays mattered little to him. She'd thought about asking him if he wanted to come with her, just so he wouldn't be alone, but she axed the idea as soon as it formed. As careful as he was to avoid anything personal with her, he'd have backpedaled so fast at the invitation that he'd have been a mere blur.

As for Louie Lindstrom, she knew he'd spent the holidays with his nephew's family watching them argue over television programs and eating turkey as dry as moose hide. He'd told her so himself.

The old ex-sailor, mechanic and stevedore continued to show up at the shop with some regularity after those first unanticipated visits. Hannah knew that, not because she always noticed him when he shuffled around the corner in the snow, but because, for well over a month, she ran into him nearly every time she went down to the freezer or to her herb garden.

One afternoon, however, she realized Mr. Lindstrom hadn't arrived as usual. Damon appeared at her door to use her phone to check on him after he had failed to show up three days in a row.

Damon didn't want to look concerned about the elderly man's welfare as he headed for her office. But Hannah knew he was. As soon as he'd told her that Louie had simply stopped coming, she was concerned herself.

"He said his gout is acting up and he can't walk this far," he told her, after he'd hung up. "Said he'll take his medicine and watch what he eats for a few days, then come back, if I want him."

"What did you say?"

"It's up to him."

The shrug accompanying that flat statement made it appear that Damon didn't care one way or the other if the guy came back. What it really meant was that he didn't *want* to care. Wondering if he knew the difference, suspecting it wouldn't matter, all she said was, "He shouldn't be walking alone in this wind, anyway."

The weather was particularly blustery. But that January day was merely a harbinger of what came in its wake. Having lived all her life in Minnesota, Hannah was no stranger to cold winters or the dangers that came with their isolation and beauty. There were days when the high never rose above thirty below zero. The wind howled like the wolves in the forests. And the danger of freezing to death was an everyday reality. But the bitter cold was no more remarkable to the people who lived in lake country than the walls of snow that eventually lined shoveled sidewalks, or the mountains of the interminable white stuff the snowplows scraped from the roads and dumped on the frozen lakes and ponds on the far side of the highway. On days when the wind was particularly stiff, people added another layer under their muffin-man clothes and went about their work and play as best they could encased in down.

When the weather turned bad enough to keep people indoors, the locals simply snuggled in with their crafts and books and projects, then dug themselves back out when it cleared.

Instead of curling up with a book, what Hannah found herself doing on those days was thawing and feeding tired, stranded travelers and sending them two blocks over to the Shorecrest Motel for lodging. In turn, the motel's owner sent his hungry, stranded guests back to her café to be fed. For the most part, though, the short days and long nights were quiet and blessedly uneventful—except where Damon was concerned.

The first clear day after Louie Lindstrom's attack of gout subsided, the determined old guy was back at the shop. The day after that, Damon started leaving midmorning to pick the man up, and taking him back home in time for his game show. Damon never did say whose idea the arrangement was. When she asked, he just gave her a look that made it clear he didn't want her reading anything into the gesture, then simply said he could use the man's expertise. In return, because the old guy had refused his offer of payment, he bought Louie's lunch. From Hannah. The way Damon saw it, as long as she was bringing one lunch, he might as well get his from her, too. He even specifically requested chowder, sourdough and pie, which she'd once given him, as if he'd been thinking about them a lot but had refused to indulge himself.

The thought that he'd deliberately denied himself something he could have easily had for the asking made her wonder what else he was denying himself. But the thought that he was denying himself *her* was too absurd to consider. He didn't touch her. He didn't come anywhere near her unless he had to. And the only time he really talked to her at all was when Mr. Lindstrom was around. Or if Louie had one of his "spells."

Hannah had nearly forgotten how confused Mr. Lindstrom could get until Damon returned alone late one morning in March. He'd gone to pick Louie up, and had found him as disoriented as he'd been the day they had found him on the dock. Mr. Lindstrom hadn't recognized him and turned him away at the door. The second time it happened, over a month later, Damon talked him into leaving with him, only to spend the day answering the same questions a dozen times and taking him home early because Mr. Lindstrom wanted to take a nap.

When Hannah asked Damon if he'd noticed anything unusual with Mr. Lindstrom before the episodes, Damon said he'd seemed fine. He'd been a little achy was all, he'd told her, as if his arthritis was acting up. Or maybe it was his gout. But other than that, he'd noticed nothing unusual.

Damon was lying under the stopped-up sink in her kitchen when he told her about the third spell. He'd come up to help her after she'd come downstairs to get a pipe wrench.

"It was really strange," he said, his deep voice muffled. "We were fitting the seals around the prop shaft and he kept rubbing at his knee. He said he was aching more than usual because the weather is turning. I guess now that we're warming up, the damp bothers him more than cold," he added, patting the area by his hip for the tube of putty he'd left there.

Thinking that *warming up* was a relative term, though forty above was definitely warm compared to forty below, she handed him what he was groping for.

"Anyway," he continued as his hand disappeared, "he took a couple of pills and we kept working, but he was hurting so much that I finally told him to just sit down and rest for a while. He fell asleep in that old chair we brought from his house, and when I woke him up to take him home, he was out of it."

"What kind of pills?"

"I don't know," he mumbled over the sound of metal pieces being threaded together. "I didn't ask. He's got a regular pharmacy in that fishing vest of his."

Because his head, shoulders and half of his chest were under her large industrial sink, she could only see him, more or less, from his waist down. One long, jeans-clad leg was stretched out. The other was bent so that his boot was planted by his opposite knee. The view wasn't bad. It was just distracting. Especially when he would shift positions and his black sweatshirt would ride a little higher above the buckle of his leather belt.

Leaning against the edge of the sink, she studied a chip in her nail. It seemed preferable to staring at the strip of rock-hard abdomen and the dark hair arrowing beneath the waist-band of his jeans. "He takes a lot of medicine?"

"I guess."

The chip failed to hold her interest. Kneeling down by his hip, she deliberately focused on the dark head under the curved pipe. "Maybe you should mention this to him."

"Mention what?" he muttered, grunting a little as he turned the wrench and metal squeaked. "He *knows* he has spells where he gets confused. It's not as if he isn't aware of it." His stomach muscles tightened as he gave the wrench another turn. "I don't know what one has to do with the other, but he says the only time he gets them is when his joints get to aching bad."

"And that's when he takes those pills?"

He gave one last turn on the metal ring joining the pipes, then she saw his big body go still. A moment later, he was scooting out and sitting up beside her, the pipe wrench dangling from where his wrist balanced on his upraised knee.

"You think his medicine makes him weird?"

"I don't know. It could be. Or maybe it doesn't mix well with something else he takes. People have bad reactions to drugs all the time." She tipped her head, her smooth brow furrowing. "Don't you think you should mention it to him?"

She rested on her heels, her small hands curled against her apron and her eyes steady on his. There was nothing but genuine concern in her expression. None of the wariness that so often guarded her manner when they were together. At that moment, she was totally open to him, totally receptive, and that was when Damon always found her the most dangerous.

His glance skimmed the gentle contours of her face, the delicate wings of her eyebrows, the fullness of her peach-tinted and very kissable mouth.

He didn't usually let himself get this close because he simply didn't trust himself around her. He was restless and edgy enough being cooped up inside the shop so much of the time. What made coping so much harder was being cooped up with her right upstairs, and knowing that all he'd have to do was knock on the door, pull her into the stairwell and he could have her in his arms.

When he'd get to thinking like that, he'd usually quit early and go ice-fishing with Louie, or drive to Two Bays to take care of errands he'd put off. The one time he'd caved in and climbed upstairs to her apartment, telling himself he was near enough to finishing his boat that getting involved with her now wouldn't matter, she'd opened the door and he'd found his intentions promptly doused with ice water. Behind her, Brenda and a woman Hannah introduced as Brenda's sister were curled up on the sofa with scraps of fabric they were all quilting.

The sight of those women, the homey atmosphere Hannah always created and her soft smile immediately jerked him back to reality. He'd been thinking with his body instead of what was sitting on his shoulders, and he'd forgotten that getting involved with him would do her far more harm than good. So he'd muttered something about wanting to know if she needed anything from Duluth, then headed out to his truck wondering if he should stuff snow in his pants or his head into a snowbank.

He did go to Duluth that night, too, fully intending to find a bar and a woman and spend a couple of days getting Hannah out of his head. He'd found the bar. He'd found a willing distraction. But all he'd been able to think about was the woman who refused to see him the way everyone else did, whose voice could soothe and arouse in the same instant, whose smile touched the heart he swore he didn't have, and he'd headed back to Pine Point feeling frustrated as hell and praying for an early thaw. Once he moved the boat out of the shop and he was away from her, he would forget her. Right now, she was like some virus he just couldn't quite shake.

"Will you?" she repeated, the wariness he hated growing evident with his silence.

Shades of fire glinted in her hair. Her scent surrounded him. With her lake blue eyes seeking an answer in his, the desire to reach for her was like a living thing inside him.

"I'll talk to him," he murmured, and stuffed himself back under the sink.

"When?"

"I have to drive to Two Harbors for oil and more sealer. I'll stop in the morning and see if he's up to going with me."

"Why don't you take the day off and go fishing with him instead? You work too hard, Damon."

"I need to get the boat finished."

She knew that. Damon was obsessed with getting his boat put back together by the end of the month. The ice in the inlet was already breaking up. But she'd thought the outing might be good for both him and Mr. Lindstrom. As hard as they'd worked all winter, they seemed to work even harder now. But, working or relaxing, Damon seemed to enjoy the older man's company as much as Mr. Lindstrom enjoyed his—even though Damon still insisted he was only picking the guy's brain because he knew so much about boats.

The claim didn't fool Hannah in the least. The friendship that had grown between the two men was as obvious to her as the melting snowdrifts piled around every building and tree in northern Minnesota. In a way, they were two of a kind. Louie had family, but they didn't seem to want him around. Damon had no one, but no one wanted him around, either. They were indeed an odd couple, the old man and the reclusive hellion, but they were good for each other. At least, that was what Hannah thought. But not everyone saw it that way.

"Afternoon, Neil." Sam Thorson wrapped a stout fist around his coffee mug and raised it toward the man shrugging out of his raincoat by the café's front door. At Sam's elbow, Ellen, Sam's wife of thirty-two years, dabbed soup from her mouth and smiled, too. "Bit damp out there, I'd say."

Neil's affable, golden-boy features were red from the cold. "Sure is," he agreed, chafing his hands and knocking slush from his boots. "Miserable time of year, but have to get through it to get to summer now, don't we?"

Neil gave Sam a friendly slap on the back as he headed for his usual table by the front window. On the way, he popped Grady Olson, who was sitting at the counter, on the shoulder and nodded to Dorothy Yont and one of her daughters-in-law at the table ahead of him. He didn't know the two other customers occupying a table by the side window, but he smiled at them, too, just in case they knew who he was. As one of the town's most prominent citizens, in his estimation, anyway, he took his roll of representative quite seriously.

He was meeting Gunnar Erickson for lunch. Gun was already at the table, rubbing the wheat-colored, walruslike mustache that hid his overbite as he scrutinized Hannah's pared-down winter menu. Bracing himself when Neil approached, he received a whack, too, and determinedly suffered the jarring sensation that undoubtedly rattled his back teeth. Men always got the enthusiastic, good-old-boy slap; women, the conciliatory nod and toothy smile.

Hannah had often wondered if the once-almost-pro hockey player didn't realize his strength, or if he used the greeting as a way to prove how macho he still was. As for the smile, its wattage had dimmed considerably lately when she was on the receiving end of it.

Her own attitude was friendly as always. Especially since she looked first to Gunnar, a leaner, quieter man, to take his order. The carpenter's pleasant, down-to-earth manner had always appealed to her. She liked his wife, too, though she didn't see her as much. She wasn't so sure, anymore, how she felt about Neil.

"I'll have the usual," Neil told her, smoothing his sandy hair back from his high, square forehead. Beneath heavy, pale blond eyebrows, his blue eyes darted to his watch. "I'm pressed for time today, so I'd appreciate it if you'd hurry with that. After I talk to Gun here about that bleacher problem we had during Snow Daze, I have to take my youngest to get her braces adjusted. After that, I have a meeting with one of our suppliers at the store."

He turned a beleaguered look to the man across from him, certain he'd find understanding in a counterpart. "Kirsty went to Duluth to shop," he went on, explaining why he'd been stuck with the run to the orthodontist. He rolled his eyes toward the ceiling and lowered his voice just enough to make people strain a bit to hear him. "I can't begin to imagine what that's going to cost me."

Neither his mumblings nor his itinerary had been for Hannah's benefit. They were to impress anyone within earshot, which happened to be everyone there since the room was small enough for every word to be heard.

Trying hard to not roll her eyes to the ceiling herself, not so sure that Dorothy didn't, Hannah headed for the swinging doors to the kitchen. As she did, she heard Gun reply.

"Say, Neil, I saw your uncle," he said, tactfully avoiding comment on Neil's last remarks. "He and Damon Jackson were out front of the auto supply store in Two Harbors last week. It looked like they were buying cases of motor oil or some such. How's Louie doing these days? Has he had any more problems?"

Hannah knew by now that Gun wasn't a gossip. Since he had an elderly parent he routinely checked in on, his interest in how Neil's uncle was faring was genuine. But as she stood in the heat of the stove dishing up hearty yellow pea soup for Neil and chili for Gun, she couldn't help smiling at his first question. Mr. Lindstrom's memory actually seemed better than hers most of the time. His biggest complaint these days was that his pants were getting snug from her cooking. At that very moment, he and Damon were downstairs polishing off the lunch she'd taken them.

The conversation continued, her smile fading at the sound of Neil's voice. She truly wasn't trying to eavesdrop, but standing at the service window made it impossible not to hear Neil's reply. Though the clatter of the pot lids made her miss the first of what he said, the gist of it was that he was really getting worried about his uncle Louie. The rest, she heard perfectly.

"His judgment is getting more questionable every day," he declared, as she garnished Gun's chili with sour cream, onion, grated cheddar and parsley. "And that makes him as easy a target as you're likely to find. You hear all the time about scams against old people, and you've got to know that Jackson's pulling one on him. Why else would someone like him befriend a senile old man?

"You know as well as I do that Jackson can't be trusted," he hurried on, seeing no need for other input. "That's why I make him pay cash for everything at the marine supply store. You have to know he's up to something," he muttered, getting back to how untrustworthy Damon was. "I bet I know what that something is, too."

The sharp clink of forks and spoons settling against dishes filtered in to Hannah. Grabbing the paprika, considering cayenne, she sprinkled the top of Neil's soup, and heard the soft-spoken carpenter ask what that "something" was.

Neil's voice lowered further. Not enough to make his words confidential. Just enough to make them sound that way.

"Everybody in town knows how tight Louie Lindstrom is with a buck. My uncle's got more money than Croesus stashed away in his savings accounts. I'm willing to bet Jackson's getting ready to hit him up. If he hasn't already," he muttered ominously. "It has to cost a fortune to refit that wreck of his, even with my uncle supplying free labor."

"If you're so sure of that," Gun interjected, truly concerned, "shouldn't you talk to Louie? Keep him away from the man?"

"How can I keep him away?" he asked, sounding helpless. "I can't lock him in his house. And I have talked to him. All he does when I bring it up is stare at his television and tell me I don't know what I'm talking about. I'm sure he doesn't," he conceded with a snort. "He doesn't know what anyone's talking about anymore. He even tried to blame his medicine for making him senile."

Hannah made it as far as the swinging door, bowls in hand and anger on slow simmer. From the moment she'd first met Neil, her impression of him had been that he'd always felt he'd deserved more than he got, and that he rather relished feeling put upon. He constantly hinted about how hard it was to work for his demanding, unappreciative father-in-law, how his wife and daughters were spending money faster than he could make it, and what a burden it was keeping an eye on his old bachelor uncle. Hannah knew Mr. Lindstrom didn't care for Neil and what he called Neil's "uppity" family, and with no other family on his side in town, that had to make things difficult for his nephew. But it was hard for Hannah to feel charitable toward the man. Not when his speculation about two people she cared very much about was so disparaging.

Conversation stopped completely when she backed through the door and slid the men's meals in front of them. She asked Gun if she could get him anything else, and after he said everything looked fine, she turned to the man reaching for the salt. She didn't ask what else she could get for him.

"Be careful, Neil."

"I know," he muttered. "It's hot."

"I'm not talking about your soup."

She met his quick frown evenly and turned back to Gun. "I couldn't help overhearing what you asked Neil about his uncle," she said quietly. "I visit with Mr. Lindstrom a lot and our conversations are quite rational. He enjoys working with Damon, too.

"As for what Neil said about Damon scamming him," she continued, knowing at least three people watching them would repeat every word they heard, "Damon would no more do something to hurt Louie Lindstrom than you or I would. They're friends."

Neil gave another snort. "You've just caught him on a couple of his good days," he pronounced, dismissing her observation with the snap of his burgundy napkin. "I know you've taken an interest in my uncle, too, but I see him at least once a week and he's definitely deteriorating."

She saw his uncle nearly every day, and she didn't agree with his assessment at all. But this was neither the time nor the place to floor a debate over the difference between deterioration and cantankerousness, or to suggest that he take the conclusion Damon had obviously mentioned to his uncle about his medication more seriously. She just wanted to make sure Grady, Dorothy and Dorothy's daughter-in-law had another side to tell when they recounted the conversations they'd heard—and to let Neil know she wasn't going to put up with comments about Damon in her café.

"I'd be more than happy to talk to you about your uncle later," she informed him, quite politely. "In fact, I'd really like to. What I don't care for are unfounded conclusions that start rumors."

Neil's face turned the color of his napkin, his glance darting to Gun, then back to her. He was definitely peeved. She just couldn't tell if he was because she'd disagreed with him, or because she'd called him on what he'd said about Damon.

Thinking it best to let everything drop for the moment, she

turned to ask Dorothy if she'd like more coffee. As she did, Neil's arrogance got the better of him.

"I've known Damon Jackson since I was a boy," he informed her. "So has Gun. And Grady," he continued, rising from his chair, "you and Dorothy and your families have known him longer then we have. Knowing what we all know about him, I have good reason to question his agenda with my uncle. No man with his lack of moral fiber ever does anything without an ulterior motive.

"Now, if I were you, Hannah," he warned, planting his hands on either side of his soup to lean toward her, "I'd be real careful about what you say and do around here. The God-fearing, law-abiding folk I know have already questioned your judgment about renting space to such riffraff. From the way you're always coming to Jackson's defense, I'm inclined to question a couple of other things about you, too."

A soft gasp sounded from the ladies' table. Hannah just wasn't sure if it had been precipitated by the suggestive look Neil ran over her body, what he'd said, or the fact that the man he was talking about was standing with his hand braced on the open swinging door of the kitchen.

Damon hadn't caught the whole conversation. He'd walked in at the God-fearing part. Actually, that was the part he'd heard when he'd pushed open the door into the café and eight pair of eyes swung toward him. The part that had stopped him was what Neil had said about her being careful.

Neil straightened. Curious to see what had pulled the attention from him, he glanced over his shoulder.

Damon scarcely noticed the way Neil's bluster faded. All he cared about was Hannah. Framed by a pair of frilly curtains, she looked as pale as the snow melting outside the window.

"What's going on?"

The question was a low rumble of demand, directed only to her. He didn't even look at any of the other people scattered around the cozy little room. His eyes bore into Hannah's, the latent tension in his powerful body defying anyone else to speak while he waited for her to respond.

She drew a steadying breath as Neil sank into his chair and everyone else suddenly became enamoured with whatever was on their plate. But before she could offer a word of assurance or explanation, the bell over the door cut through the air with a cheerful tinkle that sounded as out of place as laughter at a funeral.

Brenda didn't notice the six feet of wire-taut muscle at the kitchen door. Busy stowing her dripping fuchsia umbrella, she saw only that her boss was waiting on the customers she should have been tending herself.

"Oh, Hannah, I'm sorry I'm late, but I got stuck at the gift shop. Hi, Dorothy." The aside was as natural as her smile as she started edging sideways toward the kitchen, her attention again on her employer. "I stopped to pick up a card for the Sondheim's new baby, but the only one I liked was the same one you sent. So I ran across the street to the pharmacy to see what they had," she continued, working at the buttons of her red slicker as she kept backing up, "and Holly Miller started telling me about Arvida Sieverson's accident at the grocery store this morning. I guess there was glass and pickled beets everywhere...."

Confusion suddenly washed over Brenda's pixieish features as she cut herself off. The odd atmosphere in the room must have finally registered. Either that, or she'd just felt the presence of the rugged, rough-hewn man behind her.

She glanced over her shoulder, then promptly cranked her head up when all she could see was a corrugated wall of black T-shirt.

Hannah knew the petite woman's wide-eyed expression was more surprise than disquiet. Brenda regarded Damon with the same benign skepticism he regarded her, but the waitress knew as well as Hannah did that he deliberately avoided being anyplace where he could run into the people cautiously eyeing him now.

"Would you bring the bread for this table when you get your apron on?" Hannah asked her, managing a wan smile for an uneasy Grady at the counter as she passed behind him. "And refill everyone's coffee?"

"Sure," Brenda replied, looking a little worried as Hannah slipped past her and the big man still holding the door.

Damon waited until Brenda had entered the kitchen, too, then let the door swing closed behind them all. In the time it took for whispers in the café to escalate to a low buzz, Brenda had hung her slicker on the hook by the back door, washed her hands and was tying on a burgundy bib apron like the one Hannah wore while she hurried back out. Damon wasn't sure if the diminutive waitress hadn't stuck around to ask questions because of his presence, or because of what her boss had asked her to do. He didn't care. All that mattered to him was that Hannah kept making their situation harder than it needed to be.

"Did you or Mr. Lindstrom want something else?" she asked, heading toward the lunch tray he'd set on the counter.

She was trying to pretend that nothing extraordinary had happened. To push the unpleasantness out of the way and continue on as if this, too, would pass. The woman was like an ostrich.

She'd taken two steps past him when he caught her by the apron strings at the back of her waist. Tugging her around, he immediately let go. If he touched her anywhere else, he'd get grease on her—or wring her lovely neck.

"You can't go around doing that anymore," he informed her, banked fury shimmering in his low, certain voice.

"Doing what?"

"Defending me. Dammit it, Hannah. In the first place, I can take care of myself. I've been doing it all my life. What's more important," he grated, "is that people are going to get the wrong idea if you keep it up and start thinking we're something we're not.''

The harsh words jolted her back. Grappling with what Neil had said, not sure how much Damon had heard, she simply hadn't been prepared for the sting that came with his bluntness. She already knew he'd dismissed any possibility of them as a couple. She'd dismissed the idea herself. Regularly. But in the past months, their relationship had grown into a wary sort of friendship. One that she'd come to count on a little too much. One she'd thought, hoped, Damon had come to count on a little, too.

At the moment, upset with Neil for what he'd implied, and with Damon for doing what he did best by pushing her away, she could only think that she'd been wrong to assume Damon would let himself count on anything at all.

''I'll defend whomever I choose,'' she informed him, forcing calm over anger and hurt. ''Especially when I know someone doesn't deserve the treatment he's getting. As for giving anyone the wrong impression about us, I can't imagine how much more wrong people around here can get.'' She lifted her arm in an arc. ''Half this town already thinks we're sleeping together. The other half suspects it. Since we seem to be the only two who know we aren't, I don't see that it makes any difference what I say.''

Through the service window came the distinct sound of someone choking on her coffee. Aware that their conversation was far from private, she saw Damon turn his turbulent scowl to his hands. A heartbeat later, with a look that seemed to say ''what the hell,'' he grabbed her arm, turning her so quickly she nearly lost her balance, and steered her into her office.

He'd barely booted the door closed when he turned her back to the wall and planted his fists on either side of her head.

''I heard Neil, Hannah.'' His granite-hard face was inches

from hers, his eyes glittering with anger and some emotion she couldn't begin to name. "I heard what he said about what people are saying about you, and about how their attitudes will affect your business. There isn't a hell of a lot that I'm inclined to agree with when it comes to that man, but I'll back him on this. It doesn't matter that your sense of fairness is insulted by the way things work around here. You'd damn well better start taking my reputation seriously before the good citizens of this town stop patronizing your establishment completely and you lose everything you're working so hard to get."

Hannah's shoulder blades bit into the wall. His anger was a physical force that pushed her back as surely as if his hands had been locked on her arms. He wasn't touching her. Even if he had been, he would never hurt her. Yet the way she shrank from him made him think she didn't know that for certain.

The thought sickened him. He'd cut off his own hand before he'd harm her. It hadn't been his intention to badger her into backing down. All he wanted to do was make her understand how foolish it was of her to befriend him. But if he had to make her fear him to accomplish his goal, then he'd just have to live with her being as apprehensive of him as everyone else. He could give her nothing. But he could keep her from losing what she had.

He could also make sure that Louie's jerk-of-a-nephew understood who was fair game in this town, and who wasn't.

Breathing in the impossibly erotic scents of cooking spice and herbal shampoo clinging to her, he raked one last glance over Hannah's delicate features. He halfway expected to see her tip that stubborn little chin up and challenge his demand. For once, she didn't push back. Her usual composure had shattered. She looked bewildered, confused, hurt. He hated that she'd chosen to button herself up in a place that would surely extinguish the fire inside her. But it was her choice. And he'd see that no one deprived her of it.

He pushed himself from the wall, shaking inside. From fury with bigots like Neil who were allowed to be insufferable because they'd been born into the right family, from a sense of loss he didn't understand. Jerking open the door, he stepped into the kitchen and caught Brenda's eye through the service window.

He didn't give himself a chance to consider what he intended to do. That alone should have told him not to do it. But he motioned her into the kitchen, then stayed behind the swinging door after she came through so no one could see him or hear what he said.

"Is Lindstrom still out there?"

The petite woman with the dark, curling hair hesitated, then gave him a nod.

"He said he'd lost his appetite and paid his bill. He's just getting ready to leave." Suddenly leery, she stepped closer to the door. "Look," she whispered intently. "I have no idea what's going on yet, but if you're going to cause Hannah trouble, I can't let you go out there."

Had Damon been in the mood to smile, he would have just then. The woman was barely five feet tall, mostly smile and hair. Yet she was looking as proprietary and protective as he felt himself.

She was also standing in his way.

"I'm not the one who started this," he muttered, and reached over her head to push open the door.

The melodic tinkle of the entrance bell had just faded when Damon jerked the front door back open, causing the bell to peel more wildly. The rain wasn't much more than a steady drizzle, but the air was so cold his agitated breathing looked like smoke from a dragon.

He scarcely noticed the cold, or the fact that he was going to get soaked.

"Lindstrom."

In the process of pulling a brown cap over his ears, Neil jerked to a stop and spun around. His disgruntled expression immediately went cautious.

"I have nothing to say to you, Jackson." His chin came up, his courage fueled by the knowledge that everyone in the café or driving down the street could see every move the bigger, less-civilized man made.

Damon took a menacing step forward. "That suits me fine. All I want you to do is listen."

"There's nothing you can say that I want to hear. And by the way, I'm on to you and your phony concern for my uncle. You might as well know right now that I intend to make certain you don't take advantage of him, either."

He started to turn away. Damon's hand on his arm stopped him.

"How dare you—"

"I dare anything I please," Damon informed him, his voice dangerously tight.

He immediately let the man go, though it would have given him enormous satisfaction to wipe the arrogant glare off his face. The last thing he needed was the town's golden boy screaming "assault."

"You'd better keep that in mind, too, Lindstrom. I don't know what you mean about your uncle, but nobody's taking advantage of him. And I don't give a damn what you think about me. But I'm the one you'll answer to if you say anything to harm Hannah's reputation." He took another step forward, certain he was missing something, but too angry to care as the fuming man backed up. "You got that?"

He didn't wait for a response. He'd delivered his message. All he was interested in now was going home, getting dry and doing what he should have been doing all along. Keeping completely to himself.

* * *

Any other day, news of Arvida Sieverson's encounter with the display in front of aisle five would have received top billing as a topic of conversation. The demise of forty-two economy-size jars of pickled beets was quickly overshadowed, however, by accounts of Damon Jackson manhandling Neil Lindstrom in front of the Pine Café.

What Hannah found most interesting about the two versions she heard was that one was amazingly accurate. It included everything from Neil's inflammatory conclusions about Damon's motives regarding Mr. Lindstrom and Neil's not-so-veiled insults toward Hannah, to Hannah's remarks to Damon in the kitchen prior to Damon following Neil out to "cause a ruckus" before they parted in opposite directions.

Hannah figured either Dorothy or Gunnar was responsible for the accurate accounts. Her money was actually on Dorothy. The ex-postmistress wasn't known to embellish, and Gunnar, if he ran true to form, wouldn't get around to saying anything about his interrupted lunch for another couple of days.

The other version, the one Hattie called from the florist shop to confirm, would have had Hannah fuming if she hadn't already been so upset.

"I won't say I told you so," the woman graciously allowed the moment Hannah had answered the telephone. "But now you know why everyone's been so concerned about you renting to that man. Do you need any help cleaning up over there?"

Hannah didn't know if the matter had become confused with the pickled beets incident or if someone had decided the truth just wasn't juicy enough on its own. Hattie had heard that a fight had started inside the café when Neil confronted Damon about stealing from old Mr. Lindstrom and ended with broken glass everywhere and both men yelling and shoving at each other on the street.

Anyone walking into the café could see that no damage

had been done. No physical damage, anyway. Brenda said she swore the few locals who came in that Saturday stopped mainly to inspect wreckage. Sheriff Jansson was the only one who didn't seem disappointed when he walked in and found the quaint interior as clean and inviting as always. But, then, he'd received a call from Neil about what had happened, so he knew the altercation hadn't led to bloodshed. Damon had threatened Neil, though, so his day wasn't a total loss.

For once he didn't warn Hannah, or chastise her. He just gave her a look that echoed Hattie's I-told-you-so sentiment and asked if she had overheard the threats. He posed the same question to Brenda, though his manner was considerably friendlier when he addressed her. After all, Brenda just worked there. It wasn't her fault that her boss had such lousy judgment.

Like everyone else who'd gaped out the café's windows when Damon had stormed out, Hannah had seen him and Neil for the brief moments they'd been outside together. She'd also seen Damon walk back through the café without saying a word to a soul. Five minutes later, his black truck had rounded the corner. She told the sheriff as much, then attempted to relate what Neil had said about Damon, since she was pretty certain Mr. Lindstrom's nephew had omitted the parts that hadn't served his purpose.

The sheriff wasn't interested in what Neil had said, however. All he wanted from her was to know if she'd actually heard Damon's threats—which reduced her response to a simple, decidedly terse "No."

"I guess that wasn't what he wanted to hear," Brenda mused after the sheriff had walked out with the muscle in his jaw jumping. "But maybe something good did come of all this."

Agitation had Hannah grabbing a sponge to attack a soup spill on the stove. "I can't begin to imagine what that would be."

"Well, you did put a few rumors to rest with that remark about how the two of you aren't sleeping together."

Hannah simply couldn't appreciate Brenda's optimism at the moment. Keeping her neighbors apprised of her nonexistent sex life wasn't exactly what she'd had in mind when she'd moved here.

"Of course," Brenda continued when Hannah just kept scrubbing, "the way Damon acted does leave a lot of room for speculation. He was sort of…well, kind of chivalrous, I guess. When he was yelling at you in the kitchen, he sounded like he was only thinking about you. And the look on his face when he left your office…" she mused, absently thumbing her wedding ring. "You know, Hannah, it's not every day that a woman has a man looking like he'll draw blood to defend her honor."

"You make it sound as if he was suited in armor and mounted on a white horse when he tore out of here."

"I wouldn't go that far," she countered, defending her observation. "Damon's not knight-in-shining-armor material. He's more the rogue knight on a black stallion. But it's like you tried to tell the sheriff. I think he was upset with what Neil said about you. I don't think he heard the other part you told me about. The stuff about him trying to get Mr. Lindstrom's money. The way you say he is about not defending himself, I almost think he'd have ignored that."

Hannah couldn't discount her friend's conclusions. They were pretty much her own, anyway. She'd felt certain from the moment she'd seen Damon that he hadn't heard what Neil had said about him scamming his uncle. He'd looked far more protective than insulted and, as much as he thought of Louie, he'd certainly have said something to her about Neil's remarks if he'd been aware of them. That had to mean he'd taken after Neil only because of what Neil had said about her.

She didn't know what to make of him coming to her defense that way. Considering that all he wanted was for her to forget she even knew him, and as adamant as he was about having people forget he was around, what he'd done made no sense at all.

"I think he was trying to help, Hannah."

Beneath the anxiety, the trepidation and the odd, lingering sense of hurt, Hannah had that feeling, too. "If he was, he went about it all wrong."

"I hope you'll tell him that the first chance you get. Just so he doesn't get himself into trouble, I mean. Or cause any more for you."

Brenda's sweet concern only reinforced what Hannah had been thinking all afternoon. And the more she thought about it as evening approached, the more imperative seeing him became. She didn't know what he'd said to Neil, or what he was capable of where the man was concerned. And even though it would only make him angry, she needed to tell him that Neil thought he was after Louie's money, just so he didn't say or do anything to Louie that could be misconstrued. But Neil wasn't her biggest worry.

She knew how reclusive Damon was, and how he could cut someone out in the blink of an eye. If he was feeling as defensive as she suspected he might, she didn't doubt that he'd cut himself off from everyone—and that meant ending his relationship with his elderly friend.

He'd be hurting himself as much as he would Louie if he did that, but he wouldn't care about himself. She needed to make him understand what it would do to Louie, though. Letting the old guy down now would be harder on him than if Damon had never let him work with him at all. Whether he liked the idea or not, Louie needed him.

As for what she might need, she didn't dare let herself consider it as she pulled her little blue sedan between the melting mounds of snow on either side of his driveway and ran through the dark to his porch.

Chapter Ten

Damon's ramshackle house sat south of the inlet, nearly obscured by the deep woods that ran right up to the edge of a sheer, forty-foot cliff. The dense stands of pine protected the place from the worst of the winds that swept across Lake Superior, but the ravages of time and the elements had long ago taken their toll on the old Jackson place. With the snow melted from the roof, the sag over the garage was clearly visible in the light anchored below its peak. The weathered siding, even illuminated only by the porch light, was splintered and peeling, trails of rust tears running from its nails.

The only thing that didn't look in danger of tumbling down was the stone chimney rising beyond the dormers and the new glass storm door. The place was as decrepit as his boat had once been, but Hannah was fighting the cold and nerves and it wouldn't have mattered if the inheritance he was so determined to keep was a pea green teepee as long as he hurried up and opened the door. All she wanted was to get this over with.

He answered on her third knock. She didn't take it as a good sign that he took one look at her, then closed his eyes and lowered his head as if he wished he'd hadn't answered the door.

He'd changed clothes after getting soaked that afternoon. A stark white undershirt stretched over the broad expanse of his chest, exposed by the sides of the denim shirt hanging open over it. Jeans, washed nearly white in places, clung to his lean hips. He hadn't bothered with a belt. Or to comb his hair. From the way the dark strands spiked up in places, however, it did seem he'd run his fingers through it a few dozen times.

"May I come in?"

He seemed to know she wasn't going anywhere until she'd stated her piece, but there wasn't a shred of invitation when he unlatched the storm door and pushed it open. When he hadn't said a word by the time he turned away, leaving her to close the doors behind herself, Hannah knew that the calm she'd hoped for would not prevail.

Tension radiated from him in waves as he moved to the middle of the small, neat little room. She stayed back by the door, lowering the hood of her blue slicker and slowly popping its snaps while she dripped on the rug. The brown carpet was worn, in need of replacing, but the tan sofa looked new. So did the television that displayed a wild car chase and the word *mute.* On the end wall, a fire crackled in the stone fireplace. The painting above it was of a huge schooner under full sail. It battled a foaming sea as hostile as Damon's expression when he turned back to face her.

"You don't listen very well, do you?"

"I was just wondering if you would listen at all."

He eyed her evenly, gray eyes distant. He was in no mood to spar. "I'm not going to argue with you, Hannah. You shouldn't have come here."

Even prepared for it, the cold rejection stung. "I don't want to argue with you, either," she quietly informed him, drawing her own defenses around herself. "I just want to talk to you about Neil. And Louie."

"What about Louie?" he muttered, clearly preferring to ignore the man's nephew.

"Are you going to pick him up in the morning?"

Had Damon looked at all confused, Hannah would have conceded that her concerns were completely misplaced and that she really didn't know him at all. But he didn't even blink. He just stood watching her, solid and immovable as a mountain, his jaw working furiously.

She had no idea what thoughts warred in his mind before he glanced away and motioned toward a small table visible through the narrow doorway. It was covered with brass fittings he obviously intended to polish.

"I'm going to do what I can here for a while. Alone," he carefully emphasized. "I have to wait for the sealer to dry before I paint, anyway. There isn't that much for him to help with."

There was no satisfaction at all in having her suspicions confirmed. "He doesn't always help you now," she pointed out, refusing to condone his rationale. "Half the time, he just watches you, or sits and visits. It's your company he wants." She motioned toward the table herself. "You could bring him here if you don't want to go to the shop."

"And what do you suggest I do with him after the boat's finished? Take him out on the lake with me every day?"

His sarcasm was wasted. He was pretending to be practical. Hannah knew he was only being self-protective. "We both know he wouldn't be up to that," she informed him flatly. "But I know he's offered to come down to the dock after you've unloaded your catch in the afternoons and help you get ready for the next day. You're not being fair to him, Damon. He doesn't want to stop spending time with you."

His gray eyes locked on hers, as cool as quicksilver, as

hard as diamonds. "You're still expecting fair? Haven't you figured out by now that 'fair' isn't something that happens around here?"

He jammed his fingers through his hair, looming closer as her accusation festered. "And just for the record," he said, seething, fury tightening his voice, "I'm being a lot more fair to him than that nephew of his is being to him, or you or me. Neil was badmouthing you right in front of your customers, and I'm the one," he grated, jabbing his finger at his chest, "who got blamed for causing trouble because I told him to back off. I'd say that's about as fair as him accusing me of planning to hit an old man up for his money when all I've been doing is minding my own business. Wouldn't you?"

Hannah didn't realize how she'd dreaded raising the subject until she realized she wouldn't have to. "I didn't know you knew about that."

"Oh, the sheriff made sure I did. He wanted me to know that I'd be the first person he looked to if Louie is missing so much as a dime. Anything happens to bruise Neil the Wonder Boy's pretty face and I'm on the block for that, too."

He had every right to the anger burning inside him. The accusation, the rumors, the suspicion. None of it was justified. Not anymore. He'd grown beyond the man he'd been ten years ago. But feeling his quiet rage slither along her nerve endings, she didn't know who was more at fault for not seeing that. The town. Or him.

"I'm not talking about everyone else, Damon. All I care about is you and how your actions affect one old man. He needs to help you. You won't be protecting yourself at all by staying away from him, either. It'll just look as if Neil was right and that he scared you off before you could do anything."

She knew by the dark flicker in his eyes that she hadn't phrased something quite right. Either that, or he was about to take exception to her insinuation that he was running away. Too upset to care, she held her ground and matched his glare.

"And one other thing," she said, cutting him off before he could get started and make her forget what all she'd come to say. "I know you were trying to help this afternoon when you took off after Neil. I appreciate it. I really do. But you're not the only one who can take care of himself. I can take care of myself just fine."

The sound he made as he scanned her upturned face was nothing short of rude. "How? By living in a state of perpetual denial?"

She'd sounded so certain seconds ago. At his unexpected attack, her voice lost its strength. "I don't live in denial."

"It's exactly what you do," he snapped. "You rationalize and justify and refuse to see anything that threatens you or your idea of what your life is supposed to be in this place. If you can't overlook it, you make excuses for it. You did it when those waitresses quit, and when you've tried to explain why your business is slow. You were ready to do it when you went into the kitchen after Neil popped off in the café."

His voice grew lower, rougher. "The way you deny things is what I was talking about when I said you have to take the effect I have on your business seriously. You never have done that, Hannah."

There was a difference between denying something and trying to make the best of a situation. Hannah would have pointed that out, but she had the feeling Damon would only insist it was the same thing, and she didn't care to defend the only way she'd ever had of coping with what life dumped on her.

"I know what you were talking about," she said, feeling exposed and vulnerable and desperately afraid that she was losing the emotional shield that guarded her feelings for this man. "You don't need to get angry with me or use your reputation as an excuse to push me away. You've made it clear enough that you don't want me, Damon. If you don't even want to be friends, then at least have the decency to be as up-front about that as you have been about everything else."

She had the horrible feeling that he heard the shaking in her voice. But she kept her chin up, her stance defying challenge. As long as she could meet him head-on, he'd never know how vulnerable she was to him. He'd never know how it broke her heart to see him holing up inside himself when he had so much to offer. Or how she ached for him in ways she had no choice but to deny.

Defiance was her defense. But it taunted Damon like the proverbial red flag being waved in front of a bull.

He stepped closer, his anger coiling around her as he came slowly forward, knotting her stomach, testing her courage. He didn't stop until his body blocked sight of the fire, the room, everything but the breadth of his chest and the storm clouds darkening his eyes.

"I don't use excuses," he informed her, his voice rumbling like distant thunder over her nerves. "I don't need them. I've honestly tried to do what was best for both of us by staying on the fringes of your life. And you think it's because I don't want you?"

Any incredulity in his expression was masked in the fierceness of his carved features. His glance darted over her face, touching her hair, the part of her mouth when she drew in an uncertain breath. "I want you so badly I ache, Hannah." His arm swept behind him, his eyes glittering hard on hers. "I lay in that room night after night imagining how it would feel to have you under me. I imagine how your hair would look spread out on my pillow, how you would taste and move and feel. It takes every ounce of willpower I have to keep my hands off you. Don't you realize that?"

Like a starving man faced with a banquet he couldn't consume, he forced his glance from her mouth and turned his back on what he'd told himself he couldn't have.

Hannah's heart pounded as she focused on his rigid back. His heated admissions robbed the strength from her voice. "Did it ever occur to you that I'd rather you use your willpower for your temper?"

"I don't *have* a temper."

"It certainly sounds like you do."

He wheeled around, expecting recrimination, finding instead a reflection of his own desires.

Need hit him like a fist.

"There's a difference between irritation and frustration, Hannah."

She swallowed, her chin coming up, her defenses shot. "Then, show me the frustration."

The inequities he'd been dealing with for hours already had him feeling as if he wanted to explode. Now the naked challenge in her eyes taunted his restraint. If she wanted to know what he was dealing with, he'd be more than happy to show her.

He took a step closer, crowding her, and pushed his hand into the hair at her nape. The circle of gathered fabric holding back her hair hit the carpet about the time he molded his hands to her skull and lowered his head.

"You want to know how frustration feels?" he taunted.

His mouth came down hard on hers, his hands pulling her head back, tilting it at an angle. His tongue swept her lips, making them part before she could let him in on her own. He wanted her open to him, as vulnerable to his invasion as he was to her smile, the sound of her voice, her scent. If she wanted to understand what he felt, then she needed to know how it felt to have control wrested away and constantly teetering on its edge, to be burning up on the inside and having no way of slaking the heat. Even now, especially now, the desire clawing in him was a physical thing. Demanding. Taunting. Threatening.

He dragged her forward, wanting her body vulnerable to him, too, but her raincoat was in the way. Shoving his hand between the open sides of the slick fabric, he swallowed her faint moan when he deliberately dragged his palm up and over the roundness of her breasts.

His heart was hammering when he finally pushed her coat over her slender shoulders and let it fall in a heap at her feet. She was trembling like a leaf in a stiff breeze, her fingers coiled around his neck as if she would fall without his support. He wanted her mindless, limp with need. He wasn't sure what was pushing him. He just knew it was no longer anger. That had died the instant he felt her mouth soften beneath his.

He knew, too, that he was beyond proving a point. With Hannah's soft hands working under his shirt, her mouth seeking him as hungrily as he sought her, he simply couldn't remember why he should care.

He wanted her.

The knowledge flowed through Hannah like the headiest wine. She yearned for this man who tried to do what was right; this scarred, angry man who felt compelled to hide how truly decent he was. He made her feel things she'd never known existed, and now, she feared, she couldn't live without. She'd never known, never believed, she could experience such reckless need. That she could crave a man with such desperation. But, then, she'd never been desired the way Damon desired her. No man had ever told her he'd imagined her in his bed. No man had ever touched her with such possession.

His big hands molded her, shaped her hips, drawing her intimately against him. It wasn't enough.

"I want you," he murmured, sliding his hand under her sweater. He rubbed the silky fabric of her camisole over her ribs, her breasts. "You want me to stop, say so now. I can fight myself. I can fight you. But I can't fight both of us." The satiny fabric slipped up, exposing her skin to the tantalizing roughness of his callused palm. "Another minute, and I'm not going to try."

The thought of him stopping nearly undid her. "Then, don't. Where's your room?"

His eyes glittered like polished pewter in the moments before he bent to catch the back of her legs. He didn't answer. He just lifted her in his arms as if she weighed nothing at all, and swung her through the doorway behind him.

He didn't bother with the lamp by the bed. The golden light spilling in from the living room made it easy enough to see when he lowered her to the rumpled sheets, then reared back to unbuckle his belt.

Over the erratic pounding of her heart in her ears, Hannah heard the harsh rasp of his zipper and the impatient rustle of fabric as he shed his denim shirt. Gathering his T-shirt in a wad between his shoulder blades, he dragged it over his head, revealing the corrugated muscles of his stomach and chest, the dark thatch of hair under his powerful arms. His wide shoulders glowed like hammered bronze, the narrow, dark tattoo circling his left bicep making him look like a primitive warrior about to stake his claim as he came forward on his knee.

The mattress sagged with his weight when he reached for the hem of her sweater.

Damon's impatience aroused Hannah as much as the possessiveness in his eyes when he skimmed sweater and camisole away in one tangle. His mouth came down on hers the instant the fabric hit the floor, pushing her head into his pillow while he pulled her under him. She felt his hand slide under her back and the flick of his fingers when the clasp of her bra gave. An instant later, she felt the brush of cool air on her breasts, and the moist heat of his mouth when he trailed his debilitating kiss from her lips to the pebbled hardness of her nipple.

She didn't know if the moan she heard was his or her own. Tangling her fingers in his amazingly soft hair, pressing him to her, she knew only that she had been missing him for her entire life. She had fallen in love with him. Hopelessly. She didn't know when it had happened. But she could no more deny that simple fact than she could deny the fire he ignited deep inside her. Everywhere he touched, she burned. And he was touching her everywhere.

His mouth was still on her when he peeled away her slacks and underwear. On her breasts, her stomach, her thighs. She could feel him trying to slow down, to curb the impatience and heat that drove him. But she gloried in the knowledge that it was she who had put the stark need in his beautifully tortured features; that it was his want of her that coiled the raw tension through his magnificent body. Slowing down was the last thing in this lifetime that she wanted.

She reached for the loosened waist of his denims. He caught her wrist, stretching out over her, nuzzling her neck. "You take them off and I'll be inside you."

"I know."

He lifted himself on his elbows. His expression feral, he smoothed the dark silk of her hair from her face, fanning it on his pillow.

"The way I feel right now, I don't know if I'll be able to take it easy. I don't want to hurt you."

Every nerve in her body was vibrating when she moved her hand shamelessly beneath his briefs. "I want you the way you feel right now." She wanted him exactly as he was. The rough edges. The unbridled passion. He held too much of himself back from her in too many other ways. Here, now, she could refuse his restraints.

Her eyes steady on his, she pushed at the fabric. His jaw locked, but he lifted his hips, letting her shove jeans and briefs as far as she could before he pulled back himself and kicked them away. In an instant of sanity, he fumbled open the drawer of the nightstand and ripped open a small foil packet with his teeth. She barely had time to feel grateful that at least one of them had been thinking before his hands were in her hair, his mouth crushed hers and he'd covered her slender curves with his hard, hot body.

From beyond the window by the bed came the patter of rain on the sill. The gentle sound was muffled by their ragged breathing, the soft rustle of skin brushing skin and the heated honey of Damon's dark voice. He murmured to her, inflaming her with a graphic description of what he wanted to do to her as his big hand slid under her hips, his legs wedging hers apart. He told her exactly what she did to him, too. A tiny moan escaped her lips at the knowledge, then she gasped at the feel of his fingers seeking her dampness before he proved that she made him every bit as hard as he claimed and he began sinking into her.

Damon's hand fisted at the side of her head. He was hanging on to his control by a hair, and the sensations surrounding him as he entered her were almost more than he could bear. He knew she didn't want him to hold back. She gave as well as she got from him even now. But she wasn't a big woman, and he was a big man. So he inched forward, dying a little death each time she lifted her hips higher, taking him deeper, until he was aware of little beyond his need and her heat.

She rose to him like a siren coming out of the sea, melding her body to his, matching his rhythm. He had never wanted a woman the way he wanted this one. She was like a fever in his blood, a delirium that could well drive him mad. Part of him wanted to purge himself of her, to drive her out of his system with each thrust she so willingly met. Another part drove him to make her part of him, to brand her as his. Torn by the storm raging in his body, he ignored the one raging in his mind and let himself be swept away by the feel of her in his arms.

"That's it," he whispered, coaxing her higher. His hot breath feathered against her skin as he traced the delicate shell of her ear. Her skin felt like satin. She tasted like sweet wine. "Let go, honey. Do it. Let go."

His name was a ragged plea on her lips when he felt her convulse around him. Burying his face against the side of her neck, he lifted her with one last, powerful stroke, and emptied himself into her body.

The fire in the other room had burned to embers, its flickering glow long gone. In his spartan bedroom, with its dresser, nightstand and queen-size bed that lacked both headboard and bedspread, the air was considerably cooler than it had been hours ago.

Damon lay in the semidarkness, listening to the constant drumming of rain on the roof. The television was still on and he should turn off the lights, but the thought of disturbing the woman tucked spoon-fashion against him made him stay right where he was.

Even if Hannah hadn't been curled so trustingly in his arms, he wouldn't have wanted to move. Always before when he'd wakened with a woman, an odd, gnawing emptiness would be in his gut. The feeling would drive him from the bed and, ultimately, out into the night. The fact that he was in his own house gave him nowhere else to go. But leaving was the last thing on his mind. The emptiness wasn't there. He'd been waiting for it, expecting it. Yet, as he lay holding her, it simply hadn't come.

He held her left hand in his. Slipping his fingers from hers, he pulled the blankets and sheet down far enough to expose the smooth curve of her shoulder. Easing forward, he kissed her nape, the warm curve of her neck. He'd taken her twice, the second time with the patience he'd lacked the first. But he wanted her again. And again.

But there were a lot of things he'd learned to live without.

With a soft sigh, she shifted against him, then turned in his arms.

"Hi," she murmured.

"Hi, yourself."

"What time is it?"

"Nearly five." He drew his finger along the delicate line of her collarbone, his shadowed features revealing nothing. "What time do you have to be at the café?"

The sweet lethargy filling Hannah began to fade with the rude tug of reality. With the memories of the night flooding back and Damon's hand skimming possessively down her body, the café was the last thing she wanted to think about.

"It's still closed on Sundays."

His response was to let his hand roam over her bare stomach.

Encouraged by his touch, she reached for him, too, skimming her hand over the hard muscles of his shoulder. She could scarcely believe she was finally free to touch him.

Her fingers trailed to the tattoo circling his bicep. She remembered it being a deep indigo blue. But the intricate patterns in the inch-wide band looked black in the light filtering through the bedroom door.

Realizing what had her attention, the strong line of his jaw hardened.

"Does that bother you?"

His question held a note of defense. Hannah had a pretty good idea why it was there. In a place like Pine Point, a tattoo was considered a sign of rebellion, an in-your-face way of defying convention. In the city, people often regarded them as decoration, or art—or the signs of a gang or cult. Damon wasn't the art type. As much of a loner as he was, she couldn't imagine him belonging to a gang, either.

She shook her head, still tracing the patterns. She wasn't put off by the markings at all. Not on him. "I was just wondering what it's supposed to be."

It was his turn to hesitate.

"They're symbols," he finally said, sounding as if he had considered some less revealing response. "From the Samoan *tatau,* except a true *tatau* covers a Samoan chief pretty much from the middle of his back and sides to his knees."

He'd learned of the elaborate body tattoo when he'd worked tankers in the Pacific, he told her. The whole thing was about religion, individual integrity and the honor of the Samoan people. As he spoke, she could hear respect in the low, smoky tones of his voice. She could hear caution, too, as if he wasn't quite sure he wanted to admit that he cared about anything so redeeming or noble as honor.

"These are just the symbols from it I thought I could use."

He'd accused her of living in denial. Perhaps, she thought, slipping her finger along the intriguing shapes, he'd recognized that because he did such a remarkable job of denying things, too.

"What do they mean?"

"The long spear around the top is for bravery in fishing deep waters."

She smiled at that, easily understanding why he'd chosen it. "And these?" she asked, moving the tip of her nail along the undulating line and what looked like the ribs of a feather beneath it.

"That's the centipede. It's to remind a man that he won't feel pain if he's hurt."

She lifted her eyes to his as her hand slowly slid to his muscular forearm. She suspected she understood why he'd chosen that one, too. But she didn't ask if it was only for physical hurts, or if it reminded him not to feel emotional pain, as well. He'd closed himself off in so many ways over the years. Just for now, she wanted to believe that whatever cracks she'd made in his wall wouldn't be so easy for him to repair.

Her voice was quiet, gentle, like the patter of the rain on the windowsill. "And here I thought tattoos were just something a sailor got after a few too many in an accommodating port."

He placed a kiss on the skittering pulse at her wrist, then flattened her hand beside her head when he rolled over her. "Shows how little you know, huh?"

She smiled at that. He smiled back, looking just a little dangerous as his free hand skimmed her breast, her nipple instantly blooming against his palm. The way she responded to him drove him crazy. He'd told her so himself.

Carrying that touch to her hip, he fitted her to him as easily as if they'd been lovers forever, rather than only for a night.

"How am I ever going to keep my hands off of you?" He growled the question against her ear, stealing her breath as he slipped inside her. "How can I work knowing you're just a flight of stairs away? This isn't going to be easy, baby." He began to move, slowly, his voice growing husky. "Being together won't be easy."

Damon knew he was right. But he also knew Hannah would choke before she'd admit it. She refused to back down when she believed in something, but the thought that she believed in him destroyed any thought of pressing the point.

They spent Sunday together secluded at his place, making love, walking in the rain. By tacit agreement, neither spoke of what had happened the day before, or of the town. He had learned to live on its fringes, and his world was a quiet one of deep woods and open waters. That was what he shared with her. Reluctantly at first. More easily when he realized she wasn't put off by the meagerness of his existence. He wasn't a sentimental man. He wasn't even sure he knew what sentiment was. But he knew he'd never forget the way she looked smiling at him from the edge of the cliff overlooking the vast lake.

The rain had stopped, and a shaft of sunlight backlit the hair the wind whipped around her head. She turned to watch him walk toward her, her smile soft, inviting.

"I wish we never had to leave," she said, fitting her back to him when he put his arms around her. "It feels so peaceful here."

He didn't trust the way her quiet words pleased him. Nor did he trust the thoughts that came unbidden that evening when they prepared dinner in the kitchen he'd refloored but hadn't yet painted, or when they later lay curled in front of the stone fireplace that had once been covered with years of soot. He was slowly cleaning up the place, making it livable, but he hadn't really considered why he was doing it, other than it needed to be done.

He couldn't let himself consider any other reason now, either. He was an outcast, and, whether she wanted to believe it or not, if she stayed with him, she would be, too.

Arguing with her about that would be pointless, though. She'd never listened to him before, and, stubborn as she was, he had no reason to think she'd start now. Once he put the boat in the water, he could go back to his old routine and he would be out of her life. In the meantime, he'd just work a little harder, and learn to live with the fact that, inevitably, the day would come when he would walk away from something he'd truly hate to leave. Since his job would go faster working in the shop, and with help, he'd do what she wanted and have Louie work with him. The old guy was slow at times, a little forgetful, but he was worth his weight in advice.

The incident with Neil still had Damon concerned, though. He just hoped that Hannah was right. When they returned to reality the next morning and he asked if she'd be all right in the café, she seemed to think that Neil's insinuations about her were dead already, since everyone had heard what the two of them had said to each other in the kitchen. That circumstance amused her since they now *were* lovers, but as she pointed out, gossips rarely got anything right, anyway. She was also of the opinion that a woman named Dorothy and a guy named Gun would keep the more outrageous versions of what happened between him and Neil in line.

As for what Neil had said about him scamming Louie, she had an opinion about that, too.

"I think he's feeling defensive about your relationship with his uncle," she explained later that night when she brought him a bowl of stew she saved for his supper. The café was closed, her apartment quiet except for the groans and creaks of the building settling in for the night.

"Brenda was talking about how competitive Neil has always been," she continued, sitting across from him at her small table, "and she thinks he did it because you embarrassed him. It doesn't reflect well on him that his uncle gets along better with you than he does his own nephew. Saying what he did makes it look like you've duped a defenseless old man into liking you. It's his way of saving face."

Hannah had a few things she'd like to say to that face herself, but she didn't want to burden Damon with those musings. He would never have asked what she thought of the incident if it hadn't been weighing heavily on him already.

When his brooding expression indicated that he didn't buy that bit of admittedly amateur psychology, she pushed the rolls toward him and moved on. "So how was Louie today? When I brought your lunch, he seemed kind of quiet."

"He's been sort of preoccupied lately." He poked at a chunk of potato. "Neil's trying to talk him into moving to a retirement center."

"You're kidding."

"No," he returned, echoing the flatness of her tone, "I'm not."

"Is he considering it?"

"That, I don't know." Damon's eyes met hers over the steam rising from the bowl. He no longer tried to hide the concern in the hard lines of his face. Only the magnitude of it. "He said he's not leaving his garden, but it's almost like the idea's got him too depressed to put up much of an argument."

That didn't sound like Louie at all. "The retirement center on the north end of town is actually very nice. But I can't picture him there." She could hear him now, saying it was full of nothing but old people. "And I can't picture him giving up his home without a fight. Not as feisty as he can be."

"It doesn't seem like something he'd do, does it."

The flatness of his tone made his words a statement. Louie had his moments, but they had both come to know him as a rather spirited man who was decidedly set in his ways and who returned favors wherever he could. Because Hannah made him his favorite soup, he tended her herbs, something he enjoyed enormously. And after she'd sewn a dangling button back on his shirt cuff so he wouldn't lose it, he brought her an African violet from his living room. They had also discovered a certain logic to his eccentricities.

The fishing vest he always wore did look a little strange. Especially when he'd worn it under his heavy winter coat. But Hannah didn't consider that his odd way of dressing meant he was as daft as his nephew insisted he was. When Damon, blunt as he was, had asked him why he wore it, Louie had maintained that by the time a man was in his eighties, those with any smarts at all opted for practical over conventional. Aside from the tackle he carried for lake or ice fishing, he found the little pockets handy for carrying everything from his tobacco pouch to his medicine, and the loops were good for hanging things when he was gardening. It was sort of like wearing a purse, he'd claimed, except he'd look like an idiot doing that, so the vest worked for him just fine.

She still smiled every time she thought of how Damon had cut his finger on a hacksaw and Louie had whipped an adhesive strip out from one of those little pockets. But the smile that threatened now immediately faded.

With the boat nearly finished and his nephew talking of a retirement home, maybe that spirit was beginning to wane. She felt fairly certain that Damon hadn't responded to the remark he'd made about meeting him on the dock this summer. Maybe not knowing he could look forward to that was contributing to Louie's odd mood, too.

She mentioned that to Damon, quietly asking if he'd considered Louie's offer, but he evaded her, saying he simply wasn't letting himself think that far ahead. His focus was on finishing the boat.

No one was more aware of that than she was. Damon worked fourteen hours a day—six of those with Louie—to accomplish his goal. The only time she had to be alone with him was after she closed the café. Then he came up every evening to share the supper she'd set aside for them. Sometimes they ate in her comfortable apartment, sometimes in the café's kitchen. But he never failed to thank her with a kiss that turned her knees to water, which inevitably meant he had to carry her up to her bed. And always, always, he left her arms to go home before they fell asleep, just so his truck was never behind her building overnight.

He was only thinking of her, she reminded herself each time he left—and would try very hard not to believe he was leaving because waking up next to her implied more of a commitment than he was willing to make. But rationalizing no longer worked the way it once had. She was painfully aware of the distance in him. Despite all that they shared, there was still a part of Damon she simply couldn't reach. A part that seemed to draw farther away the closer he came to finishing his task.

That distance was never so great as the morning she went

downstairs to see what he and Louie wanted for lunch, and found Damon preparing to pull the gleaming white boat out the open doors.

Damon was working alone. That was unusual in itself because she knew Louie had planned to launch the boat with him. But it was the fierceness of his movements as he jerked on a rope that warned her something was very wrong. He wasn't just cinching the rope; the abrupt motions were a way to vent anger.

The boat and trailer were already hooked up to the black truck he'd backed up to the gaping doorway. She didn't know what sort of equipment he had under the tarp at the front of the bed, but that was where he'd lashed the rope he yanked on. Apparently deciding it was tight enough, he finished off the free end in a knot, shoved his fingers through his hair, then visibly forced himself to slow down.

"Damon?"

The sound of her voice caused his head to jerk toward her. The rain had stopped for the moment, but a frigid spring wind blew in from the lake, fluttering his dark hair around his head. He wore no coat. No hat. Just khaki cargo pants and a long-sleeved black T-shirt that made his chest look a mile wide.

"What's wrong?"

His response was to glance from her and stalk the length of his beautifully restored boat, with its gleaming hardware, new propellers and bright blue *Naiad* painted on the stern. When he reached the empty boxes behind it, he started filling them with the paint and thinner cans he'd stacked there. His motions were deliberate, but she could see him consciously slowing them as he brought himself under control.

He had the first box filled and started to reach for another when he stopped. All Hannah could think was that he'd needed to calm himself down before he spoke.

"I went to pick up Louie just like I usually do," he finally said, his words terse and biting. "But he wasn't there. Neil was waiting for me, though. With the sheriff." He lifted his foreboding glance to her, the chill in his voice visible in his eyes. "It seems Louie didn't get to spend his Sunday resting. Neil moved him to a retirement center. And I'm to stay away from him."

A knot had formed in her stomach the instant he'd mentioned Neil. It had doubled itself on the word *sheriff*. "The retirement center isn't that much farther than his house. They can tell you to stay away, but they can't stop him from walking down here. He's probably on his way right—"

"That's not where he is." His skin drew taut over the bones in his face, carving his angry features tighter. "They moved him to Brainerd. That's over a hundred miles away."

For a moment, Hannah didn't know what to say. She could only stand in the chill of his glare, hoping this was someone's idea of a sick joke. Until a couple of weeks ago, she couldn't have imagined Louie caving in to Neil's unnecessary suggestion. But she'd watched him grow more melancholy with every bit of progress Damon had made on his boat, and she could see where he might have finally allowed it. It had been as if he was watching his usefulness come to an end, and his dejection over that made him care about little else. She'd thought there would be plenty of time for Damon to see how important he'd become to him, and for Louie to see that he had friends in her and Brenda, too. She'd just never dreamed Neil would move him so far away.

"Did they say why?"

"I didn't stick around to ask."

She didn't imagine that he would. Knowing Damon, he'd banked his rage beneath an exterior of pure ice, subjected both men to the glare that could cool a jalapeño and walked away. The answer seemed obvious, anyway.

"What can I do?"

She started to reach for him, only to find her hand stalling before she touched his arm. Whether consciously or not, Damon had retreated a step, denying her the contact, and himself the support. She could practically see him pulling into himself, locking his emotions down, cutting himself off.

Praying it was only his feelings about what had just happened that caused the withdrawal, she crossed her arms over the knots in her stomach and watched him turn from her.

"You can't defend me on this one, Hannah." He lifted the box he'd filled, set it aside and started another. "This one's all mine. Tell me," he said, silencing any disagreement she might have had, "how much more has your business dropped off?"

She didn't trust the change of subject at all. Especially to that particular topic. But attempting to figure out how he'd tied what had happened with Louie to the decline in her business wasn't a priority. At the moment, she didn't trust him, either. His tightly spoken words held as much self-blame as anger, and that anger now seemed directed at himself.

She'd apparently hesitated a little too long.

"Forget it," he muttered, heading for the door with a box. "You'll just feed me excuses. I'll ask Brenda."

That was obviously what he intended to do, too. He walked away before she could say another word, not that he'd left her anything to say. And when he returned that evening after launching the *Naiad* and bringing her around to dock, he headed straight up the stairs to the kitchen. Hannah heard him coming up the stairwell even as Brenda was coming through the swinging door.

Brenda didn't work on Mondays. But that was the day she dropped her nieces off at the dance studio for her sister, then came to the café to kill the time waiting for them. Since business was slower than a geriatric snail on Monday evening, Hannah enjoyed the company.

Tonight, however, Brenda didn't appear at all her usual, smiling self. Between the oddly worried expression on her face when she saw the man who'd just opened the stairwell door, and the tension so apparent in Damon, Hannah didn't know which direction to head, or who to greet first.

Damon saved her having to decide. Framed by the doorway, he gave a tight nod toward the service window.

"Is there anybody out there?" he asked Brenda, since she'd just come through.

She shook her head, curls bouncing. "No. But listen, you guys, did you know Neil moved Mr. Lindstrom to Brainerd?"

Hannah cut a cautious glance toward Damon. "We heard."

"Did you know he's talking about having a competency hearing so he can take over his affairs?"

"What?"

The thunder in Damon's voice set Brenda back a step. The cold fury in his eyes made her take one more.

"Alice over at the dance studio just told me," she said, clearly distressed by the news herself. "One of the Lindstrom girls takes dance over there, and she's telling her friends that her dad had to hire an attorney because their Uncle Louie is demented."

Hannah's eyes had fastened on the broad back disappearing from the doorway. "Where are you going?" she called, darting across the polished beige linoleum.

Damon's low, heated rasp rose from the stairwell. "This isn't about anybody being demented."

"Damon," Hannah called, a little frantic when he didn't slow his stride. "Where?"

"To have a little talk with Neil."

"There's a pastor selection meeting at the church," Brenda advised over Hannah's shoulder. "I saw his car over there."

"Brenda!" The glare Hannah aimed at her friend was diluted considerably by apprehension. "You didn't have to tell him that."

With a helpless gesture, Brenda murmured a quiet "Sorry," then jumped at the slam of the stairwell door.

Seconds later, a second, more muffled report sounded as the entry door of the shop was subjected to Damon's exit.

Apprehension turned to pure worry as Hannah glanced back to Brenda. She didn't know whether to lock up first or just leave.

Brenda was already ahead of her. Grabbing Hannah's coat and pocketbook from her office, she pushed them into her hands, gave her a shove toward the door and simply said, "Go."

Chapter Eleven

The members of the pastor selection committee were just taking their seats when Damon strode down the brightly lit hall of the church basement. Over the roar of blood pounding in his temples, he could hear the scrape of chairs, the murmur of conversation and a sharp bark of laughter.

Straining at the reins of self-control, he stopped in the open doorway. There had to be fifty people in the room, many of them the town's more prominent movers and shakers. The knot of people near a wall of colorful children's drawings included a face or two that looked familiar. The one he recognized for certain was Hannah's old cook. Caught midsentence when she noticed him, the big woman with the coiled braids went dead silent.

By the time his glance sliced past the Feldsons, Ernie Pederson and the back of Sheriff Jansson's head, the noise level in the room had subsided considerably. When his eyes finally locked on Neil chatting amiably with a couple in the front of the room, the sandy-haired ex-athlete was the only person still talking.

Even Neil finally shut up when he realized the people he spoke with were no longer looking at him. There wasn't a soul in the place whose attention wasn't focused on the man looming in the doorway. Damon's face was as impassive as rock. It was the leashed fury coiled in his body that had everyone glancing around so uneasily.

Neil appeared to suffer a brief moment of distress himself—just before he slapped on a bored expression that might have worked had the veins in his forehead not suddenly popped out.

"We're having a meeting here, Jackson."

Eight months ago, Damon would never have exposed himself to such potential for trouble. The thought wouldn't even have occurred to him. But as often as Hannah had stuck up for her principles, for him, the least he could do was stick up for his old friend.

Friend, he thought, the muscle in his jaw jerking. Before he'd met Hannah, he'd never even had one. And look what he'd done to him.

"This won't take long," he assured Neil, his voice tight with control. "Come out here for a minute."

Neil was not a fool. The idea of stepping out into the hall, alone with two hundred pounds of banked wrath, was not only preposterous, it was suicidal. Though the movement was barely perceptible, he edged toward the man rising importantly from an end chair. Sheriff Jansson had turned around and was tucking the back of his plaid sport shirt into his slacks, his chest out and his expression a mix of resignation and dislike.

"We don't have time for this," the sheriff informed Damon, as determined to be rid of this particular intruder as he was to keep the peace. "I don't know what your problem is, but I can't have you disrupting—"

"The *problem* is what he's done to an innocent old man," Damon shot back. "I know you hate my guts, Sheriff, but if you're going along with him about Louie just to get back at me, then you're as big a hypocrite as he is. What he's doing to his uncle is downright criminal."

"Wait a minute," Neil sputtered, his skin turning red.

The sheriff's arm barred Neil's chest, his eyes fixed on Damon. He looked a tad pink himself. "You be careful who you accuse, Jackson. Neil moved his uncle for the man's own good. We all know Louie is old, and his mind and his judgment aren't what they used to be. Neil did what any of us would do to see that an elderly relative isn't taken advantage of."

"By his judgment, I assume you mean his association with me."

"It was certainly a consideration," Neil blustered, pushing the sheriff's arm away.

Fueled by the same sense of inequity that had always haunted him, Damon stalked forward. It was one thing to swallow prejudice when it was aimed at him. He knew defending himself was so much wasted energy. But when bias against him hurt someone else, no way would he let it pass.

"Do you want to tell your friends here what the other considerations were?" Like Moses parting the sea, he moved steadily down the center aisle, the people on either side edging back as he passed. "Do you want to tell them who you were really thinking about when you talked an elderly man out of his home and stuck him away from everything familiar?"

"I have no idea what you're talking about."

"The hell you don't," Damon growled, oblivious to the widened eyes and gaping mouths. "The only person you're thinking of is yourself. You never took any interest in Louie until you thought the man's money was threatened. Money you'd probably get someday. Which was it that you really thought?'' he demanded over someone's gasp at the audacity of the suggestion. ''That I'd con him out of it? Or that he'd give it to me and cut you out?''

Neil's mouth opened, closed and opened again. Looking like a fish out of water, he sputtered something that sounded like a protest.

''Deny it,'' Damon demanded, edging forward, eyes even with Neil's. ''Deny that you were only thinking of yourself. You don't give a damn about him. You wouldn't even listen when he told you we thought one of his prescriptions was causing him to be confused. You blew it off as an old man's ramblings. If you'd bothered to check it out, you'd know he called his doctor and his doctor changed the medicine. He hasn't had a bad spell since.''

Groping for a comeback, Neil glanced to the sheriff for help. Jansson's brow was furrowed, his stony glance bouncing between the two glaring men.

''He has different kinds of spells,'' Neil retorted, grasping for something to fight back with. ''Every time I went over there to talk to him lately, he'd just be sitting in his chair, wearing that stupid fishing vest and staring off into space. If he bothered to answer me at all, he'd mumble about not caring where I moved him. Most of the time, he'd just look at me like I wasn't even there.''

''He's depressed, you idiot.'' That's what Hannah had said, anyway, and Damon figured she knew what she was talking about. She was good with people, compassionate and caring. He figured, too, that if Louie looked at Neil as if he weren't there, it was probably because he wished he weren't. ''How would you feel if you didn't have anything to look forward to and your only relative wanted you out of the way? There's nothing wrong with him that a little time and attention wouldn't cure. He just needs a purpose,'' he insisted, getting in the guy's face, blocking him completely with his body. ''He doesn't belong where you stuck him. If he gets to the point where he really needs to be in a home, then put him in one in a place he knows. Protecting him from me was just an excuse to move him far enough away that you wouldn't have to be bothered with him anymore.

"And stop worrying about his money," he snarled. "You'll get it soon enough."

His own culpability where Louie was concerned was biting hard when he saw Neil retreat another step. By sheer force of will, or divine intervention, Damon hadn't touched him, but Neil had backed into a folding chair and was about to go over it.

Instinctively, Neil groped for the nearest support, which happened to be the front of Damon's shirt.

It was sheer perversity. Damon knew it, he even took time to acknowledge it. But since he wouldn't let himself deck the self-righteous son of a sea witch, he did the next best thing. Stepping back before Neil's hand could clutch fabric, he let him crash in a heap under the podium with its carving of a dove and an olive branch.

The clatter of collapsing metal had given way to gasps when Neil grabbed his right wrist and scrambled to his feet. Swearing a blue streak, he rounded on the sheriff. But Damon was already backing away, vaguely aware of a man in a clerical collar admonishing Neil to watch his mouth. He was more conscious of the collective murmurs coming from behind him—and the feel of worried blue eyes on his back.

He didn't know what it meant that he could sense her the way he did. But he knew Hannah was there even before he turned and saw her clutching her coat around herself at the back of the room. Her face was pale, and her eyes filled with anxiety as they darted from him to the man loudly insisting that he be arrested.

"That's assault!" Neil fumed. "He pushed me!"

The burning in Damon's gut instantly changed quality. He'd been so far into the guy's face that no one could possibly have seen what had happened. For all anyone knew, he'd bumped him with his chest. He hadn't, but that didn't matter. Not when it came to him.

He was already halfway to the door. Since no one tried to stop him, he kept going. Past the people gaping at him. Past the whispers, the stares. Past the only decent thing that had ever happened to him.

It was only his desire to protect Hannah that prevented him from grabbing her arm and hauling her out with him. She didn't need him acting possessive around her. That would only fuel whatever speculation was still going on about them. He'd already done enough damage to an innocent old man. All he could do now was minimize the damage he'd done to her.

If she'd just let him.

The commotion he'd caused was still audible when he heard her quick, light footsteps hurrying up the stairs after him. He didn't slow for her and he didn't turn around, but he did hold the door when he reached the end of the upper hall until she could grab it, then headed down the wet walkway to where he'd left his truck at the curb.

"Damon, don't do this." Hannah's hand curved over his shirtsleeve, her touch as insistent as her voice. "What happened back there?"

The night was quiet and cool, the air damp from the earlier rain. The breeze rattled the budding birch trees, the sound as brittle as his voice when he finally spoke.

"I didn't touch him."

He could see her relief in the pale light from the street lamp, her unquestioning acceptance of his word visible in her eyes. But the worry straining her delicate features remained, torturing him as much as the odd, empty ache in his chest.

"Come back to the café. I'll lock up and we can talk. Or not talk, if you don't want to." Her glance searched his, offering reassurance, asking for the same. "We'll figure out what to do for Louie. We'll go see him tomorrow."

"I already know what I need to do."

The rage had leaked out of him. The fire that had burned in his eyes extinguished as if the wick had been cut from a candle. Hannah could have dealt with his anger. She'd been prepared for that. But its sudden absence frightened her even more than Damon's abrupt withdrawal this afternoon. All that remained in the shadowed angles of his face was distance, and resignation.

Slowly, deliberately, he reached for her hand and moved it from his arm.

"I can't do this anymore, Hannah. If Louie hadn't been helping me, he'd be in his house right now going through his gardening catalogs. I hurt him. And I'm hurting you," he added, as if the deed were a simple, irrefutable fact. "Your business is already suffering because of who I am."

The temptation to argue his conclusion wasn't there. His strange calm precluded excuses. But it was the way he'd cast off her touch that robbed the strength from her voice. "It's not that long until summer," she said, folding her arms over the awful knot in her stomach. "You know it'll be better then."

"This isn't about just scraping by. That's not why you came here. You want to belong, and that won't happen if you're with me. You know as well as I do that reputation is everything around here. This town isn't going to change the way it thinks, and I can't do anything to change my past. Hell, it's my present," he said, his voice starkly devoid of emphasis. He motioned toward the church, looking as if he expected the sheriff to come bolting out any minute. "Even when I try, I can't stay out of trouble."

He turned, heading for the driver-side door of his truck. Hannah stepped in front of him, blocking him at the fender but careful not to touch him. It almost seemed as if he were pushing her away to protect her. But it wasn't his protection she wanted. She just wanted his heart.

"You didn't do anything wrong. You didn't say anything in there that I wouldn't have said if I'd thought of it."

The plea in her voice was for understanding, and for the chance she could feel slipping through her fingers like wet glass. She'd known it was only a matter of time before he pulled completely away from her, but she'd let herself dream, anyway. And the pain of those shattering dreams was fierce.

She wanted his heart. But he wasn't offering that. He never had.

"As for changing the way people think about you," she continued, trying to break through any way she could, "you've never given them reason to change their minds. You're a good man, Damon. You've got so much to offer if you'd just let yourself. All you've ever let them see is what they expect to see."

She knew now why he did that. It didn't hurt as much when he could push someone away before they could push him. It was the same defense he used for people he might care about, the one he was using now as he cut his glance from her as if there was no point discussing the obvious. He simply abandoned people before they could harm him. The way his mom had done. The way his father had emotionally abandoned him. The way the system and the community had cast him aside. All his life, he'd been doing the only thing he'd ever been taught to do. That had to be why he didn't try to give himself a chance by moving someplace else. It didn't matter where he lived. No matter where he went, he wouldn't let himself risk being anything other than alone.

"I'll clean out the shop in a couple of days," he said, stepping around her to open the truck's door. "What I have to do shouldn't take much longer than that."

She didn't let herself ask what it was he intended to do. But Damon knew it had her concerned. He caught a glimpse of that worry in her eyes, along with the hurt he'd put there, before she turned and walked away as the first drops of rain began to fall.

There was nothing he could do about that hurt, except live with the same feeling himself. Seeing light spill from the doorway when the side door of the church opened, he started the engine and pulled out onto the dark, damp street. The only way he could stay out of trouble was to keep to himself. He'd known that. And he'd been doing fine…until Hannah. But he'd broken his own rules and stepped beyond the boundaries he could control. It was time he returned to his own world. It was where he belonged. But first, he had to do what he could do for Louie.

The rain that started that night never let up. For two days, the dismal gray sky leaked a constant supply of the wet stuff—which meant every person darting through the door of the café had a comment about how nasty it was outside. The remarks were invariably followed by mention of the only other topic worth discussion—the now-infamous scene at the pastor selection meeting at the Good Shepherd church.

"That wind!" Brenda exclaimed, pulling down the hood of her wet raincoat as she closed the café's front door. "I haven't seen it like this since last fall."

Hannah was well aware of the wind. Between the ache in her chest she was trying hard to not think about and a nagging sense of worry she couldn't ignore, she was agitated enough without Mother Nature getting in on the act. "Do the spring storms get as bad as the fall ones do?"

Hannah watched Brenda bat at her curls as she cleared plates from a table. Considering the weather, it had been fairly busy until a few minutes ago. Given that the rain was now blowing in sheets, the midmorning lull was likely to be even quieter than usual.

"They can. That's one of the reasons I'm here. You might want to put up your shutters."

Hannah had already thought about that. But since she hadn't noticed any of the other merchants boarding up, she'd decided to wait herself. "What's the other reason?"

"To check on you."

A soft smile touched her lips. "I'm fine, Bren. Really," she lied, knowing she wasn't fooling her friend. "I just wish I knew where he was."

"Did Dorothy tell you she thinks Damon is right?"

Hannah nodded, carrying dishes to the kitchen. "She was in yesterday."

Dorothy, who hadn't been at the meeting but had certainly heard about it, also thought Damon could have exercised a little more restraint by not shoving Neil. But, like several others who'd generously shared their opinion with Hannah— every one of whom she tried to set straight on the shoving issue—any criticism of him had been tempered with respect. Damon hadn't caused the disruption to defend himself against Neil's accusations. He hadn't attempted to benefit himself at all. Everything he'd said had been in defense of Louie Lindstrom.

It was Damon who needed to hear their remarks, though. Not that he'd think they made any difference. And not that he was where anyone could talk to him. He hadn't moved his things from the shop. He hadn't been home when Deacon Jim had stopped by his house yesterday and this morning. And his truck wasn't at the dock.

"Hannah?"

"What?"

"I think we ought to get the shutters up. The welcome sign from the Curl Up and Dye just blew by the newsstands."

Hannah couldn't see the dislodged sign, but when she glanced back through the service window, she could see the trees behind the appliance store across the street bowing sharply to the left. Brenda was right. But even as she grabbed her slicker and she and Brenda hurried down the stairwell and wrestled the first board out the silent shop's door, the concern that had nagged at Hannah all morning took firmer hold.

They had that board up and were starting back to the shop for the other when Hannah caught Brenda's arm.

"Go back inside," she insisted over the drumming of the rain. "And don't you dare try to finish this yourself."

"Where are you going?"

"To Damon's boat."

"What?"

"If his truck is there, I'll be right back." She could see vehicles in the lot at the end of the narrow street, but with the rain blurring everything, the shapes all looked the same. "If not, I'll be back in ten minutes."

The sound of thunder rumbled in the distance. Bracing herself against it, she took off down the hill with her head bent against the sheeting rain. If his truck was in the lot, it would mean he was taking care of his boat. If it wasn't, she'd have to do what she could. After all the work Damon had put into the *Naiad* and as much as it meant to him, she couldn't bear the thought of anything happening to it. She could hardly keep it from being tossed out of the water if the waves got that high, but she could make sure the windows were covered and the extra bumpers tied on.

The windshield wipers were barely keeping up with the deluge when Damon pulled away from the café to head for the dock. He couldn't believe Hannah had left her windows half shuttered to take care of his boat. But that was exactly what Brenda had said she'd done, just before he'd jammed the other board into place himself and jumped back in his truck.

Swiping water from his face, he focused on the road through the blur of water pouring against the windshield and the frantic slap of the wipers. He didn't know which was pushing him more at the moment, anxiety, irritation or some feeling he was truly afraid to name. Hannah hated storms, and the thought of her being out there for him only added to the turmoil he'd fought relentlessly for the last two days.

A pine bough tore past his fender as he bumped into the gravel lot. Slowing, he fastened the top toggle on the long yellow slicker he'd pulled on before he'd boarded Hannah's window. Wanting only to get the job done so he could get to the dock, he hadn't bothered with the sou'wester that had fallen to the floorboard. He didn't bother with it when he pulled up by the white van with the fish logo, either. As he cut the engine and opened the door, his only thought was to get Hannah into the truck and to secure his boat. At the moment, anything beyond that didn't matter.

Leaving the keys dangling in the ignition, he bent his head against the whip of wind and rain and bolted for the wooden stairs. Only the knowledge that the steps could be slick as ice when they were wet slowed him down, but even then he was at a steady jog.

The dock normally sat a couple of feet off the water, but waves were sloshing across the planks as he passed the other big boats being jostled against the wharf. Those other vessels had already been secured with extra ropes and protected by the long, cylindrical foam bumpers that buffered their beating against the pilings and, at times, one another. But what made no sense to him when he spotted the bright blue of Hannah's slicker near his stern was that three men from those other boats were just leaving his.

The first of those yellow-slickered men came over the stern just as Hannah turned toward him. The wind caught her hood with her movement, blowing it back from her head, but she seemed so startled to see him that she didn't think to snatch it back. In seconds her hair was soaked, and her skin looked like pale, wet marble.

"She's as secure as she's going to get. You did a nice job on her, too," Ernie Pedersen said, slapping him on the shoulder before he jogged off in the rain.

The guy behind him, a man Damon recognized as one of the Feldsons' deckhands, gave him a thumbs-up and took off after the man who, until that moment, hadn't spared him more than two words in the past ten months.

Axel Feldson jumped off right behind him, wiping water from his mustache with one hand and pointing across the stern with the other. "I couldn't find a rope to tie off on that port cleat, so I used one of mine. You can get it back to me whenever you get a chance."

Head ducked against the torrent, he followed the others, anxious to get out of the storm.

Through the gray downpour, Damon watched Hannah move toward him. She looked a little hesitant, and a lot uneasy. He wasn't sure how much of that had to do with the weather and how much with him, but he was guessing it was a toss-up right about now.

He motioned to the boat. "What's going on?"

Hannah stopped an arm's length away. Watching the rain sluice over the confusion in his rugged features, she crossed her arms and fought a shiver that had nothing to do with cold and everything to do with nerves. "Mr. Feldson wanted to know what I was doing down here. When I told him, he said he wanted to help. Ernie said he wanted to help you, too."

"The wanted to help *me?* I can't believe they'd do that." He shook his head, his eyes narrowing on hers. "I can't believe you came down here in this, either."

The disbelief in his voice made Hannah's heart ache. It was as if he couldn't believe anyone could care about him at all.

"They did it to show their support for what you did for Louie," she told him, wondering if that was why he'd had such compassion for the old guy. Louie hadn't had anyone who really cared about him, either. "I did it because I love you."

She had no idea how Damon reacted to that little revelation. Or if he even cared. Ducking her head, she started past him, wanting badly to get out of the wind and the rain, and to avoid the thunder that she just knew was going to come booming across the lake any second.

She'd taken two steps when she felt Damon's arm come down around her shoulders. Her third step faltered, but he was pushing her on, apparently as anxious as she was to get away from the cold rain whipping sideways through the air and the white-capped waves lapping at their feet.

Hurrying along with him, she jogged up the stairs, lifting her head only long enough to see where he was angling them. Not until he'd practically shoved her inside his truck and climbed in on the other side did she consider that he hadn't seemed surprised to find her there.

"I put your other board up," he said, which explained why he'd known where she was. "You don't need to worry about something coming through that window."

Hannah's response was a quiet "Thank you" as he wiped rain from his face and reached for the steering wheel. He didn't turn the ignition, as she'd thought he would, however. With her focus on the droplets of water puddling around a silver toggle on her coat, she felt him hesitate just before he hooked his wrists over the steering wheel and turned his head toward her.

Damon knew what he'd heard moments ago on the dock. He also knew Hannah wasn't terribly happy with what she'd said. She looked defensive and faintly combative. The way she had the day she'd admitted she'd fired her cook in defense of him. Then she'd been defending a principle, and she'd all but dared him to challenge her right to do that. She had that same look now, complete with the same uneasiness she'd felt about the storm.

Maybe that was when he'd fallen in love with her.

The realization might have come with more of a jolt if he hadn't already accepted how much he needed her. For the past two days, he'd thought of nothing but her and Louie. About how empty the old man's life was, and how empty his own would be without her in it. He just wasn't sure now how he could do what was right for either of them.

Wind buffeted the truck. Rain pounded the roof and windows. Every breath they expelled fogged the windows a little more. He could turn on the heater. He could take her home. But he didn't want to move. The silence stretching between them felt brittle enough to shatter.

"Do you mind if I ask where you were?" Her glance bounced off his chin, totally avoiding his eyes as she wiped water from her cheeks.

"I went to Brainerd to find the home Louie's in," he replied, taking another swipe at the drips leaking down from his hair. "Neil left word that I wasn't to get anywhere near him, so we didn't talk, but I hired him an attorney in case Neil tries to challenge his competency." He caught a rivulet racing down his neck. "The guy's supposed to meet with him tomorrow."

He'd hired Louie an attorney. The knowledge did something strange to the ache in Hannah's chest. "Louie won't be there," she replied, wondering what it would take for Damon to realize how good he truly was. "The deacon from the church went to see him yesterday. He wanted you to go with him, but you weren't home."

"Why did he want me to go?"

"Because you're Louie's friend," she said simply, daring a quick glance at his profile. "Everyone could see that." She returned her attention to a toggle on her coat, flicking at the puddle around it. "A group of men are going down tomorrow to move him back to his home. The sheriff's one of them. I don't think you'll ever be his favorite person, but he respects what you did for Louie."

"Then he didn't think I shoved Neil?"

"Deacon Jim told him you didn't. I guess he was sitting where he could see everything. Even if you had, I don't think the sheriff would have cared. He was feeling pretty bad about having gone along with Neil. People take care of their own around here. They were appalled that Neil would have done something like that."

"Like he admitted it," Damon muttered.

"It's more like he can't convincingly deny it," she replied, ignoring the chip on his shoulder as she so often did. As long as it had been there, it would take forever to whittle it away. "He's still trying, but people remember all his grumbling when he'd have to do something for his uncle. The part about him worrying about the money can't be proved, but it's what you said about his medication that has people really upset with him. Neil was too willing to label him senile and tuck him out of the way." She caught a drip at the end of her nose. "At least you were willing to stick up for him." Her voice quieted, becoming barely audible over the pounding rain. "You were a good friend to him, Damon."

From the corner of her eye, she saw the telltale muscle in his jaw tighten.

"If I'd been that good a friend, I'd have asked him to help me repair nets or something this summer instead of ignoring his offer. He loves working around boats. It would have given him something to look forward to."

He'd been beating himself up ever since he left. She was sure of it. The self-recrimination lacing his tone made it clear that he blamed himself on several levels for what had happened. "You can still ask him to help."

"I don't know if I can or not, Hannah. Associating with me only causes problems." His hands tightened on the wheel.

"I don't know what to do about him." Hesitating, he glanced toward her. "Or you."

The tension in him found its counterpart in her. A knot the size of a lemon lodged beneath her breastbone. "You don't have to do anything about me."

"Yeah, I do. I love you. I just don't know what I can do about it."

Hannah's heart slammed against the knot. Scarcely believing what she'd heard, she slowly, finally, looked over at him.

He was soaked. His dark hair was so wet it looked black in the gray light of the truck's cab. He'd nicked his chin shaving. And he looked as if he hadn't slept in two days. Lines of strain were etched around his beautiful mouth and fanned from the corners of his cloud gray eyes. He seemed more weary than defensive, and far more uncertain than she'd ever known him to be.

That weariness deepened when his hands slid from the wheel and he pushed his fingers through his hair. "No matter how hard I try, I can't seem to figure it out."

Afraid to let hope build, unable to stop it, she willed her voice not to tremble. "Have you considered that maybe this isn't something you're supposed to figure out by yourself? I know you're used to making decisions on your own. But, Damon," she murmured, "you're not alone anymore."

She didn't think the thought had occurred to him. She knew for certain it hadn't when she saw incomprehension wash over his expression. An instant later, pain replaced it.

She hadn't expected that pain. Or the wrenching sensation she felt when she saw it. She knew he'd chosen his isolation. She just hadn't suspected how deeply he longed for what he denied himself. In his eyes was the anguish of a man who'd never had reason to believe life could be any way other than what it was.

That tortured look remained as he slowly lifted his hand to her jaw. The way he hesitated before he skimmed his finger over her skin made her think he was almost afraid to touch her, afraid that if he allowed himself to reach, she might disappear.

Damon's heart hurt. He'd never known the feeling before, but the bruised, too-tight feeling had been there ever since he'd walked away from her at the church. As he touched her now, seeing the concern and the anxiety in her eyes, his chest ached so badly it was almost hard to breathe. He'd never felt so vulnerable in his life as he did just then. Before she had come along, he'd kept to himself, and his armor had been firmly in place. He'd known how to protect himself, how to keep from caring. But he'd allowed her to draw him out, and the crack in that armor was huge.

He slipped his finger down the side of her neck, her soft skin warm and slick from the rain. "When we were talking about Louie..." he said, his voice rough with thoughts he hadn't been able to shake. "You said the positive changes in him might be because he finally felt necessary...like he was part of something. And that taking that feeling away from him was probably what made him feel like giving up." He knew exactly how Louie felt. Before Hannah had come along, he'd never thought of how lonely he'd been. Emptiness had simply been part of his life. Having known her, the thought of going back to what he'd had was almost more than he could face.

"You made me feel part of something, too," he told her, the ache in his chest starting to burn. "I don't want to leave that. I want to marry you. I want us together. But I can't just ask you to give up what you've worked so hard for and go away with me somewhere. And if we stayed here, your life wouldn't be anything like what you wanted."

He was still doing it. Pulling her to him with one hand, pushing her away with the other. Only now he was talking about her entire future.

"And what if what I want is you?"

She couldn't remember the number of times they'd admitted that to each other. *I want you.* They couldn't be in each other's arms without the thought, the words, passing between them. Those thoughts and words were in Damon's eyes now as his glance moved over her rain-slicked skin and the droplets clinging to the ends of the hair the wind had wrested from its clip. The "want" she meant was so much more than physical need. It always had been. And she suspected he'd always been aware of that as he slowly pushed her wet hair back from her face.

"Then I'd have to say you've got me," he murmured, drawing her closer.

Thunder built, seeming to hover in the distance before it raced across the lake with the wind. Hannah scarcely noticed its jarring boom, or the apocalyptic crash of waves and rain surrounding them. What made her heart lurch was the feel of Damon's mouth settling over hers in a kiss so tender she couldn't tell if the dampness on her cheeks was rain, or tears. He touched her as if she were made of crystal, taking small sips from the corners of her mouth, gently opening her to him to seek her warmth. He drew her against him, deepening the kiss as if he'd really meant to pull back, but now that her taste was on his tongue, he had to have just a little more. It was always like that with him. He could never quite get enough.

There was no mistaking the hunger in him when he pulled back. But the worry was still there, too. She had no trouble sensing it as he rested his forehead against hers.

"So." He breathed out the word, his voice oddly husky. "What are we going to do?"

Willing her own breathing to slow down, Hannah stared down at where his big hand rested on her thigh. "You said something to me once...about how a person had to make a place for himself if he didn't fit in anywhere." With the tips of her fingers, she touched the heavy yellow cloth of his coat where it covered his heart. "This is where I belong," she murmured. "And this," she added, moving his hand from her leg to hold it against the beating in her chest, "is where you already are.

"I'll be your wife," she told him, lifting her head to meet his eyes. "And I'll go anywhere with you. Or we can stay right here. Let people know you," she asked, touching her palm to the chiseled angle of his cheek. "You've already given them a glimpse of who you are, and a lot of them like what they've seen. You already have Louie and Brenda on your side. And the deacon and the fishermen. And Dorothy and Gun," she added, though she wasn't sure he knew who they were. "Erica and Eden's mom even—"

"Okay," Damon said, cutting her off with what threatened to be a smile. "I get the picture. It's just hard getting used to the idea of having friends." He turned her hand to his lips, placing a kiss in her palm. "How do you think Louie would feel about being my best man?"

The thought of their irascible friend brought delight to her eyes. "I think he'd tell you he already is."

Damon pulled her closer, absorbing the smile moving into her eyes before he drew her into a kiss that would have rocked the heavens, had the heavens not been rocking already. He never would have believed anything would change in Pine Point. Or how much he could change, himself. But he had, because of the woman in his arms. And because of her, he was no longer alone. He'd stopped being alone the day he'd met her.

* * * * *

Don't miss Silhouette's newest cross-line promotion

Five stellar authors, five evocative stories, five fabulous Silhouette series— pregnant mom on the run!

October 1998: **THE RANCHER AND THE AMNESIAC BRIDE** by top-notch talent **Joan Elliott Pickart** (Special Edition)

November 1998: **THE DADDY AND THE BABY DOCTOR** by Romance favorite **Kristin Morgan** (Romance)

December 1998: **THE SHERIFF AND THE IMPOSTOR BRIDE** by award-winning author **Elizabeth Bevarly** (Desire)

January 1999: **THE MILLIONAIRE AND THE PREGNANT PAUPER** by rising star **Christie Ridgway** (Yours Truly)

February 1999: **THE MERCENARY AND THE NEW MOM** by *USA Today* bestselling author **Merline Lovelace** (Intimate Moments)

Only in—

▼ *Silhouette Books*

Available at your favorite retail outlet.

Look us up on-line at: http://www.romance.net

SSEFTB

Silhouette

SPECIAL EDITION ®

™

That's My Baby!

Don't miss these heartwarming stories coming to
THAT'S MY BABY!—only from
Silhouette Special Edition®!

**June 1998   LITTLE DARLIN'
          by Cheryl Reavis (SE# 1177)**

When cynical Sergeant Matt Beltran found an abandoned
baby girl that he might have fathered, he turned to compassionate foster mother Corey Madsen. Could the healing
touch of a tender family soothe his soul?

**August 1998   THE SURPRISE BABY
          by Nikki Benjamin (SE# 1189)**

Aloof CEO Maxwell Hamilton married a smitten Jane Elliott
for the sake of convenience, but an impulsive night of
wedded bliss brought them a surprise bundle of joy—and a
new lease on love!

**October 1998 FATHER-TO-BE
          by Laurie Paige (SE# 1201)**

Hunter McLean couldn't exactly recall fathering a glowing
Celia Campbell's unborn baby, but he insisted they marry
anyway. Would the impending arrival of their newborn
inspire this daddy-to-be to open his heart?

THAT'S MY BABY!
**Sometimes bringing up baby can bring surprises...
and showers of love.**

Available at your favorite retail outlet.

Catch more great

◇ HARLEQUIN™ **Movies**
™

featured on the movie channel tmc

Premiering July 11th
Another Woman
Starring Justine Bateman and
Peter Outerbridge
Based on the novel by Margot Dalton

Don't miss next month's movie!
Premiering August 8th
The Waiting Game
Based on the novel by *New York Times*
bestselling author Jayne Ann Krentz

If you are not currently a subscriber to
The Movie Channel, simply call your
local cable or satellite provider for more
details. Call today, and don't miss out
on the romance!

the movie channel tmc ◇ HARLEQUIN®
®
100% *pure movies.* ✍*Makes any time special* ™
100% *pure fun.*

An Alliance Television Production

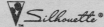

The World's Most Eligible Bachelors are about to be named! And Silhouette Books brings them to you in an all-new, original series....

World's Most Eligible Bachelors

Twelve of the sexiest, most sought-after men share every intimate detail of their lives in twelve never-before-published novels by the genre's top authors.

Don't miss these unforgettable stories by:

Dixie Browning

Marie Ferrarella

Jackie Merritt

Tracy Sinclair

BJ James

Rachel Lee

Suzanne Carey

Gina Wilkins

Victoria Pade

Maggie Shayne

Anne McAllister

Susan Mallery

Look for one new book each month in the **World's Most Eligible Bachelors** series beginning September 1998 from Silhouette Books.

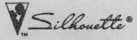

Silhouette®

Available at your favorite retail outlet.